The New York Times

CHANGING PERSPECTIVES

Populism

EDUCATIONAL PUBLISHING
BOOKS

I0879000

THE NEW YORK TIMES EDITORIAL STAFF

Published in 2020 by New York Times Educational Publishing
in association with The Rosen Publishing Group, Inc.
29 East 21st Street, New York, NY 10010

First Edition

The New York Times
Alex Ward: Editorial Director, Book Development
Phyllis Collazo: Photo Rights/Permissions Editor
Heidi Giovine: Administrative Manager

Rosen Publishing
Megan Kellerman: Managing Editor
Michael Hessel-Mial: Editor
Greg Tucker: Creative Director
Brian Garvey: Art Director

Cataloging-in-Publication Data
Names: New York Times Company.
Title: Populism / edited by the New York Times editorial staff.
Description: New York : New York Times Educational Publishing, 2020. | Series: Changing perspectives | Includes glossary and index.
Identifiers: ISBN 9781642822335 (library bound) | ISBN 9781642822328 (pbk.) | ISBN 9781642822342 (ebook)
Subjects: LCSH: Populism—Juvenile literature.
Classification: LCC JC423.P678 2020 | DDC 320.56'62—dc23

Manufactured in the United States of America

On the cover: U.S. Senator Bernie Sanders speaks during a rally in Providence, R.I., April 24, 2016; Scott Eisen/Stringer/Getty Images.

Contents

CHAPTER 5

Global Right-Wing Populism Overtakes the Establishment

Introduction

THE WORKER, THE FARMER, the "commonweal," the "silent majority," the "ninety-nine percent": the people. The "idle holders of idle capital," the railroads, the banks, the "pointy-headed intellectuals," the "one percent": the elites.

These names come from one of the most significant political styles of modern democracy: populism. Unlike other "isms," populism is not a particular platform but is instead a pattern political movements follow. Populist appeals have appeared all around the world from a range of positions, pitting "the people" against "the elites" — however vaguely defined. Today, we encounter populism yet again, directly challenging established political processes.

The populist movement began in the United States after the Civil War, a period of rapid industrialization and social change. The Farmers' Alliance and unionized laborers organized against social inequality and the concentration of economic power in railroads, banks and corporations. This movement made aggressive and plainspoken appeals for policies that would attend to the needs of "the people." These included antitrust and worker protection laws, inflationary monetary policies and other goals later taken up by the progressive movement. Populism soon reached the major political parties but was often divided over race, immigration and religious difference. These challenges raised the core problem of populism: does "the people" truly mean everyone?

After World War I, the competing ideologies of communism and fascism appeared, channeling populism into political power. Communism called for workers to overthrow the capitalist system, while fascism called for militant authoritarian nationalism. When the Great

Depression struck, many believed that one of these two alternative political systems would replace traditional democracy. In the United States, populists flirted with both of these ideologies. Some, like Huey Long and Earl Browder, advocated for socialist policies; others, like "radio priest" Charles Coughlin, began to veer toward a fascist model. The United States sided against fascism during World War II, and populism's reputation became associated with totalitarian ideology.

After the war, American public intellectuals examined populism with a critical eye, and it became common to muse on populism's history and causes. These writings were occasioned by independent politicians like George Wallace and Ross Perot, whose populist styles made headlines despite their electoral failures. At the same time, two very different populist movements appeared in the world: anti-immigration politics in Europe and political Islam in the Middle East.

At the turn of the 21st century, the economy was globalized by new technologies. This process echoed the 19th century in its enormous growth and increased income inequality. In response, populism again took center stage. A revived left-wing populism included protests against the World Trade Organization and a "pink tide" of Latin American populists like Hugo Chávez and Evo Morales. These movements culminated in the Occupy Movement, which popularized the concept of the wealth gap between the "ninety-nine percent" and the "one percent." At the same time, the Tea Party movement gave a populist basis to Republican criticisms of Barack Obama and government spending. In parallel, European populists criticized the European Union's enforced austerity policies, which cut social services.

By the end of Obama's presidency, populist movements had shifted rightward and begun winning elections around the world. In Europe, smaller parties gained influence by appealing to voters' fears of refugees from Syria and the greater Middle East. In the United States, the 2016 presidential election was a dramatic play of conflicting populist visions. Bernie Sanders, a self-avowed socialist, based a popular but ultimately unsuccessful primary campaign on criticizing the billionaire

MARK MAKELA FOR THE NEW YORK TIMES

Bernie Sanders supporters at a presidential campaign rally in 2016. Sanders, like Donald Trump and other recent populist politicians, drew large crowds to hear his speeches.

class. Donald Trump surprised the world by winning the presidency with a populist attack on immigration and on establishment rival Hillary Clinton. As a result of these elections, populism became a dominant force in global politics.

As the world is shaped by the visions of these many incarnations of populism, there is simultaneously a danger and an opportunity. At the heart of it, populism represents an enormous burst of energy into the democratic process. The results of that often unfocused energy lie not just in the people but in whoever channels that energy for political power. For those seeking to use that energy for their own ends, the result is often paranoia and misdirection, where legitimate grievances are channeled into fears, leveraged for the pursuit of power. For those seeking to share that power with the people they represent, the result is a renewal of democracy itself.

CHAPTER 1

Farmers and Laborers Build a Movement

The populist movement was based on agricultural and industrial labor movements — alongside other spontaneous demonstrations — that appeared after the Civil War. These movements were critical of railroad monopolies, trade tariffs and the gold standard, all of which were seen as favoring the wealthy over the poor. The populist movement found initial success in the Democratic Party but lost momentum due to internal divisions on race and foreign policy. Eventually, the Republican Party would win elections on a platform first proposed by the populist movement.

The National Grange: Declaration of Its Objects and Purposes.

BY THE NEW YORK TIMES | FEB. 12, 1874

ST. LOUIS, FEB. 11. — The National Grange, to-day, after the transaction of some minor business, received the report of the Committee on Resolutions presented by Mr. Wardlow, of Florida, and adopted it unanimously. It is as follows:

Profoundly impressed with the truth that the National Grange of the United States should definitely proclaim to the world its general objects, we hereby unanimously make this declaration of the purposes of the Patrons of Husbandry:

First — United by the strong and faithful tie of agriculture, we mutually resolve to labor for the good of our order, and country, and mankind.

Second — We heartily indorse the motto: 'In essentials unity; in non-essentials liberty; in all things charity.'

Third — We shall endeavor to advance our cause by laboring to accomplish the following objects: To develop a better and higher manhood and womanhood among ourselves; to enhance the comforts and attractions of our homes, and strengthen our attachments to our pursuits; to foster mutual understanding and co-operation; to maintain inviolate our laws; to stimulate each other to hasten the good time coming; to reduce our expenses both individual and co-operative; to buy less and produce more, in order to make our farms self-sustaining; to diversify our crops, and crop no more than we can cultivate; to condense the weight of our exports, selling less in the bushel and more on hoof and in fleece; to systematize our work and calculate intelligently on probabilities; to discountenance the credit system, the mortgage system, the fashion system, and every other system tending to prodigality and bankruptcy; we propose meeting together, talking together, working together, buying together, selling together, and in general acting together for our mutual protection and the advancement the association may require; we shall avoid litigation as much as possible by arbitration in the grange; we shall constantly strive to secure entire harmony, good will, and vital brotherhood among ourselves, and to make our order perpetual. We shall earnestly endeavor to suppress personal, local, sectional, and national prejudices, all unhealthy rivalry, all selfish ambition. Faithful adherence to these principles will insure our mental, moral, social, and material advancement.

Fourth — Our business interests. We desire to bring producers and consumers, farmers and manufacturers, into the most direct and friendly relations possible. Hence we must dispense with a surplus of middle-men — not that we are unfriendly to them, but we do not need them. Their surplus and their exactions diminish our profits. We wage no aggressive warfare against any other interests whatever. On the contrary, all our acts and all our efforts, so far as business is concerned, are not only for the benefit of producers and consumers, but also for all other interests that tend to bring these two parties into speedy and economical contact. Hence we hold that transportation companies of every kind are necessary to our success; that their interests are intimately connected with our interests, and harmonious action is mutually advantageous. Keeping in view the first sentence in our declaration of principles of action, that individual happiness depends upon general prosperity, we shall therefore advocate for every State the increase in every practicable way of all facilities for transporting cheaply to the sea-board or between home producers and consumers all productions of our country. We adopt it as our fixed purpose to open out the channels in nature's great arteries that the lifeblood of commerce may flow freely. We are not enemies of railroads, navigable and irrigating canals, nor of any corporations that will advance our industrial interests, nor of any laboring classes. In our noble order there is no communism and no agrarianism. We are opposed to such spirit and management of any corporation or enterprise as tends to oppress the people and rob them of their just profits. We are not enemies to capital, but we oppose the tyranny of monopolies. We long to see the antagonism between capital and labor removed by common consent and by an enlightened statesmanship worthy of the nineteenth century. We are opposed to excessive salaries, high rates of interest, and exorbitant percentage profits in trade, as they greatly increase our burdens, and do not bear a proper proportion to the profits of the producers. We desire only self-protection, and the protection of every true interest offered by legitimate transactions, legitimate trade, and legitimate profits. We shall advance the cause of education among ourselves and for our children by all just means within our power. We especially advocate for our agricultural and industrial colleges that practical agriculture, domestic science, and all the arts which adorn the homo be taught in their courses of study.

Fifth — We emphatically and sincerely assert the oft-repeated truth taught in our organic law, that the grange, national, State, or subordinate, is not a political or party organization. No grange, if true to its obligations, can discuss political or religious questions, nor call political conventions, nor nominate candidates, nor even discuss their merits in its meetings; yet the principles we teach underlie all true politics, all true statesmanship, and if properly carried out will tend to purify the whole political atmosphere of our country; for we seek the greatest good to the greatest number. But we must always bear it in mind that no one by becoming a grange member gives up that inalienable right and duty which belongs to every American citizen to take a proper interest in the politics of his country. On the contrary, it is right for every member to do all in his power legitimately to influence for good the action of any political party to which he belongs; it is his duty to do all he can in his own party to put down bribery, corruption, and trickery, to see that none but competent, faithful, and honest men, who will unflinchingly stand by our industrial interests, are nominated for all positions of trust, and to have carried out the principles which should always characterize every grange member, that the office should seek the man, and not the man the office. We acknowledge the broad principle that difference of opinion is not crime, and hold that progress toward truth is made by differences of opinion, while the fault lies in the bitterness of controversy. We desire a proper equality, equity, and fairness; protection of the weak; restraint upon the strong — in short, justly-distributed burdens and justly-distributed power. These are American ideas, the very essence of American independence, and to advocate the contrary is unworthy of the sons and daughters of an American republic. We cherish the belief that sectionalism is, and of right should be, dead and buried with the past. Our work is for the present and the future in our agricultural brotherhood and its purposes. We shall recognize no North, no South, no East, no West. It is reserved by every patron, as his right as a freeman to affiliate with any party that will best carry out his principles.

Sixth — Ours being peculiarly a farmers' institution, we cannot admit all to our ranks; many are excluded by the nature of our organization; not because they are professional men or artisans or laborers, but because they have not a sufficiently direct interest in tilling or pasturing the soil, or may have some interest in conflict with our purposes; but we appeal to all good citizens for their cordial co-operation to assist us in our efforts toward reform, that we may eventually remove from our midst the last vestige of tyranny and corruption. We hail the general desire for fraternal harmony, equitable compromise, and earnest co-operation, as an omen of our future success.

Seventh — It shall be an abiding principle with us to relieve any of our oppressed and suffering brotherhood by any means at our command.

Last, but not least, we proclaim it among our purposes to inculcate a proper appreciation of the abilities and sphere of woman, as is indicated by admitting her to membership and position in our order. Imploring the continued assistance of our Divine Master to guide us in our work, we here pledge ourselves to faithful and harmonious labor for all future time to return by our united efforts to the wisdom, justice, fraternity, and political purity of our forefathers.

ADDRESS TO THE SOUTH.

A memorial to the Patrons of Husbandry in the cotton States was also presented, and unanimously adopted. It is an argument in favor of mixed husbandry in the South, instead of expending the energies of the people in raising a single crop. It says:

> *During the past seven years our cotton fields have added to the wealth of the world $2,000,000,000 and caused prosperity to smile upon every one who has handled our crops, save those who struggled for its production annually. The energies of the cotton planters have been exhausted in attempting to produce a maximum crop of a single staple, while quite as frequently he has reduced his means in supplying his necessary wants.*
>
> *A system based upon such a policy and producing such results must be radically wrong, and if persisted in will lead to bankruptcy and ruin. No people can ever become prosperous who are not self-sustaining. Our fertile soil, exhaustless mineral wealth, abundant water power, and general salubrious climate avails us nothing if annually we expend millions for subsistence. It is generally conceded that home-grown bread is cheaper than purchased supplies, and the observation of every planter is that those Southern farmers who live within themselves are more independent and less encumbered with debt than those who have relied solely upon the cotton crop. Were it otherwise, it is hazardous for any people to rely upon others for a supply of those articles which are necessary for their consumption.*

It then refers to the famine which more than once has occurred in India, owing to the efforts of the people to grow cotton to the exclusion of breadstuffs, and adds that

> *During the past year portions of Iowa, Minnesota, and Dakota have been invaded by grasshoppers, which destroyed every vestige of vegetation. Imagine your condition should a similar invasion become general in the Northwest. Couple with this idea the total failure of a cotton crop, either from the worm, from drought, or any other unavoidable cause, improbable as such visitations may appear. Have we the power to prevent them? And is it wise to subject ourselves to the possibility of becoming the victims of such calamities? Our wisest and safest policy is, as far as practicable, to produce at home our necessary supplies. Is there a farm in the South upon which this cannot be done, and at the same time produce an average cotton crop as the net result of the farmer's annual labors? We believe there is annually 4,000,000 of bales of cotton produced upon Southern soil. But what proportion of this vast amount is retained to*

indicate our prosperity? One-half of it is expended for necessary supplies, while the remainder is divided between labor and taxes. Hence, the cost of production has exceeded the value of the article produced. Shall this policy continue? Extensive cotton crops have evinced our unity of purpose and entailed poverty upon us unequally. Uniform adhesion to mixed husbandry would secure our recuperation. Cotton is a necessity, and the extent of that necessity can be calculated with exactness. If 3,500,000 bales are grown they will be consumed before another crop can be gathered, and a remunerative market price will be sustained by the consequent demand. If 4,500,000 bales are grown, the large marginal excess will control and depress the market. Alternatives for success are numerous, but we rely upon the single one of co-operating in the determination to subsist at home. With this end attained, there is no reason why we should not be the happiest, most independent, and prosperous people on earth.

The memorial is signed by the masters of State granges of South and North Carolina, Alabama, Mississippi, Florida, Arkansas, Louisiana, Georgia, and Tennessee, and was not only heartily approved by the Committee on Resolutions, but indorsed by every member of the National Grange.

The Great Railroad Strike

BY THE NEW YORK TIMES | JULY 21, 1877

IT IS NOT CERTAIN whether the feebleness of the West Virginia authorities, or a previous understanding among railroad employees, is at the bottom of the present general railroad strike. The disaffection, which is almost a rebellion, is spreading. From the Baltimore and Ohio Railroad, the trouble has been communicated to the Pittsburg and Fort Wayne Road, and to the Western Division of the Pennsylvania Railroad. The Western Division of the Erie Railway, with head-quarters at Hornellsville, is also in a state of insurrection, and there are rumors of similar difficulties on the Lake Shore Road. There are indications that the rebellion, if such we may call it, will affect most of the lines of railroad travel between the East and the West, and will seriously impede the movement of freight, which, at this time, is a matter of very great importance. If the strikers have been watching for an opportunity to strike when they could most seriously embarrass the roads, they have certainly hit on the right time. On several lines the passenger business is also interrupted or wholly suspended.

Generally speaking, the interruption of freight and passenger traffic would not be great if the strikers simply quit work without ado. But, as in the case of the Baltimore and Ohio Road, the strikers, not content with leaving their posts without warning, oppose the employment of men who would take their places, on any terms. This is the fatal weakness in the cause of the strikers. So far as heard from, in every case of insubordination, the issue is merely a question of wages. The firemen, engineers, and brakemen insist upon being paid a certain rate of wages. If they are not paid at this rate, they will not only quit work, but they will prevent others from taking their places on any terms. This is the tyranny of trades-unionism. There is something about it which is so antagonistic to the proverbial Anglo-Saxon love of fair play that most fair-minded men refuse at once all sympathy with the movement. If these so-called strikers can buy flour cheaper in Hornellsville than they can in Martinsburg, other things being equal, they will buy in Hornellsville. They would think it monstrous if anybody should attempt to compel them to buy dear flour when they can buy cheap flour. But they now, by force of arms, are trying to coerce railroad managers into employing them at rates which only they, the insurgents, are willing to accept.

Back of this, of course, lie many questions of the general management of railroads which cannot now be discussed. It is said, for example, that some of the men who struck on the Baltimore and Ohio Road have been earning a sum hardly sufficient for subsistence, and that the proposed reduction would leave them less wages than are adequate for the support of life. If this is true, it is deplorable, both as regards the condition of the men and the condition of the railroad corporation. It is no less deplorable that men needy enough to accept the reduced terms can be found. Just now, however, this is not the question. Ours is a free country, and the right of a man to get the best price he can for his work necessarily involves the converse of the proposition: a man or corporation may procure labor at the lowest possible cost. It is a pretty bad state of things when able-bodied men are obliged to work for three or four dollars a week, and pay extra expenses for board out of that. It is worse, however, when any considerable body of men, armed, belligerent, and violent, insist, at the pistol's muzzle, that they shall be paid certain wages, and that no man shall work for less at the peril of his life. As well might a striker go into a grocery store and insist, that the dealer sell him provisions at a certain price or have his head shot off.

As it is, the passenger and freight business on several great roads is impeded and confused by the unlawful acts of men who insist on being employed at certain wages. The corporation for which they have worked, though it may be ill-managed, and even dishonestly managed, is under no obligation to employ them at any rate of compensation which is not acceptable to both parties. But a strange hallucination seems to have seized the men, who fancy, because they have worked for the corporation, that they have a standing claim for employment at wages which they may dictate. The hallucination, unhappily, extends to many unthinking people outside of the ranks of the employed. In Baltimore, for example, a regiment marching to the scene of disorder was fired upon by a crowd of sympathizers with the strikers. The fire was returned and several people were killed. This is simply a revolt against law and order. How soon it will end, we cannot tell. That it can only end in one way is absolutely certain. The railroad companies are entitled to the protection of the law in the pursuit of their lawful business. Nobody has a claim upon them for employment. Any interference with them, or with their employees, must be prevented, whatever it may cost.

Bigots in a Legislature: The Farmers' Alliance Idea of Lawmaking.

BY THE NEW YORK TIMES | APRIL 1, 1891

RALEIGH, N. C., MARCH 31. — If anything can put life into the hitherto moribund Republican Party of North Carolina, the acts of the Legislature recently adjourned will have that effect. The members as a body were the most ignorant that ever assembled in the Capitol. They were narrow-minded, bigoted, niggardly, and without public spirit. They were wholly in favor of class legislation and were intensely hostile to all corporate interests. If six men had been taken from each house it would have been impossible for the remaining members to have prepared any legislation, because they could not have drawn the simplest bill.

The whole session of sixty days was a continued assault upon the railroads and other corporations. It was with the greatest difficulty that a charter for any purpose could be gotten through in any shape. The introduction of a bill to incorporate a railroad company was like shaking a red flag before an infuriated bull. Numbers of charters were rendered entirely useless to the incorporators by the senseless amendments of the committees.

The Farmers' Alliance organization of the State had a steering committee in this city during the session of the Legislature, and no legislation of a public character was acted upon until this committee had decided what should be done. The session was void of any measure of great public interest. The most important matter which came before the Legislature was the question of renewing the charter of the Petersburg and Weldon Railroad Company. This road is sixty miles long, but only twelve miles is within the State of North Carolina. This road was originally exempt from taxation, and the charter has just expired by limitation. It is owned and operated by what is known as the Atlantic Coast Line, a part of which line is the Wilmington and Weldon Railroad Company. The latter road's exemption from taxation is to continue in perpetuity until the dividends from the road reach 8 per cent on the capital stock. It is contended by the State that this amount has been exceeded for many years. This company is building branch lines and desires other legislation. It therefore offered to surrender its right to escape taxation on property valued at $3,000,000 and to pay in cash $12,000 in settlement of all back taxes. The taxes arising from the three millions of property would have brought in to the State $20,000 per year. This arrangement was to have continued for ten years and then the amount of taxes was to have been increased to $30,000 a year.

The bill as introduced to recharter the Petersburg and Weldon Company contained no exemption clause, but distinctly provided for taxation. The Alliance members were determined to force the Wilmington and Weldon Company to surrender its exemption from taxation, inasmuch as its charter was perpetual. On this line D. H. Rittenhouse, while private secretary to Col. L. L. Polk, President of the National Farmers' Alliance, had written a letter to the company reciting the fact that the Petersburg and Weldon charter had expired by limitation, and that its renewal would be resisted unless the exemption from taxation was surrendered. If the company desired to have a conference with him, it was more than probable that an arrangement could be made that would prove beneficial to both parties. This letter was read and denounced as an attempt to extort money, and it gave the Alliance people a deal of trouble to explain it away. Finally, the proposition of the Wilmington and Weldon Company was rejected, and the Petersburg and Weldon charter was renewed for only two years.

While attempts to coerce the Wilmington and Weldon Company were going on, another bill was introduced, (it passed the Senate on the Friday before the Legislature adjourned,) repealing the charters of the Seaboard and Roanoke, the Raleigh and Gaston, the Raleigh and Augusta Air Line, the Carolina Central, and the Georgia, Carolina and Northern Railroad Company. These are the roads that constitute the seaboard system, and of which Col. John M. Robinson of Baltimore is President. This system is now building a road from Monroe, N. C., to

Atlanta, Ga. Six millions of dollars will have been spent in the building of this new road and yet the repeal of its charter was treated as flippantly by the Legislature as if the repeal had applied to a toll gate. The excuse for this action was that the Seaboard and Roanoke and the Raleigh and Gaston Companies were exempt from taxation.

Such extraordinary legislation was never before heard of in this State. Senator Butler, who was the Alliance leader in all this warfare on the corporations, said in the Senate "that it would not be long before the people would sweep any court out of existence that would uphold the contract of the State with this company, and that the Dartmouth College case, as decided many years ago by the United States Supreme Court, was not the law now." The repealing act as it passed the Senate only failed in the House because no quorum was present.

The law establishing the Railroad Commission is an iron-clad measure, calculated to harass and injure the roads as much as possible. It contains many unjust features and was framed out of hostility to the railroad companies. The Commissioners are James W. Wilson, Chairman; Thomas W. Mason, and E. C. Beddingfield. The first is a railroad man of experience and is regarded as a fair and just man. The second is a good lawyer. The third is the Secretary of the Farmers' Alliance. The impression prevails that Mason and Beddingfield will overrule Wilson and that the iron-clad measure will receive an iron-clad construction.

The most stupendous blunder of all is the change of the revenue law, so as to tax incomes and profits derived from property not otherwise taxed, and incomes derived from salaries and fees. The new law taxes every cook who gets weekly wages; every farm hand and laborer who is paid by the month; every clerk who gets salary; every officer whose compensation is by a salary or by fees. On incomes and profits the tax is 1 per cent; on incomes arising from salaries and fees the tax is one-half of 1 per cent. The former exemption of $1,000 was stricken out. It is calculated that this tax will bring to the State $3,000,000 each year, more than twice the cost of running the State Government.

There is consternation in the Democratic camp over this law. The press of the State, without regard to politics, is unanimous in its condemnation of the measure. But what is very exasperating to the Alliance men and very amusing to all others is the fact that the tax on incomes does not reach any person who receives fees except public officers. The hated lawyers with all their fees are exempt, as are physicians and all other professional men.

Merchants are greatly dissatisfied at the failure to amend the revenue law. The law as it now stands requires every merchant and trader to give in on the 1st day of July and January the gross amount of his purchases made in and out of the State and to pay tax on the same. Whatever is left unsold on the 1st day of June is taxed as other personal property is.

Now as to the political effect of these matters of commission and omission: The railroad people and other corporate interests are thoroughly alarmed; the merchants are up in arms; the lawyers and professional men generally are proscribed by the Alliance, and they are hostile thereto; the various classes who are to be taxed on their incomes are thoroughly aroused. At least one-half of the Democratic Party is included in the several classes mentioned. Leading men representing each of these classes declare that they intend to promote an organization, independent in character if possible, to stamp out this new Communistic spirit. This can be done unless the Republicans undertake to take advantage of this condition in the Democratic Party by nominating a straight ticket for every office next year. There would be no trouble of this kind but for the Federal officers. They are opposed to any combination with the Democrats. The real leaders of the Republicans are in favor of any combination that has for its object the defeat of the Democratic Party as at present dominated and controlled by the Alliance.

The Republican opposition to the present system of county government — designed to keep counties with negro majorities from having negro officers — has enabled the Democratic Party to draw the color line and appeal to the white men to stand together and prevent negro domination. The people have heeded this appeal, and the Republicans have been defeated at every election on this issue. It is now proposed by the Republicans to abandon the fight on county government and to pledge themselves not to disturb the present mode of allowing the Legislature to select the various county officials should they obtain control of the State. The leaders also say that the Republicans will not nominate any negro to office in this State. In this way they hope that the Democratic element, which is now dissatisfied, will form an independent movement and bolt the regular Democratic organization next year. The Republicans do not propose to take any part in this movement other than to support the ticket that may be put out by the independent Democrats.

The movement will take shape unless the Alliance nominates candidates for President and Vice President. Should that be done, the Republican office holders will try to hold the negroes in line.

There is a very strong and growing sentiment among the white Republicans, especially in the western counties, to call a State Convention and organize a White Man's Republican Party. Every white Republican declares that it is impossible ever to win on present lines.

It is believed to be more than possible at this time that the Alliance organization will prove to be the means whereby the solid South will be broken up and the dominant party will be composed of Democrats and Republicans and be known as the Democratic-Conservative Party. And in this organization the negro will be protected in his right to vote, but he will not be appointed or elected to any office. The White Republicans of the western counties say that it is of no use to start this movement unless it is a cardinal principle that no negro is to be appointed or elected to office.

Coxey Without His 'Army': He Comes to New-York as a Horse-Dealer.

BY THE NEW YORK TIMES | APRIL 22, 1894

"J. S. COXEY, Massillon, Ohio, Room 271," on the register of the Sturtevant House recorded yesterday the arrival in this city of the leader of the Commonweal.

Mr. Coxey is the proprietor of the Coxey Stock Farm, at Massillon, and President of the J. S. Coxey Good Roads Association of the United States. He came to New-York to attend the sale at the Madison Square Garden of a consignment of trotting stock from his farm, and to treat for privileged transportation, not only for his "main army," which he left at Hagerstown, Ind., Friday, but for accretions from all points up to May 1.

To this end Mr. Coxey, having registered at the hotel at 11 A. M., breakfasted and went to the office of the Trunk Line Association to see Commissioner Farmer. Failing to see Commissioner Farmer, he visited Tattersalls, at Fifty-fifth Street and Seventh Avenue, to see how his consignment of stock was getting along.

Here Mr. Coxey was greeted by many experts in road stock, including Hamilton Busby and Majors Abercrombie and Quinby, and he went to luncheon at the Hotel Grenoble. He would not talk of the Commonweal then, but showed to a reporter for The New-York Times his string of horses and expatiated on their "points." His stock consists of seven trotters, a pacer, and a pony.

Mr. Coxey is short and wiry. Exposure has bronzed a broad and intelligent face, and his bearing is that of an active man who is in touch with his convictions. He wore a brown Fédora hat, a neat suit of blue-gray, and a black overcoat, and was entirely at his ease.

After looking at his horses, Mr. Coxey went to the café of the Grenoble to talk about the Commonwealers.

"I got away from the main army," said the "General," "at Hagerstown, Md., yesterday, after paying 98 cents toll for the horses of the contingent." I rejoin the main army at Ridgeville, Md., Tuesday. I shall wait here over Monday evening to see my horses sold. They will be the property of the highest bidder.

"Now, as to the Army of the Commonweal. The main army will march to Washington and meet there other divisions that will march in and a multitude that will have come by rail.

"All will march and assemble and demonstrate to give to the American public an object lesson in political economy. We will rivet public attention on this relief question.

"The labor of 4,000,000 men has been lost to the Commonweal of America, and the Commonweal during the past nine months has lost $3,000,000,000 through this loss of services. It would have been wise politics to have utilized that labor and have paid for it by money issued through the Government.

"I mean that these men should have been employed on public improvements and paid by money coining from the Government, in payment of services rendered in the shape of public improvements.

"Take it another way. Suppose the Non-Interest-Bearing Bond bill now before Congress passed. The people are most interested in how to get work for the unemployed and, incidentally, in good roads. The City of New-York has a bank account in the City of Washington, subject to call to half the assessment value of its entire property.

"By issuing non-interest-bearing twenty-five-year bonds upon the whole wealth of the city, to make all the public improvements that are needed here, New-York would get the improvements and employ the unemployed.

"The City of New-York would pay back all this with 4 per cent, but the money would come to this city at cost — that is to say, the Government would simply retain 1 per cent, for the actual cost of creating the money. Thus the City of New-York could make all her public improvements that are needed without paying one cent of tribute in the shape of interest to any one.

"This is the law we are endeavoring to have passed in the District of Columbia:

> *Be It Enacted by the Senate and House of Representatives, in Congress Assembled:*
>
> *That whenever any State, Territory, county, township, municipality, or incorporated town or village deems it necessary to make any public improvements, it shall deposit with the Secretary of the Treasury of the United States a non-interest-bearing twenty-five-year bond, not to exceed one-half the assessed valuation of the property in said State, Territory, county, township, municipality, or incorporated town or village, and said bond to be retired at the rate of 4 per cent per annum.*
>
> *Whenever the foregoing section of this act has been complied with, it shall be mandatory upon the Secretary of the Treasury of the United States to have engraved and printed Treasury notes in the denominations of one, two, five, ten, and twenty dollars each, which shall be a full legal tender for all debts, public and private, to the face value of said bond, and deliver to said State, Territory, county, township, municipality, or incorporated town or village, 99 per cent of said notes, and retain 1 per cent for expense of engraving and printing same.*

"Now, as to the 'army,' so called. There are no restrictions on recruits, except insistance in the matter of good behavior and American citizenship — nothing on the old lines of Know-Nothingism or bars based on nationality or religion. There is no 'native-born' requisition to be met.

"Of course, we have to have faith in the statements the applicants make. We cannot exercise deeper scrutiny. We have to be satisfied with what they say.

"As to the demonstration at Washington, it is hard to say what numbers of adherents we may expect, but the cause grows like an epidemic. It is all over the country.

"I believe that when we enter Washington my followers will number 10,000, and there may be as many more who will march there under different leaders. There may be from 100,000 to 500,000 go there by train.

LIBRARY OF CONGRESS PRINTS AND PHOTOGRAPHS DIVISION

"More Money! Less Misery! Good Roads!" Coxey's army approaching Washington.

"At any rate, our 'object lesson' will be imposing. It is a necessity of the times. It may be the averting of trouble, this pacific demonstration. We have heard much talk lately of the West and South being arrayed against the money bags of the East.

"Any way, the employment of the unemployed is the burning question of the day. We've got to face it, and meet it, and dispose of it. Philanthropically speaking, it is a duty; politically speaking, it is a necessity.

"As to the expenses so far? Well, we get donations of food and of clothing and some money. What disbursements we need I have to make, and I have no financial 'backer.' We are not looking to anybody for reimbursement. We are not with or against any political party. We have adherents who are both Republicans and Democrats.

"My 'army' is not a collection of 'bummers.' No man in it but is closely watched, and punishment for begging, intimidation, and peculation is swift and decisive.

"The newspapers poke fun at us, but we keep as clean as the newspaper correspondents. There is no smuggling of rum into camp, for instance. Take the case of a man who started in our ranks from Massillon. At Uniontown, last week, he was warned for inebriety. At Cumberland he erred again, and was locked up. I thanked the Sheriff, and ordered the man kept off the boats. He hid away, and I found him with the mules on the towpath, and he was compelled to leave the contingent. You'd be astonished to see how the men follow the line of ethics drawn up to keep the Commonwealers fit to represent their cause."

Mr. Coxey spoke as a man having the courage of his convictions, and appeared pleased to exhibit the nine badges of the Commonweal, which include those of "Group Number," "Commune Marshal," "Surgeon Marshal," "President," "Honorary," "Commissary Marshal," "Commonweal Marshal," "Canton Marshal," and "Community Marshal." All are printed on white muslin, and; while bearing different devices, have the motto, "Peace on Earth, Good Will Toward Men, but Death to Interest on Bonds."

Bryan the Demagogue: Career of the Man Who Will Lead the Silver Fanatics.

BY THE NEW YORK TIMES | JULY 11, 1896

WILLIAM JENNINGS BRYAN enjoys the distinction of being the youngest man ever placed in nomination for the Presidency by a great political party in this country. He has passed by only one year the Constitutional age for eligibility for the Presidential office. He was born in Salem, Marlon County, Ill., March 19, 1860. His father was a public man. He had come from Virginia when a youth, and, after a course at college and at law, he settled at Salem. The district sent him to the State Senate, and he became a Judge of the Circuit Court of Illinois. The Salem home was a farm. Several acres were always reserved for romping by the children, of whom there were nine. William was the fourth. He attributes his robust health to his early life and to the vacations on the farm. Until he was ten years old he was taught at home by his mother. His first ambition was to become a Baptist minister, but his preference switched over to the law before he began to attend school and that determination remained unchanged. After a few years at public school he entered Whipple Academy at Jacksonville, Ill., and at the age of seventeen years he was admitted to Illinois College, also at Jacksonville.

He took much interest in debating and declamation. In 1880 he represented his college in a State contest at Galesburg, and won second prize with an oration on "Justice." His father died that year, but William contrived to finish his college course and to study law. He was an athlete in college, and in his last year he won a prize for a standing jump of 12 feet 4 inches.

While at Jacksonville he met Miss Mary E. Baird, who attended the female academy at that place. Her father was a merchant at Berry, Ill.

They were graduated from their respective schools in June, 1881, she being the valedictorian of her class.

When he went to the Union College of Law at Chicago, Miss Baird decided that if she was to be a lawyer's wife she ought to know something of that profession. Accordingly, she took up the study, and a few years later, when they moved to Nebraska, she was admitted to the bar. She had no thought of practicing, but she wished to be fitted to assist her husband. He has always cheerfully acknowledged that her aid and advice have been invaluable to him. He remained at the law school for two years, at the same time studying in the office of Lyman Trumbull. He returned to Jacksonville to practice, and was married there to Miss Baird Oct. 4, 1884. In 1887 one of his clients sent him into Kansas and Nebraska to look after some land suits. He visited Lincoln, where his law-school chum, A. R. Talbot, resided. The place pleased him, and when Talbot offered him a partnership he accepted it. His family demurred, except his father-in-law, Mr. Baird, a Republican, who said he would be glad to go, because Nebraska was so strongly Republican that Bryan would have to keep out of politics. He soon made headway in Lincoln, and when his family joined him, early in 1888, he had many friends to welcome them.

His public career began in Lincoln, when the Democrats, July 30, 1890, nominated him for Congress. He said he got the nomination because no one else wanted it. Already he had become known in politics from having stumped the district in 1988 for J. Sterling Morton for Congress. The same year he was a delegate to the State Convention, and declined the nomination for Lieutenant Governor. He had also made a few tariff speeches, and was regarded as a well-informed young man. When he stood for Congress he wrote a platform for free wool, free lumber, free salt, free sugar, free iron ore, and free coal, and he challenged his opponent, W. J. Connell, one of the best Republican speakers in Nebraska, and then member of Congress from the district, to joint debate. The tariff was the only issue, both men being strong for free silver. The district included Lincoln and Omaha. Connell was well liked in both places, and Bryan's friends criticised the proposition for joint debates. He persisted, however, and the debates attracted great attention. The issue of them, was that Bryan overcame an adverse majority in a Republican stronghold, by making the tariff the issue before the people of his district. He succeeded in Congress, by 6,700 majority, a Republican who had been elected by 3,400 majority.

Bryan received the largest majority any candidate ever had in the district. He went to Congress in December, 1891, was appointed by Speaker Crisp to the Ways and Means Committee, and, March 12, 1892, he made the tariff speech in the House which called the attention of the country to him as a rising man.

The Republicans reapportioned Nebraska for the next campaign and able and popular men were nominated against Bryan by the Republicans and the Populists. Efforts of the Republican State Committee were also concentrated against him. Bryan called for joint debates, canvassed the district thoroughly, and was elected again. His party otherwise suffered defeat, but he ran 5,800 votes ahead of his ticket, and won by a small plurality. He served again on the Ways and Means Committee and devoted himself assiduously to the preparation of the Wilson Tariff bill. At the extra session of Congress in 1893 he was conspicuous in opposition to the repeal of the Sherman silver purchase law.

He took a prominent part also in advocating the income tax, the coining of the seigniorage, and the Anti-Option bill. Election of United States Senators by the people was espoused by him. The Carlisle Currency bill, the Morgan-Belmont bond contract, railway pooling bills, and other important measures engaged his active interest.

Early in 1894 he informed his constituents that they must not consider him a candidate for a third term in Congress. The State Convention of that year, following his project for an election of United States Senators by the people, named him for the Senate by unanimous vote of the delegates. He chose to enter the campaign on general issues and gave little attention to candidates for the Legislature. He challenged Gov. McKinley and John M. Thurston to meet him in joint debate on the

THE NEW YORK TIMES

William Jennings Bryan, nominated for President by the Chicago Convention.

tariff. Gov. McKinley declined. Mr. Thurston was clearly worsted by him, both at Lincoln and Omaha. There were 15,000 persons at the Omaha meeting. Although Mr. Bryan gave little attention to legislative candidates, the people were allowed to express by ballot their preferences for United States Senator. There are 50,000 Democrats in Nebraska. More than 80,000 voters indicated him as their choice, and only 1,866 voted for Mr. Thurston. The Legislature ignored this expression.

On his return home from Washington, in March, 1895, the people of Lincoln gave him a reception, with bands, parades, and exercises, at the Opera House. The day he returned he was thirty-five years old, and the turnout of citizens, regardless of party, gave to that birthday a demonstrative ending. He said he intended to devote himself to his profession. Calls for his services as a speaker for silver were too strong for him to resist, however, and he has given much time in that field, speaking in Ohio and nearly all the States westward and in the South. He has also expressed himself vigorously on that and other public topics in the columns of The Omaha World-Herald, of which he was for a time the editor.

He has a pleasant home in Lincoln, his family consisting of his wife and three children. The family attends the Presbyterian Church, to which denomination Mr. Bryan was formally admitted when fourteen years old.

It was his speech in reply to Senator Hill in the convention that undoubtedly secured for Mr. Bryan the nomination of the Chicago Convention. The securing of such a prize by such means has probably only one precedent in our history, namely, the nomination of Garfield in 1880, when he attended the convention of his party as the representative of John Sherman. It was Garfield's general tact and discretion in the discharge of his trust, however, that impressed that convention into believing that the agent would be a more eligible candidate than his principal, and that made the delegates forget for the time the ugly blots upon his record. It was by no means any single burst of eloquence such as that with which the Nebraska Populist electrified the Chicago

Convention. In fact, Garfield did not, as Bryan distinctly does, belong to the class of electric orators, who have the psychological, one might perhaps say the physiological gift of arousing the enthusiasm of a sympathetic and of conciliating the sympathies of a hostile audience.

There never was a more propitious moment for such an orator than that which fell to Bryan. The minority had just been pleased and the majority had just been depressed and mortified by the appearance, as the champion of free silver, of Tillman, whose manner and whose matter were those of a recently emancipated, untaught, and underbred cracker, whose ruling motive was revenge upon the better-bred and better-taught people of his own neighborhood and acquaintance, who had held him and his ancestors in a subjection almost as degrading as slavery. It was this vindictive freedman who had undertaken to be the mouthpiece of an assemblage of which only a small part could really accept such as him for their spokesman, of which the greater part was composed of freeborn American citizens, as little used to bully as to cringe.

After that came the shrewd, acute, lunge-like dissection by Senator Hill of the platform recklessly thrown together by the penmen of the motley crew, and undertaking to combine their incompatible heresies. The minority had indicated its position. The majority felt exposed, crestfallen, and humiliated. And it was at that critical point that there appeared to give articulate expression to their inarticulate sentiments a man who had the air and manner of a freeman, and not of a spiteful freedman who, moreover, seemed to speak with the fervor of conviction, who enabled them to hold up their heads a little after Tillman had shamed them and after Hill had showed them how they had shamed themselves. Bryan's was the eloquence of "the many long-dumb voices." It was the expression in safe generalities of human sympathy with human trials and human sufferings. In safe generalities, for it was the fervent cry of the patient. It was the eloquent description of his symptoms, and it did not go into enough detail about the patient's own prescriptions of a remedy to show how utterly foolish and futile they were. No wonder that the delegates voted so readily for a man who had done so much for their own self-love!

But, in truth, Bryan as an orator is on quite a different plane not only from the snapping spite of Tillman, but from the perfunctory and florid oratory of the "Col. Bungstarters" of the convention, from the empty rhetoric of Senator Daniel, which preceded his speech, and from the equally empty rhetoric of Senator Vest's presentation of Bland, which succeeded it. In the first place, it is not empty. He had something to say, as he generally has had. In the second place, he has, as Clarendon admitted of John Hampden, a "strange power of making himself believed," at least of convincing his hearer that he believes himself. He occasionally overdoes it, as in that speech which excited the House of Representatives to unsympathetic laughter by declaring that he would willingly lay down his life to prevent the repeal of the Silver Purchase act. But even about that it is not necessary to accuse the speaker of conscious insincerity. A man who has the oratorical temperament will be carried very far by his own momentum, and even further by the assurance of a sympathetic audience, until, as in this instance, he may return its sympathy.

But upon the whole and upon a study of the published speeches of Mr. Bryan, one gets the impression that, if he is to be called a demagogue he is a convinced demagogue. The history of the French Revolution shows that this is the most formidable type of all. By the way, it is not true, as has been said, that his oratory is of the kind that involves careful preparation, that he is capable of the "good continued speech, without a good speech of interlocution," which, according to Bacon, "shows slowness." To say nothing of the joint debates in which Mr. Bryan has been so uniformly successful, the speech in the convention would have disproved that. It could not have been "cut and dried," for the speaker took up the points of Senator Hill, and traversed them one by one in a manner which argued Mr. Bryan was probably not a very valuable member of the Ways and Means Committee. His speeches are not to be compared with those of Mr. Wilson, either in a grasp of economic principles or in mastery of commercial detail. They are evidently the work of a clever man, who has "crammed" for the occasion, and who has started with the general conviction that protection is of no benefit to the farmer, for whom Mr. Bryan always seems to himself to hold a brief. But in the matter of readiness, of the kind which a successful advocate possesses, they show no deficiency — on the contrary, a rather exceptional proficiency. This is even more strikingly illustrated in the speech in favor of the Anti-Option bill, delivered in June, 1894, in the House. Nobody can read the speech without seeing that it is much more the effusion of sentiment than of reason. The speaker does not understand the economical laws that underlie the question. He was subjected, however, to such sharp and searching interruptions that half the report is taken up with them. His replies were always ready and superficially pat, and showed the lawyer's skill in great perfection. But the "nagging" was so persistent and so pertinent, especially on the part of Mr. Goldzier of Illinois, that the speech was by no means a triumph for the orator. He was at last driven to declaring that the onus of proving that the bill was unnecessary rested upon its opponents. "It is necessary for the people who are opposed to this bill to prove that gambling does not affect prices."

In the course of his speech on the Wilson bill, Mr. Bryan made use of an illustration to show the futility of trying to legislate against natural laws, which we may leave to him to reconcile with the "demands" of his platform:

> *We had a man in Nebraska who professed to be able to bring rain, and after there had been a short dry spell this man was engaged by a few citizens to call down a refreshing shower. He was to receive $500 for his services provided an inch of rain fell within four days. He went to work, and within four days the rain came — an inch of it. Not only did rain come, but wind came with it, and blew down signs and broke off trees, so that the citizens threatened to sue him for bringing wind with the rain. But when the man tried to collect his $500, the men who had employed him said: "It not only rained here, but all over Nebraska, and we do not believe that you caused the rain at all. It was a natural rain." And they refused to pay him. And yet there was a man who was hired to bring*

rain. He tried to bring rain. The rain came within the promised time, and exceeding the promised amount; yet they doubted his being the cause. What a rainmaker a protectionist would be!

It will have been seen that the effect of Mr. Bryan's speeches is the effect rather of rhetoric than, of logic, and, rather than either, of that strange power of making himself believed "which can scarcely come but of belief." He represents, intellectually and morally, the least discreditable elements of the Populist craze. Whether that fact makes him the strongest candidate who could have received the nomination he has so unexpectedly and fortuitously obtained may be questioned; but assuredly he is not the weakest.

Furor Over Mary Lease: The Kansas Woman Orator Has a Crowd in Cooper Union.

BY THE NEW YORK TIMES | AUG. 11, 1896

THE NOVELTY OF a woman orator drew out a big crowd to hear Mrs. Mary Ellen Lease of Kansas at Cooper Union Hall last night. There were a great many women in the crowd, and a number of them were on the stage. Men took off their coats in the hot room and the speakers and audience suffered terribly from the heat. Fans and lemonade that was more cool than sour sold at a premium.

Despite the intense heat, the enthusiasm of the audience was thoroughly aroused by the woman talker from the West, and they cheered, laughed, and hissed by turns. There was a goodly number in the crowd that did not like some of her utterances, but the mass of the meeting was with her, and cheered her almost continually.

Among those on the stage were noticed David Rousseau, Gideon Tucker, Edward King, Charles Hoadley, Senator Jones, and Clarence Todd Davis.

As is usual, there were a number of speeches that the crowd did not want to hear. They came to listen to Mrs. Lease, and were a little disappointed and out of patience as speaker followed speaker, touching on everything that has been mentioned in the campaign, from British gold and British Tories down to the poor farmers of the West, and the enslavement of them by the aforesaid Tories and gold of England.

James R. Buchanan of the Knights of Labor opened the oratorical banquet. He said he was embarrassed to stand as an expounder of the cause and principles of William J. Bryan. While Mr. Bryan, he said, stood apparently on a Democratic platform, he represented a rejuvenated Democracy. He wanted a change, and McKinleyism offered no change. "Who stands behind McKinley at this time?" he asked. A voice replied, "His creditors." He said the Republicans are trying to array the factory and the mill laborers against the farmers, whom he called "the mud sills of our country." He was a labor-union man. Every union man should be a politician — "and a Socialist!" shouted a man in the audience.

Louis Ficke of the Lithographers' Union made a short and embarrassed speech, in which he recommended some free-silver books for the audience to read, and asked for contributions to carry on the campaign.

W. P. St. John, who was referred to by Mr. Buchanan as "the one millionaire in our midst," made a few remarks on fifty-three-cent dollars. He said he was looking for them with a microscope. Paper is not money, he said, but a mere promise of money. The old Continental currency had been almost worthless because it had no real money behind it. Greenbacks had been depreciated because the people lost confidence in the ability of the Government to redeem them.

This somewhat candid statement that paper cannot be money did not arouse the enthusiasm of a crowd that had been told in the same hall a few weeks before by the great Populistic Democratic leader, Tillman, that paper was money, and that the "stamp" was able to make anything money.

After Mr. St. John's speech the Secretary read the resolutions to be adopted. These resolutions set forth that they are adopted by "the workingmen and other independent citizens composing this mass meeting, called to give public testimony to their support of William J. Bryan and the principles involved In his candidacy."

As to the connection formed with Populists, the resolutions say:

"We applaud the patriotic and progressive spirit which animated the great mass of delegates who sat in the Democratic and Populist National Convention of this year. Though the formal declarations of these two bodies are not identical, they are both founded upon principles which mean the protection of the welfare of the producers both of the city and the country.

"We stand for the supremacy of law, equal in its application to rich and poor. The epithet 'Anarchist' which the agents of organized capitalism so profusely apply to us, we hold to be most appropriately applied to these who corrupt our City Council and State Legislatures for the theft of public franchises; who use our Circuit Courts for the imprisonment, without trial by jury, of labor's representatives; who prevail upon our Supreme Court to overthrow a just law taxing capital for a small share of the expenses of Government, and who debauch our President into forging issues of bonds, upon flagrant terms, in violation alike of decency and of the plain intent of the law.

"We look with suspicion upon the sudden affection for the laborer lately expressed by those journals and men long known as the special agents of organized capitalism. We hear unheedingly their absurd warnings that free silver would mean a benefit to the capitalist at the expense of the laborer. Whether learned or unlearned, the instinctive sense of the laborer is that if such a result were to follow free coinage, the Danas, the Godkins, and the Whitneys would be its most enthusiastic champions."

Among the "demands" are the following:

"There has come to be in this Nation a question whether the Government controls the telegraphs, the railroads, and the banks, or the telegraphs, the railroads, and the banks control the Government. We demand the public ownership of the means of transmission of news and of transportation, and the replacement of bank issues of currency by Government currency solely.

"We demand the free coinage of silver at 16 to 1, and the reissue of the greenbacks locked up in the Treasury through the illegal bond issues. The need of an expansion of the currency to revive industry and restore full employment to all capable and willing workers imperative and immediate.

"We also demand a graduated income tax, the abrogation of Government by injunction, the reference to the people of all important laws, the establishment by the Government of postal savings banks for the safe deposit of the savings of the people, and we protest against the Presidential use of the military in aid of law-defying corporations."

On the issue of the campaign they declare:

"From our point of view the issue this year is clearer and more definite than it has ever been before in the history of our country. On the one side are all the exploiters of wealth, standing for doctrines that mean the final extinction of the liberties of the people. It rests with us to present to the enemies of democratic institutions a united and unwavering front, so that this Government, created 'of the people, by the people, for the people, shall not perish from the earth.' "

The resolutions were adopted amid applause.

Mrs. Mary Ellen Lease was next introduced to the audience. She was received with a wild hurrah, clapping of hands, stamping of feet, and cries of all sorts, so that she could not speak for several minutes.

She said among other things:

"I accept this splendid greeting and this splendid audience as evidence that there is no Mason and Dixon's line between the East and West, and that the people of the East and of the West are battling against a common foe. Patriotism, not patronage, is the watchword of the hour. We are at the beginning of a period of reformation and readjustment. Its problems are rendered difficult, not only because of our ignorance, but because they are new in the history of the race.

"Centuries ago the battle of liberty had been fought out against real Kings. After they have secured their civil and religious liberties, they are now trying to take peaceable possession of their own.

"The grand principles of Socialism," she began, but was interrupted by a howl of applause from the crowd. When she could be heard again, she continued: "The principles of Socialism cannot live under the tyranny of Old World royalty or of British gold."

She stated that the United States was the most prosperous nation in the world. But the giants of machinery invented by American genius had driven away human laborers.

"Increased production," she said, "without increased consumption, is valueless."

"The present condition of affairs is a parody upon the religion of Jesus Christ." She said that the condition is such as to lead men to perjure their souls in order to save their bonds from taxation.

"Under our present condition, an American millionaire pays $2,000,000 for an impoverished French Count and it permits him to give a breakfast costing thousands of dollars when hundreds are starving in this city. This condition makes it possible for a daughter of the Vanderbilts to pay millions for a scion of the British peerage whose history would be a disgrace to our civilization."

She denounced the British aristocracy and royal family, called the Prince of Wales a debaucher, and said that Victoria was no longer regarded as made even of common clay, but of common mud. The divine rights of Kings had disappeared before the use of gunpowder on the field, which made the royalty and the common people of the world equal.

"The James Brothers and the Daltons were limited in their methods. If they had operated on as large a scale as the millionaires of the country, they could have built universities like Rockefeller, or serve the people in the Senate of the United States like that old robber John Sherman."

"Redemption money and interest-bearing bonds," she said, "are the curse of civilization. We are paying tribute to the Rothschilds of England, who are but the agents of the Jews."

The remainder of her speech was a virulent and eloquent attack on England, denouncing the treatment of Ireland, Egypt, India, and declaring that the British are enslaving the people of this country through gold standards and interest-bearing bonds.

Her speech was received with close attention, and was heartily applauded.

After it, the Secretary asked the audience to sign resolutions that had been placed in the seats. These resolutions contained the following statements:

"With free coinage of silver the price of silver will advance to $1.29 an ounce in the United States, and a like price, with exchange added, in London.

"There is nowhere in the world any available surplus of silver. Its use absorbs it, always has, always will.

"When the United States remonetizes it, other nations must follow in defense of their trade and investments."

The meeting adjourned after three cheers for "Mrs. Lease and Bryan." Nothing was said at the meeting of Sewall.

Roosevelt's Issues: Ground on Which He Will Stand in Campaign.

SPECIAL TO THE NEW YORK TIMES | FEB. 13, 1904

Panama policy, coal strike attitude, "open shop" position, and Northern Securities case to be emphasized.

WASHINGTON, FEB. 12. — President Roosevelt intends to make the issues on which he will run in the coming campaign, and has already outlined them. They are four in number.

There will, of course, be others, but these are the ones on which the President intends to make his fight. No doubt they will be inserted in the platform by his friends, but in any case they will be emphasized in his letter of acceptance and in every other way open to Mr. Roosevelt by which he can shape the campaign policy. These are the issues on which the President will stand:

1. The Administration's policy in the Panama matter.

2. The attitude toward corporations taken in the Northern Securities case.

3. The attitude toward labor shown in the Miller "open shop" case.

4. The attitude toward the differences between capital and labor taken in the settlement of the great anthracite coal strike.

It will be observed that all these, taken together, make Mr, Roosevelt himself the great issue, for every one of these four achievements was his.

Two of them are labor issues. The settlement of the coal strike, the President thinks, made him popular with the union labor element, and he is willing to rest his case on that. On the other hand, the Miller case was a square declaration for the open shop, and the President's friends think that, properly understood, it should show employers that there is nothing extreme or radical in his attitude on the labor question.

The selection of these two labor planks is held to mean that the President's campaign attitude on the labor question will be that of resistance of the extreme attitudes of both capital and labor, and that he will take the position of an Executive who will not permit unwarranted aggression by either. The open shop and the victory of labor in a great strike convey, his friends think, this lesson.

The Northern Securities case, in the opinion of the President, makes the trust issue clear enough. By it the Republicans expect to steal all the Democratic thunder on the trust question. In Congress and elsewhere, the Democrats have for four years been ringing the changes on the trust question, except in the House, where more attention has been paid to the tariff. All this ammunition, it is held, will be useless in the face of a Republican campaign vigorously conducted on the Northern Securities issue.

As to the Panama issue, the President is confident that his policy in that matter is highly popular and sure to be approved by the people, and he is eager to put it to the test. He thinks the opposition to it is no more serious than what has assailed other great steps forward in the development of the United States, such as the Louisiana Purchase, for example. He is confident that the Panama Canal is a thing desired by Americans, and that his policy in getting it will be approved. His foreign policy he considers one of the strong cards in his hand.

This selection of issues, Mr. Roosevelt's friends says, will leave the Democrats practically without a gun to fire. They cannot make a convincing presentation of the trust matter, it is declared, if the Northern Securities issue is vigorously insisted upon, and will be on the unpopular side if they attack the coal strike settlement. If they denounce Mr. Roosevelt as an enemy of labor in the Miller open shop case the President's friends say that the coal strike matter will be a sufficient answer. Not only would an attack on the Panama policy prove unpopular, it is urged, but the Democrats themselves are divided on that issue.

In the House the Democrats have avoided all these issues and have sought to move upon and occupy the abandoned Republican ground of reciprocity and tariff revision. They are using the ideas of Blaine and McKinley, and are working hard to make a successful flank movement upon the Republicans.

If the Democrats of the Nation should follow the lead of Mr. Williams and his Congressional followers the President might have to shift his ground somewhat and fight on the issues made by the Democrats. His friends think, however, that there is little danger of that. They think that Mr. Gorman, not Mr. Williams, is likely to shape the Democratic platform and that they will have no difficulty in making the fight on the four planks outlined by Mr. Roosevelt.

CHAPTER 2

Mass Politics and Fascism After the First World War

Populism returned after World War I, as social upheaval was followed by the Great Depression. The political movements of communism and fascism channeled popular unrest, using mass media and public demonstrations. These movements waged a three-way struggle with established governments in Europe, while American populists considered both ideologies. The United States eventually rejected them, defeating their adherents in Europe and at home. After World War II, fascism briefly lived on in Latin America.

Bolshevism Seen as New Religion

BY HAROLD WILLIAMS | JAN. 11, 1918

PETROGRAD, JAN, 9. — The Christmas holidays passed off quietly. The Russians of all classes stubbornly celebrated Christmas, despite snowstorms and the secularism of the present rulers. I have talked with many persons during the last few days. All were trying to read the riddle of Russia's future.

One writer with a restless probing mind, who was very keen on war and who assured me at the time of the democratic conference that the Russian State had collapsed, now declares that Bolshevism is a new religion. He is not a Bolshevik, but he is extremely interested. He compared Bolshevism as a mass movement with early Christianity, and there certainly are points of semblance, for instance, in the fanatical sectarianism and marked apocalyptic tendency.

My friend admitted that Bolshevism as a religion could not last because its aims are purely material, and its material basis would inevitably fail; but he considered that while it did last it would work extraordinary changes.

It is certainly true that Bolshevism as a mass movement has an almost religious quality. I remembered a little railway man who assured me in almost Biblical phrase that Bolshevism made glad the soul, though he was doubtful of the ultimate results, and none who knows the history of Russian dissent can have failed to notice that many of the emotional tendencies of the extreme sects seem to have combined with great force in this new movement.

Given the idea of Bolshevism as good tidings to the poor, as a short cut to an earthly paradise, its infectious character and the power that lies in its childish irrationalism become intelligible. Even that extraordinary jargon with which the Bolshevist writers and speakers disfigure the Russian language, seems to have on the masses the effect of a strange ritual language in the Church service.

ANOTHER POINT OF VIEW.

Another friend, more skeptical, regards Bolshevism simply as an unwholesome product of decomposition. The revolution, he says, was not a revolution, but simply the breakdown of the enfeebled and antiquated state organism under the strain of war. The mob let loose from all authority and restraint is simply plunging on in its instinctive, restless way in search of a new equilibrium. If the war goes on much longer, he says, the same thing will happen in other States, and the explosive forces that lurk in our artificial civilization will be revealed.

He thought it very possible that when the elemental movement in Russia had spent itself and Russia was reorganized on a new basis the new State, or group of States, would be conservative and very bourgeois, and Russia as the centre of order would calmly survey the upheavals in western Europe.

Russian socialism he considered was a mere phase, a convenient label for the confused multitude of incoherent aspirations now released and revealed.

The excesses of the present movement must not, he said, be set down to any peculiar savagery of the Russian people.

The excited mob, freed from restraint, is always brutal, and under similar conditions the mob in the industrial countries of the West would probably display more violence.

An American present agreed. He remarked that considering the extent of the country and complete absence of restraint there was extraordinarily little violence, and added that a mob lynching a negro in the Southern States was just as horribly brutal as a Russian mob pogroming or lynching an officer.

OTHERS TAKE GLOOMY VIEW.

Other Russians I found were plunged in extreme pessimism and full of shame and loathing for the excesses of their own people and for the complete breakdown of all ideas of honor and right. They foresaw nothing but the partition of Russia between the powers, America and Japan, say, taking the Far East; England the Caucasus, and Germany and Austria European Russia. Many expected that the excesses of Bolshevism would culminate in the restoring of despotic rule either in the form of a monarchy or military dictatorship.

Others of a more constructive and hopeful turn of mind already perceived order coming out of the chaos. The destructive action of the Bolsheviki, they said, was painful, but it had a useful side. The old system was rotten and only a clean sweep could make possible a thorough reconstruction. The present process, in their view, is inevitably elemental. Lenine and Trotsky will have their day and cease to be, like Milukoff and Kerensky, and if ever any of these leaders reappear on the surface they will be changed and wiser men, working on changed material.

All parties, cadets, social revolutionaries, and Bolsheviki, they consider necessary in the coming mental phases that are to be superseded by new formations in new conditions. Russia must die to live, must fall apart to come together again.

One hope lies in the organisation of local centres like Ukraine, the Cossack country, the Caucasus and Siberia. An all-Russian patriotism is intelligible only to the highly educated. Local patriotisms would be much more powerful as constructive forces and might ultimately combine in a new general sense of the common interests of all the parts. The economic and political system of Russia would be entirely changed. Ukraine would develop industry and would export its products through the Black Sea. The concentration of all political and economic movement on Petrograd and the Baltic is no longer possible. The Baltic seaboard, with Riga and Reval, is now entering a new orbit; and with the Letts looking perforce towards Germany and the Esthonians pulling towards Finland, Petrograd must necessarily lose its importance as an all-Russian political, commercial, and industrial centre.

CONSTITUENT ASSEMBLY A FAILURE.

As for the Constituent Assembly, none seemed much interested in its fate. Most regarded it as the survival of an obsolete, abstract phase of the revolution. The Bolsheviki had done their best to render it innocuous from their point of view, but in any case it would have been useless. The system of proportional voting by which the central committees of the parties had made up lists of candidates for every constituency had led to absurd results. For the most part members did not know their constituents. A large number of amiable men and women who had rendered services to their party had been elected for such governments as Stavropol, Sammara, Vitebsk, and Tomsk without ever having been near their constituencies or having a notion of their needs. The result was an assembly of inexperienced theorists many of whom had spent all their adult life outside Russia.

All hope of the Constituent Assembly as the power that was to decide the future of Russia and establish a new law has vanished from the peoples' minds. That is shown by the steady expansion of the area of agrarian rioting. The peasants were willing to wait at first for the Constituent Assembly to decide the land questions. Every fresh disturbance in Petrograd by increasing uncertainty led to a fresh outbreak of attacks on estates and now that hope of the Assembly is gone and no further goal is visible, agrarian riots, stimulated by the Bolshevist agitation, disorderly demobilization and the absence of a restraining force, are spreading with an almost calculable regularity of direction and movement in the Central Governments. There will not be an estate left intact by Spring.

But that is only one detail of the vast story of suffering and ruin that accompanies this elemental process in Russia. In such reflections as these and in the fantastic exchange of fantastic stories of robberies, bank adventures, and the vagaries of the Commissaries and Red Guards many thinking Russians spent the strange, sad Christmas of 1917. What does it all mean? What does this toppling, crashing process, this welter of bizarre Socialists and novel nationalism over one-seventh of the globe mean for the future of Europe and civilization?

Italy's Frankenstein and His Monster.

BY T. R. YBARRA | JAN. 29, 1922

ITALY HAS A FRANKENSTEIN. His name is Benito Mussolini. The machine created by him, which, like Frankenstein's famous monster, is steadily getting beyond his control, is the patriotic-political movement known as Fascismo.

Scarcely a day pauses in Italy without the chronicle of somebody shot by a Fascista or a Fascista shot by somebody. Affrays between the Fascisti and their foes — Italian Socialists and Communists — are getting so common that some Italian newspapers hardly devote any space at all to them — familiarity, they argue, breeds contempt among their readers for such trifles. But when one of these fights, brought on all too often by Fascisti, results in somebody getting shot or beaten to death, even the most indifferent editors have to sit up and take notice. And scarcely a week passes in Italy without at least one of these mortal affrays.

The truce recently made between the Fascisti and their enemies has been broken again and again. The Fascisti are on the warpath. They are going about in squads, armed to the teeth, more defiant than ever, looking for trouble. Their fingers, literally, are on the triggers of their revolvers. And Benito Mussolini, the man who, more than any one else, brought Fascismo into being, is powerless to control them.

Mussolini is now a member of the Italian Parliament, elected by a tremendous majority, and he would be much happier and less apprehensive if the unruly youths who elected him would behave better. In his speeches he counsels more moderation, less promiscuous shooting; in his newspaper, Il Popolo d'Italia, he frowns editorially upon the excesses of the Fascisti, and exhorts them to be less prone to blaze away at their foes.

But they won't heed him. They keep on blazing away as promiscuously as ever. Socialists, Communists, innocent bystanders — all alike fall victims to their bullets. The machine created by the Italian

Frankenstein is on the rampage. And Italy is getting rather "fed up" with it. Yet there was a time when Fascismo undoubtedly was beneficial to Italy — practically every Italian not an extreme Socialist or an out-and-out Red will agree to that.

After the close of the war, Italian Socialists and Communists got out of hand. It is little more than a year ago since workmen took control of a number of factories, ousted their employers, made good their control with cordons of armed guards, and turned the commandeered premises into regular military strongholds, bristling with machine guns. In those days Italian Reds talked openly of overthrowing the Government and putting Italy under a Soviet regime; again and again they hung the red flag from public buildings — actually on the City Hall in some Italian cities! — as a sign that the Utopia of Lenin and Trotsky was about to extend itself to Italy. Excited Reds scribbled "Long Live Lenin!" on countless walls and public buildings and churches all over the country. (Think if you saw that on St. Patrick's Cathedral and the Grand Central Station!) Every day they became bolder, more arrogant, more filled with the spirit of violent revolution.

In Italy, as elsewhere in the distracted post-war world, it was the extremists, the preachers of change, who were the militant party; the conservatives, the believers in law and order, vehement as their words might be, were not conspicuous for action. The Government's measures were essentially for defense — timorous police work. It seemed afraid of the extremists. Those who broke heads in street brawls, who put bullets through rivals, who seized factories — those who acted, in short — were the extremists.

Then, suddenly — these extremists found themselves face to face with something quite as bellicose and lawless as themselves.

A new element of violent action stepped into the field. It presented the strange anomaly of men banded up together to uphold law and order and conservatism by methods indistinguishable from those of bank robbers and hold-up gangs. This new element was Fascismo. It was the creation, primarily, of Benito Mussolini. Originally a Socialist,

THE NEW YORK TIMES

"May well involve this Italian Frankenstein in Irretrievable Political Disaster."

he had come out of the war with a glorious record, filled with feelings of intense patriotism. At once he adjudged the Italian extremists — Socialists and Reds alike — to be Italy's greatest menace. He called upon his countrymen to organize against them, to down them by their own efforts, instead of waiting for Government action. The result of his impassioned exhortations was the organization, all over the country, of the Fasci di Combattimento — bands of men, mostly young, prepared to go to any length to save Italy from the radicals, who seemed to be bringing it constantly nearer to Sovietism.

The followers of Mussolini exacted from their foes an eye for an eye, a tooth for a tooth; they gave blow for blow, shot for shot. They did not wait to defend themselves against the aggression. They went out after the Reds, raided their lairs, broke up their meetings in halls, dispersed their gatherings on public squares, threw their processions into confusion, howled down their orators. If the Reds showed fight, the Fascisti gave them all they wanted — and a lot more, too — with fist and cudgel, cold steel and cold lead.

The Italian situation underwent a complete change. From being on the offensive, the extremists suddenly found themselves on the defensive. They who had been aggressively militant found themselves up against a force even more militant and aggressive. The most daring young men in Italy, boys who had shown themselves heroes in the battle against Austria, leaped into the new fight with all the zest and temerity which youth has so often, under other circumstances, put at the service of revolution.

The forces of Italian revolution were cowed; the extremists scuttled to cover. What with the growing belief in Italy that Sovietism had failed in Moscow and the aggressive tactics of the Fascisti, the Reds lost ground every day. The establishment of Lenin's Italian branch of Utopia was indefinitely postponed. But here things began to get more complicated. The Fascismo movement began to lose something of its spirit of patriotic crusade and got rather muddled and besmirched, to the original elements composing it a goodly percentage of mere riffraff had been added. Too many acts by Fascisti began to savor more of terrorism than patriotism; it looked as if some of the Fascisti had grown to like the exciting sport of man hunting for its own sake. Suspicion of underlying personal grudges began to tarnish some of their exploits; it began to look as if some of those whom they beat, wounded or murdered had incurred their hate, not because of seditious activities but because of the mere fact of being Socialists or Communists. Life on Italian streets and roads began to be altogether too hazardous for ordinary passersby.

"Whatever is said of Fascismo," an American who has spent years in Italy told me, "should not be too black and white. Qualifications are necessary. For example, the youths — too often mere boys of 16 or 17 — who rushed into the ranks of Fascismo did not do so in order to support of conservatism, but in that spirit of ardent nationalistic patriotism which is one of the characteristics of youth in every country. Many of them have helped win Italy's war; some have had a share in d'Annuncio's dramatic Fiume expedition. They saw their newly united Italy as a shining, triumphant figure. So that when a noisy rabble spat upon her flag, reviled her soldiers, and cursed the war, these youths rose in defense of the national ideal, not in defense of social conservatism. It was not so much the Communists as Communists, still less the socialists, who committed the excesses which these young men particularly detested, as it was the anarchistic, unprincipled, merely destructive rabble, the thieves, rowdies and gangsters, who always emerge from the slums of cities whenever a Government is weak and social change is in the air.

"A Fascista would be murdered in some town, probably by some society-hating criminal, and then the Fascisti would immediately organize a 'punitive expedition,' rush to the place on motor trucks, sack the Town Hall (if, as in many Italian localities, the town administration happened to be a Socialist one), burn the workmen's co-operative, and shoot or beat all persons in their path who were, or whom they suspected of being, Socialists or Communists. Hundreds of such raids were carried out. 'Who,' thoughtful Italians began to ask after a time, 'pays for all these expensive motor trucks and the gasoline consumed?

Certainly not these university students, these penniless ex-Lieutenants! Can it be that special interests are involved?' "

Moreover, this same observer pointed, out, while the rise of militant Fascismo undoubtedly helped to re-establish order in Italy, it was not the only, or even the principal, factor. The workmen's communistic experiment in running the factories collapsed, not because they were forcibly dislodged, but because they found the thing could not be done without capital and the whole mechanism of capital. And it must be remembered that the commission of Italian Socialists sent to Russia to investigate Bolshevism returned with a highly unfavorable report, and that Lenin, who had had great hopes for Italy, eventually 'excommunicated' the Italian Socialist Party.

"There is a basis of sound common sense in the Italian people," continued this same American observer, "and I am convinced that, even at the moment of greatest confusion, all but a small disorganized minority desired order. And in an unusually clear-thinking race — such as the Italians are not popularly supposed to be, but are — the majority certainly never desired a communistic regime for their country.

"If the Government had only been a little stronger and had only had a little more faith in the essential sanity of the Italian people, the whole extra-legal phenomenon of Fascismo might, I think, have been avoided. Fascismo played its part in the re-establishment of order, but that part, I think, has been overestimated. It was like a dash of cold water in the face of a man who is feeling faint. Though the water helps, he will probably recover of himself if left alone, while, if you continue to throw cold water on him — in buckets, in vats, in tons — for an indefinite time, he will probably catch pneumonia."

Benito Mussolini is constantly calling upon his violent followers to calm themselves. He seems to realize that the machine of his creation may eventually do Italy and himself more harm than good. But the Fascisti keep right at their lawless work.

The following tragic occurrence of a few days ago, which caused a deep horror in Italy — though it was merely one of many similar happenings — is typical of the sort of thing that is getting beyond the endurance of the great majority of Italians:

A party of Fascisti went from Cremona, in Northern Italy, to a nearby town to attend a meeting. They traveled on a big motor truck, and the Cremona authorities, fearing that they would indulge in some sort of violence unless watched, sent some policemen after them in another truck, with instructions to follow the first truck closely. The meeting passed off without trouble, and the two trucks started on their way back to Cremona. Owing to tire trouble, the truck carrying the policemen was forced to halt, and the truck of the Fascisti continued on its way, freed from surveillance.

They soon came upon three men standing in the road beside a motor car in trouble. At sight of the Fascisti, the three men started to run away as fast as they could over the fields by the road. The Fascisti pursued and overtook them. It turned out that the three were a well-known Socialist Deputy of Cremona and two other Socialists. There is conflicting evidence about exactly what happened when the Fascisti overtook the Socialists; what is perfectly clear, however, is that the Socialist Deputy was beaten to death with a club by one of the Fascisti, a boy of 16.

The Socialist newspapers of Italy howled with rage at this brutal murder. Mussolini in his paper promptly disavowed sympathy with the crime. Later, however, other versions of what happened got abroad, and Mussolini became more belligerent against the Socialists, though without expressing approval of the murder.

Mussolini certainly seems embarrassed by the doings of the more violent Fascisti. Fascismo — that is, its original, patriotic phase — helped to put him into the Italian Parliament. It may prove to have been for him the cornerstone of a brilliant political career. Its later development may well involve this Italian Frankenstein, at the outset of his career, in irretrievable political disaster.

New Popular Idol Rises in Bavaria

BY CYRIL BROWN | NOV. 21, 1922

MUNICH, NOV. 20. — Next to the high cost of living and the dollar, "Der Hitler" and his "Hakenkreuzlers" are the popular topic of talk in Munich and other Bavarian towns. This reactionary Nationalistic anti-Semitic movement has now reached a point where it is considered potentially dangerous, though not for the immediate future.

Hitler today is taken seriously among all classes of Bavarians. He is feared by some, enthusiastically hailed as a prophet and political economic savior by others, and watched with increasing sympathetic interest by the bulk who, apparently, are merely biding the psychological moment to mount Hitler's bandwagon. Undoubtedly the spectacular success of Mussolini and the Fascisti brought Hitler's movement to the fore and gained popular interest and sympathy for it. Another condition favorable to the outburst of the movement is the widespread discontent with the existing state of affairs among all classes in the towns and cities under the increasing economic pressure.

Hitler's "Hakenkreuz" movement is essentially urban in character. It has not yet caught a foothold among the hardy Bavarian peasantry and highlanders, which would make it really dangerous. As a highly placed personage put it:

"Hitler organized a small insignificant group of National Socialists two years ago, since when the movement has been smoldering underneath the surface. Now it has eaten its way through, and a conflagration of course is not only possible but certain if this now free flame of fanatical patriotism finds sufficient popular combustible material to feed on."

Hitler has been called the Bavarian Mussolini, and his followers the Bavarian Fascisti. There is nothing socialistic about the National Socialism he preaches. He has 30,000 organized followers in Munich alone. His total following throughout Bavaria is uncertain, since the movement is in a state of rapid flux. He is wasting no time working out political programs, but devotes his whole energy to recruiting fresh forces and perfecting his organization.

BLACKJACKS SILENCE OPPOSITION.

"Herr Hitler regrets he is unable to meet you as he is leaving town on important business for several days," was the answer received by The New York Times correspondent. His important business was going to Regensburg with three special train loads of Munich admirers for the purpose of holding a series of reactionary inflammatory meetings and incidentally to beat up protesting Socialists and Communists with blackjacks if any dare protest, which is becoming increasingly rarer.

His simple method is, first, propaganda, and secondly, efficient organization. He personally conducts patriotic revival meetings for this purpose, often descending from his stronghold, Munich, on other Bavarian towns with special train-loads of followers. He has the rare oratorical gift, at present unique in Germany, of spellbinding whole audiences regardless of politics or creed. The new converts made at these rallies, those who absolutely and unconditionally pledge themselves to Hitler and the cause, are carefully sifted through and the pick of them who pass the standard military muster are organized into "storm troops" with gray shirts, brassards in the old imperial colors, black and an anti-Semitic Swastika cross in a white circular field on red; armed also with blackjacks and, it is popularly whispered, revolvers.

According to a reliable specialist informant, there are probably 400,000 military rifles and 130 cannon still concealed in Bavaria. So that some fine day Hitler's legionaries might well make their debut with rifles.

Hitler's strength is in the combination of his undeniable great gifts as an orator and organizer. He exerts an uncanny control over audiences, possessing the remarkable ability to not only rouse his hearers to a fighting pitch of fury, but at will to turn right around and reduce the same audience to docile calmness and good order. A typical instance is related by the informant mentioned:

"At the height of the recent Bavarian Government crisis Hitler was holding a mass meeting in Munich and had worked up the big audience when a rumor spread through the hall that he had planned a coup and that he would overthrow and seize the Government that night and was about to give the signal at this rally. His followers burst into an enthusiastic uproar, drew and brandished blackjacks and revolvers, and with shouts of 'Hell, Heil, Heil' prepared to follow Hitler and storm anything.

"With a few electric words he worked a magic change in the audience. Their duty, on which the success of the cause depended, he said, was iron discipline and implicit obedience to orders when orders were given. The time for action had not come yet. And the riot was nipped in the bud."

A DIFFERENT SHOW OF POWER.

A different exhibition of Hitler power; during a mass meeting in Nuremberg, a stronghold of Bavarian socialism, the radical elements undertook a counter-demonstration, massed outside the meeting hall and sang the "Internationale." The strains of the hated tune heard in the hall enraged Hitler's followers. At his word of command shock troops of gray shirts with fine discipline marched from the hall, pulled their blackjacks, charged and dispersed the crowd with many a broken head.

Hitler is credited with having a rapidly increasing following among the workers disgruntled by the high cost of living. It is also said many ultra-radicals, including Communists, have flocked to his reactionary banner. He is beginning to draw support from the politically sluggish middle classes, which in Bavaria, however, are not so sluggish as in Berlin. Even more significant there is some active, more passive support and to a still greater extent sympathetic interest for the Hitler movement among the Bavarian loyalists, among monarchists and militarists and in government and political circles, apparently coupled with the idea that the movement would prove a useful tool if it could be controlled by their special interests. But there is also the latent fear that the movement might wax beyond control.

Hitler, in addition to his oratorical and organizing abilities, has another positive asset — he is a man of the "common people" and hence has the makings of a "popular hero," appealing to all classes. It is reported that he was a worker before becoming leader of the Bavarian Social Nationalists. He served during the war as a common soldier and won the Iron Cross of the First and Second Classes, which for a common soldier is distinctive evidence of exceptional bravery and daring. To Bavarian mentality he talks rough, shaggy, sound horse sense, and according to present Bavarian public opinion a strong, active leader equipped with horse sense is the need of the hour.

CHIEF POINTS OF HIS PROGRAM.

Hitler's program is of less interest than his person and movement. His program consists chiefly of half a dozen negative ideas clothed in generalities. He is "against the Jews, Communists, Bolshevism, Marxian socialism, Separatists, the high cost of living, existing conditions, the weak Berlin Government and the Versailles Treaty." Positively he stands only for "a strong united Germany under a strong Government."

He is credibly credited with being actuated by lofty, unselfish patriotism. He probably does not know himself just what he wants to accomplish. The keynote of his propaganda in speaking and writing is violent anti-Semitism. His followers are popularly nicknamed "the Hakenkreuzler." So violent are Hitler's fulminations against the Jews that a number of prominent Jewish citizens are reported to have sought safe asylums in the Bavarian highlands, easily reached by fast motor car, whence they could hurry their women and children when forewarned of an anti-Semitic St. Bartholomew's night.

But several reliable, well-informed sources confirmed the idea that Hitler's anti-Semitism was not so genuine or violent as it sounded, and that he was merely using anti-Semitic propaganda as a bait to catch messes of followers and keep them aroused, enthusiastic and in line for the time when his organization is perfected and sufficiently powerful to be employed effectively for political purposes.

A sophisticated politician credited Hitler with peculiar political cleverness for laying emphasis and over-emphasis on anti-Semitism, saying: "You can't expect the masses to understand or appreciate your finer real aims. You must feed the masses with cruder morsels and ideas like anti-Semitism. It would be politically all wrong to tell them the truth about where you really are leading them."

The Hitler movement is not of mere local or picturesque interest. It is bound to bring Bavaria into a renewed clash with the Berlin Government as long as the German Republic goes even through the motions of trying to live up to the Versailles Treaty. For it is certain the Allies will take umbrage at the Hitler organization as a violation of the military clauses of the treaty and demand disbandment, even as in the case of its predecessor, the Orgesch.

Priest Defends His Radio Talks

BY THE NEW YORK TIMES | MAY 10, 1932

THE REV. CHARLES E. COUGHLIN, pastor of the Shrine of the Little Flower in Royal Oak, Mich., whose radio broadcasts on social questions drew the severe criticism of Cardinal O'Connell of Boston, arrived from a vacation in California on the Panama Pacific liner Pennsylvania yesterday.

While expressing respect and reverence toward his critic, Father Coughlin said that his broadcasts had been approved by his Bishop, the Right Rev. Michael James Gallagher of Detroit, and that he expected to continue the series unless Bishop Gallagher told him to stop them.

When first asked to comment on the criticisms of Cardinal O'Connell, Father Coughlin replied that he had nothing to say "about that." However, when pressed as to whether he considered it within the Cardinal's province to criticize his broadcasting, he replied:

"That is for the public and the higher church officials to decide. I, being an ordinary and humble priest, think that it would be out of place for me to criticize, so to speak, a general in the army.

"However, I am responsible to my Bishop, the Right Rev. Michael James Gallagher, Bishop of Detroit. Every one of my radio sermons received the approval of my Bishop, it being my custom, every Saturday evening, to show my sermon to my Bishop, and I never take it upon myself to make an utterance of national importance in any of my sermons without his approval."

Father Coughlin has broadcast sermons on economic and social problems. The former, he said, were founded on the sermons and writings of Pope Leo XIII and Pius XI, and all have been preserved in a book, 600,000 copies of which have been given away.

"I have no reason to enunciate anything radical," he said, "but I try to point out to my listeners that a disease is ravishing this country — the disease being the concentration of wealth in the hands of the few.

And, mark you, if we don't change this condition we'll have a revolution. But we should change conditions in an orderly and legal way."

Father Coughlin was accompanied by his father and mother, Mr. and Mrs. Thomas J. Coughlin. In California he stayed at the Beverley Hills home of George A. Richards of station WJR, Detroit, and at the ranch of William Randolph Hearst.

He said he had signed a contract to broadcast, beginning Oct. 16. During his twenty-seven weeks of broadcasting last season he received 2,500,000 letters from persons of all religions, the handling of which required several score clerks and typists, who are still working on replies. Although his parish contains only forty-two families, 10,000 persons come to his church on Sunday.

Fascists Plan Corporate State in Britain, Mosley Declares

BY SIR OSWALD MOSLEY | APRIL 24, 1934

The leader of the British Fascist movement, which gathered 10,000 Britons in a mass meeting in London Sunday night, tells here the aims and purposes of the movement. Sir Oswald, a wealthy aristocrat, was once a Socialist.

LONDON, APRIL 23. — Fascism, the new political creed of Europe, has reached Great Britain. The great meeting which crowded Albert Hall, the largest public hall in London, definitely marked this new phase of British political development.

It would be a mistake, however, to assume that Fascism in Great Britain must necessarily adopt the same form as under Mussolini in Italy or under Hitler in Germany. Fascism is a universal creed of patriotic reconstruction along modern lines and under the disciplined control of a powerful central government. It came to both Italy and Germany under the stress of a grave economic crisis and when those countries were trembling on the verge of communism.

Under such circumstances, its advent was inevitably accompanied by some degree of violence — but violence, it should be noted, far less than these countries would have suffered in a Red revolution.

SAYS PEOPLE WANT FASCISM.

Germany and Italy embraced Fascism because they had to. Great Britain turns to Fascism because her people want it.

The older political parties in Britain are completely discredited. It is barely two years since the Socialists (Laborites) were swept from office by a Nationalist landslide, but already the national government is covered with shame and ridicule and the pendulum is swinging back to the extreme Left.

The old political system is breaking up because the greater part of the electorate does not know to which of the old parties to turn. It cannot trust one of them. A huge mass of floating votes, amounting to from ten to fifteen thousand in each constituency, is positively waiting for new political leadership. The Black Shirt movement is out to supply this leadership and is rapidly gathering within its ranks the disillusioned members of all parties.

Our policy is one of action and we seek the complete restoration of British prosperity and prestige. The Black Shirts are determined to combat the flabby policy of surrender which is rapidly breaking up the British Empire.

OPPOSED TO BANKERS' RULE.

In home affairs we are violently opposed to the economic dictatorship of the bankers and financiers in the City of London. We plan to set up a corporate State which will place every industry in the country under the direct control of a self-governing corporation, on which will sit representatives of employers, workers and consumers. These will fix by negotiation the rates of wages, hours of work and prices and terms of competition which will be legally binding for an industry as a whole.

These corporations will send representatives to a national council of corporations which will function as an industrial parliament. Here matters of general financial policy will be settled and the operations of the various industries controlled and regulated in the interests of the nation as a whole.

The Black Shirt movement recognizes that the problem of underconsumption is the major economic problem of the day and that it can be solved only by a general raising of wages and salaries over the whole field of industry, within the controlled system of the corporate State. This will increase purchasing power in the home market and enable industry to supply cheaply by mass production methods its output for an assured market.

By these means the Black Shirts intend to bring to an end the tyranny of the vested interests and the sham democracy of politics and to restore prosperity to Great Britain.

Shadows That Fascism Casts Before It

BY C. G. POORE | MAY 19, 1935

FORERUNNERS OF AMERICAN FASCISM
By Raymond Gram Swing.
168 pp. New York: Julian Messner. $1.75.

IT SOMETIMES TAKES only a clown's hat and a piece of stale crust to give the illusion of unlimited bread and circuses. The crowd concentrates on the illusion. The critic concentrates on the delusion. By the time they are wiser it's apt to be too late. Every one remembers how funny Hitler once looked. But his promises were very rosy, and the nicked blade of ridicule cut no swath in opposing his battalions. So Mr. Swing wisely allows us little chance for superior laughter in contemplating the forces that he believes might be forerunners of fascism in America. His study is a book of the hour that really illuminates one of the murkiest questions of our strange day.

Twenty million listeners can be wrong. Yet it is a sounder plan to try to find out precisely what makes them follow their leaders than to try to dismiss them with derisive hoots. Mr. Swing's vigorous appraisals of the Messrs. Coughlin, Long, Bilbo, Townsend and Hearst give them a good many benefits of a good many doubts. Each of these men would hotly deny that he had any fascist leanings whatever. Some of them have already done so. Here they are simply called "forerunners of American fascism," not Fascists.

Mr. Swing is out to diagnose an epidemic, not to join the ranks of his protagonists. They are the ones who claim they can cure it. Several of them, we are all by now sufficiently aware, bulge with blueprints showing prodigious benefits they are ready to shower on America. Think of Dr. Townsend's pensions, Huey Long's distributed wealth, Father Coughlin's vision of a land better run than we have so far been able to run ours.

LIBRARY OF CONGRESS PRINTS AND PHOTOGRAPHS DIVISION

Huey Long addressing a crowd earlier this year.

True, experts have shot all these schemes full of holes. You would think their sponsors should feel demolished. And you know they don't. And you know their followers keep right on following. Promises are a good deal more savory than realities. And the men who make them know how to talk to the people they make them to, without talking down.

Huey Long's capital levy, for example, "may be as simple as a box of kindergarten blocks," Mr. Swing says, "but could he win mass votes, or organize nearly 4,000,000 people in eight months, by distributing a primer of economics?" Not by a jugful. And furthermore, hasn't Huey already suggested the promised land, like one of those advertising bits in a movie that show exciting scenes from next week's feature picture, by building leagues of roadways in Louisiana, distributing free textbooks, taking delighted hordes of collegians to football games?

When you contrast such undeniable boons with the way Huey runs his State you see the point Mr. Swing makes in his title. There is absolute power in action. Mr. Swing shows the scene in a session of the Louisiana Legislature when Huey is shooting his bills through the mill. He is surrounded by his bodyguards. He gets precisely what he wants done. For those who disagree with him, it's just too bad.

Fascism, Mr. Swing says, is "a reorganization of society to maintain an unequal distribution of economic power by undemocratic means." Later he drops the word "undemocratic" and adds that fascism is also "a substitution of barbaric values for individualist civilization." Well, we began to be interested in the "barbaric" notably during the post-war years, when the hard-boiled school of literature flowered, and horn-rimmed university graduates got to talking tougher than life and twice as unnaturally. So there's another omen.

Surveying his group as a whole — each one gets a thoroughly analytical chapter — Mr. Swing says he is examining them "for suggestions of their ultimate Fascist character." And the fact that we have demagogues "is not necessarily a symptom of oncoming fascism. Demagogues always have been able to function on the outskirt of American political life." Mr, Swing continues:

> *Not all our demagogues are Fascist. I have included, for example, both Dr. Townsend and Senator Bilbo. They make an instructive study in revealing the nature of the appeal any demagogue must make to build up a following. But neither can be called Fascist. Dr. Townsend is an accident as a public figure, if it can be called an accident that he hit upon a utopian solution which warmed the substratum of utopianism in most American hearts. Senator Bilbo, a master at stirring passion and prejudice, is not a national personage, or likely to become one. There is much in Senator Huey Long that is not yet Fascist, and Father Coughlin may conceivably be unaware how neatly his program fits into the Fascist pattern.*

Nevertheless, Mr. Swing is not too hopeful that fascism can be averted in America, because he doesn't think there are enough people "who care about economic democracy and individualism, in the government and outside it, to use democratic government to achieve them." So the Italian and German road to him seems wide open. It may be that at this point he does not give sufficient weight to the question of how much any government, in recent decades, has very drastically altered what you might call the total volume of a given people's civil liberties for any length of time.

Four prerequisites of fascism are given by Mr. Swing, who as a foreign correspondent during the past twenty years has studied the system in many aspects. In Europe these four have been "the impoverishment of the middle class; the slowing down of business, causing unemployment on a large scale; the paralysis of democratic government; and the threat of a strong Communist movement." We have had, Mr. Swing thinks, the first two of these, though there's room for argument about that word "impoverishment." Congress has certainly not been behaving lately as though democratic government had broken down. And we have not, Mr. Swing points out, a powerful Communist movement, Mr. Hearst to the contrary.

So the threat of fascism is not, in Mr. Swing's analysis, immediate. The identification of certain NRA agencies with fascist tendencies seems to have been done sufficiently, and in view of the deflated state of that feast of initials not a pressing matter. President Roosevelt Is given the doubtful honor of being told that he "might easily become a fascist leader if it lay in his nature to make that kind of an appeal. Fortunately, it does not." His recent break with the United States Chamber of Commerce does not bear out Mr. Swing's suggestion that business unduly influences him. And what other head of a modern State may be so freely criticized?

Mr. Swing quotes Judge Stacey of the steel board as saying that "economic power is never surrendered. It always has to be fought for." Well, that's true of practically any kind of power. It's also true of freedom, and Mr. Swing's hook is a part of the fight to preserve freedom from fascism by exploring the nature of fascism and its forerunners as he sees them.

It may come as a surprise to find that Mr. Swing considers the "Wall Street fascist conspiracy" General Smedley Butler raised a hue and cry over just "a kind of Hollywood fascism" on the ground that true fascism starts as a radical not as a conservative movement. The German and the Italian models bear him out. As to the belief that financiers are great admirers of fascism, he says; "Finance capitalism has not found fascism, either in Italy or Germany, to be the comfortable resting place it anticipated. And it is no exaggeration to say that finance capitalism is not thriving in these countries as it is in America."

The blame, then, in Mr, Swing's view, rests on men who offer the people of a country promises that cannot be fulfilled. The demand for sacrifices does not come till later. And in that case the sacrifices, unlike the promises, must be fulfilled. It is hard to see how any one who had read Mr. Swing's book could want fascism in America.

A Communist From Kansas Is a National Issue

BY F. RAYMOND DANIELL | OCT. 11, 1936

The two major parties argue about Browder, who campaigns on his own for president.

EARL BROWDER COMES FROM Kansas, too. He is a bookkeeper who years ago climbed off his high stool, rolled down his cuffs, spat on his hands and adopted the workers' revolution as his career. Much has happened since. To members of the Communist party of America, of which he is the acknowledged leader, he is their nominee for President of the United States. To many others he is an issue of considerable importance in the current struggle for power between the Democrats and Republicans.

The Browder issue resolves itself into the charge that he, an avowed Communist, is supporting President Roosevelt and that therefore there must be some truth in the allegation that the New Deal is communistic. Mr. Browder denies he is supporting Roosevelt and says he is just fighting Governor Landon — and the White House disclaims his aid. Like many another issue that has arisen in the past to plague the people of this quadrennially upset and divided land, this one is fogged in legend.

Actually Mr. Browder is the leader of an organization numbering by his own estimate some 50,000 members — scarcely a drop in the political bucket of a country which next election day probably will cast more than 40,000,000 ballots for Republican and Democratic candidates. He lives in Yonkers with his wife and three children, wears a gold wedding ring on the third finger of his left hand and commutes with fair regularity to his office in Communist headquarters at 35 East Twelfth Street.

THE BUILDING ITSELF is dingy and brooding. It exudes an air of furtive doggedness. Men and women whose solemn faces and earnest conversation mark them as individuals with a purpose in life go in and out and up and down in its swaying, groaning elevator. There on the ninth floor in a plain office at the end of a long corridor the properly introduced visitor finds the Kansas-born apostle of Marx and Engels, of Lenin and Stalin.

The office itself is small and bare. The walls are decorated with sketches of leaders of the Russian Revolution. In a corner is a magazine stand, its shelves spilling over. There is a desk and a chair for Browder and another chair for a visitor, acquired in some manner from a one-arm lunch room. Its broad flat surface is convenient for interviewers making notes.

Browder himself is a stoop-shouldered man of 45. His hair is graying and there is a stubble of sandy mustache upon his upper lip. He would resent the suggestion, but there is a faint resemblance to Adolf Hitler. He has tired blue eyes which are illuminated as though from some dynamo within when the right conversational button is pressed. After he has finished speaking the light goes out and he is silent, smiling a little, quizzically.

We talked of the campaign and the future political history of the country, and Browder's eyes narrowed and lit up at the same time. Gazing into an imaginary crystal ball, he predicted another economic toboggan slide for the country after election day no matter which side won, and he foresaw the complete disintegration of both major parties before 1940. In their place, he said, there would be a new alignment of the voters in a "people's front," against capital and the forces of reaction and fascism.

Fascism to Browder is a real bugaboo. He speaks of the rise of Fascist dictatorships, threatening Moscow with war when it wants a few more years of peace in which to build a social order to Marxist specifications. He calls attention to the fact that Hitler's rise to power was aided by Leftist sniping at a liberal government, harassed from the Right. He believes it can happen here, but he says he is not going to repeat the errors of the German radicals.

"Communist tactics at the present time," he said, replying to a question, "take into account as a fundamentally important factor the menace of fascism and the need of unity of the anti-Fascists and democratic forces to guarantee against Fascist rule in the United States and the other democratic countries of the world."

BROWDER DID NOT specifically deny that the international problems of the Soviet influenced the national policy of the American Communist party, but he said:

> *The policies of the Communist party are determined by the needs and aspirations of the toiling masses in this and every other country. Of central importance there is necessarily included the problem of fully utilizing the victories of the new socialist society in the Soviet Union.*
>
> *In this respect it is not so much that the Soviet Union needs support from the workers in the rest of the world, but rather that the workers in other countries need to use the power and example of the Soviet Union to protect and extend their own democratic rights and economic needs. The new Socialist society in the Soviet Union already is so well established that it contributes far more in the support of democracy and peace than it requires from the democratic movement in other lands in its own defense.*

In his acceptance speech delivered at Madison Square Garden last June after he had been nominated for President by the Communist convention, he said:

> *We have weighed our tasks frankly and realistically. We see that the chief enemy of the peace, freedom and prosperity of the American people is the Republican party and its reactionary allies, Hearst, the Liberty League, Wall Street.*

In the same speech he charged that William Lemke, the Union party candidate, was only "a stooge for Landon," and declared that the third party movement supported by the Rev. Charles E. Coughlin was "the product of a Hearst-Liberty League intrigue." He still feels pretty much the same about it.

The Communist leader said he believed that the struggle for the "maintenance and extension of democracy," in the face of a rising tide of fascism, would "ultimately lead the United States and the world to the choice of socialism and eventually communism." He added:

"The country does not yet face this issue concretely but it probably will in the course of the next years."

Mr. Roosevelt, by making concessions to labor and the farmer, Browder said, had "slowed down the political tempo" of the country after four years of Herbert Hoover's administration had accelerated it to a dangerous pace. Had Hoover been re-elected, he added, "public disorder would have been greater, but there would have been less public enlightenment." Likewise, while he expects Mr. Roosevelt, if re-elected, to swing sharply to the Right, Browder regards him as a lesser evil than Governor Landon, whose victory, he believes, would encourage the forces of reaction to serious excesses.

"It's possible," Browder mused during the interview, "that the reactionaries backing Landon may try to cancel the result of the election by force if they lose the election. There are open Fascists in the high command, you know. We may yet see the spectacle of the Communist party in this country rallying to the defense of a Democratic government."

BROWDER ASKS FOR time to watch the growth of the Farmer-Labor party, which he regards as "the most promising thing in American political life." In the new "people's front" he sees forming he expects his followers to play an important part. Already, he says, elements of the new alignment are rearing their heads within the Democratic party. Among them he lists Upton Sinclair's Epic movement in California and the Commonwealth Federation in Washington.

With such groups, Browder said, the Communist party is ready to cooperate, keeping its identity and aiming ultimately at control through democratic processes.

Although Browder entertains no apparent doubts relative to the inevitability of communism in America, he does not believe that the people of this country would welcome a dictatorship. At the same time, he is unwilling to admit that communism means dictatorship in the popular sense of the word. Rather, he says it means an extension of democracy in a more realistic sense than that which is enjoyed here today. This is the way in which he expresses his views:

> *I do not think democracy and communism are irreconcilable. On the contrary, I think that full achievement of democracy can come only by moving in the direction of communism. Conversely the development of socialism and eventually communism can only come through the further extension of democracy.*
>
> *In my opinion the American people have a deep-seated aversion to dictatorship, understanding that word in the sense of dictatorial rule by an individual or small minority of a parasitic ruling class.*
>
> *The American people will find in the course of their struggle to win real democracy, that it will be necessary that democracy shall function in the broad historical sense as a dictatorship of an overwhelming majority to suppress the attempted dictatorship of the minority. In this sense, however — dictatorship of the majority of the people to prevent a dictatorship of the minority — the word has quite different significance from that used in popular terminology.*

Recently Browder was arrested in Terre Haute, Ind. That is one proof to him that American liberties in practice are quite different from American liberties in theory. In Russia, he believes, there is more freedom for the worker in his daily life than in America. Yet Browder has no intention of going there to live. There is no country in the world, he says, where he would rather live than in the United States.

THE BACKGROUND OF this leading Communist of the United States is both revolutionary and American.

Earl Browder was born on May 20, 1891, in Wichita. His father was William Browder, a school teacher, who traced his ancestry back to seventeenth-century Virginia pioneers. One of ten brothers, five of whom are still living, Earl Browder left school at the age of 9 and began work as an errand boy for a department store. The elder Browder was a Unitarian with liberal ideas in politics.

The future leader of the Communist party, studying his correspondence-school course in bookkeeping and accounting, became interested in socialism before he was out of short trousers. At 15 he heard a speech by Eugene Debs, and soon afterward he was peddling copies of "The Appeal to Reason" on the streets of Wichita. He held jobs as a clerk for an oil company, bookkeeper for a wholesale drug company, and bookkeeper for a Farmers' Cooperative Store at Olathe, Kan. He left the Socialist party in 1912 because of the fight over the removal of Bill Haywood and became an active member of the trade-union group in the American Federation of Labor which was led by William Z. Foster. He held a card in the bookkeepers' union. When the war came Browder and his brother William resisted the draft and went to jail. He was sentenced on two indictments to serve a year in the Platte County jail and two years in the Federal Penitentiary at Leavenworth.

IN 1921 HE ORGANIZED a delegation of trade unionists to attend the First Congress of the Red International of Labor Unions. He attended the Third Congress of the Communist International and from 1927 to 1929 he devoted his talents to stirring up the coolies in China. He returned to the United States in 1929 just before the stock market debacle which ushered in the depression.

In the following year Browder succeeded Foster as general secretary of the Communist party in America. It was not until August, 1935, however, that he burst upon the national consciousness as a menace. That was when he appeared before the Communist International in Moscow and did some pretty tall talking about the progress of the revolutionary movement in the United States.

Following that little flight of oratory the State Department lodged formal protest with the Soviet Foreign Office. In due time the Soviet replied that it was not responsible for what went on before the Comintern, and there the matter ended.

Fascist Parallels Seen in Peronism

BY HERBERT L. MATTHEWS | MARCH 23, 1951

This is the second of a series of dispatches on Argentina by a member of the editorial staff of The New York Times.

BUENOS AIRES, MARCH 21 — Peronism is steadily moving along the road toward totalitarianism and it is because independent newspapers such as La Prensa and La Nación of Buenos Aires block the road that they are persecuted. There is a pattern of dictatorship that fits Juan Perón as it fitted Mussolini, Hitler, Stalin, Franco, Alazar and others.

Each one in his way was forced to create a totalitarian structure to maintain power, and while no two systems are exactly alike the analogies between Italian fascism and Argentine peronism are so close that they cannot be accidental. The Perón regime is easier to understand when one makes this comparison.

President Perón was a military attaché in Rome in the years before the second World War and it is obvious that Mussolini's system made a deep impression on him. Like most Argentines, especially their military men, General Perón has a profound conviction that Argentina, not the United States, is the true and natural leader of Latin America.

Some of the analogies to Italian fascism are unimportant but significant. General Perón has used the balcony of the Casa Rosada, or Government House, the way Mussolini used the balcony of the Palazzo Venezia to harangue the crowds or appear before them.

PERONISTA MARCH

Just as fascism had its stirring march of the "Giovinezza," so this movement has its "Muchachos pernoistas," the march of "the peronista boys." Oct. 28, the anniversary of the march on Rome is here "Glorious Oct. 17," commemorating the then Colonel Perón's release from jail in 1945 and the seizure of power in Buenos Aires. The use of photographs of General and Señora Perón everywhere is typical.

So is the use of the title "Líder" (Leader, Duce, Fuehrer, Caudillo). So is the slogan one comes upon at every turn, "Perón Cumple" (Perón gets things done), which is better than "Mussolini is always right." But for that matter "Perón is always right" to peronistas. Like Mussolini and Hitler, General Perón has engaged in a spate of building — new tenements, stadiums, swimming pools, parks and public buildings.

From such minor parallels one can move to more basic features. Just as Mussolini had his Carta del Lavoro or Labor Charter so General Perón has his Derechos del Trabajo or Rights of Labor.

Here one should note the important difference that Mussolini came to power in opposition to labor, which was mostly Socialist and Communist, whereas General Perón rose to power with labor support but the final result turns out to be the same. In both countries control over labor was imposed by naming union leaders faithful and subservient to the regime. Both dictators introduced "labor tribunals" to interpret contracts and settle disputes.

PERONISTA MOTTOES

Mussolini's autarchy has been paralleled here by General Perón's campaign for "economic independence" from the United States and Britain. Where Mussolini and Hitler were against "the pluto-democracies" as well as communism, General Perón is anti-capitalist and anti-Communist.

One next comes to a truly striking parallel. Mussolini invented fascism, gave it a name, seized power in 1922, gradually began integrating his power into a totalitarian structure and only then — 1925–26 — was able to come up with a Fascist doctrine.

General Perón is doing exactly the same thing with his "justicialismo" or third position between capitalism and communism, which he formulated in 1947, four years after taking power.

His original slogan, "Neither Moscow nor Wall Street," might just as well have been Mussolini's. The cloudy doctrines of justicialism such as "social justice" with the Government seeing to it that no one part of society exploits another have no practical meaning but serve a valuable political purpose. Justicialism is attractive, it sounds good and above all it serves as a cloak behind which General Perón and peronism can seize all power.

That of course is the final decisive aim, and it is where peronism resembles all other totalitarian structures. General Perón still has a certain distance to go before achieving an integral structure, but he is a long way toward it. Like all Fascist governments, the Perón regime has kept democratic forms such as separate executive, legislative and judicial powers, but they are only forms. The judiciary, for instance, is now completely purged of independent as well as anti-peronist judges and Argentine justice is now political.

General Perón abolished the liberal Constitution of 1853 based on the United States Constitution and introduced his own, which, however, is much of a dead letter. It guarantees liberty of the press, for instance, but there is no freedom of the press. In other words the rule of law has been abolished.

There is no longer genuine free enterprise because the Government exercises the widest controls including the vicious one of "intervention." The noted drug concern of Massone was intervened in the most cruel and unscrupulous fashion and expropriated because its proprietor refused to contribute to the Eva Perón Social Aid Foundation. The same thing happened to the noted candy factory Mumú. Now it is happening to La Prensa.

Civil rights are disappearing fast, with the radio completely controlled, the press almost so, public meetings circumscribed, phones tapped, letters opened and porters, servants and waiters used as Government or police spies. There is a Federal police that often knocks on doors at 2 A. M. and takes people away to be questioned or imprisoned without habeas corpus and with little hope of true justice since justice is peronist.

So one naturally finds here as in all totalitarian regimes a reign of fear. Publishers do not dare print books unfavorable to the regime's ideas; teachers carefully eschew criticism; citizens avoid discussing peronism in front of servants. A gray conformity is descending on public life.

In a speech on justicialism Dec. 19, 1950, General Perón said:

"We've no desire to make propaganda; we only desire that our truth [justicialism] should be known because we don't want to export our truth."

Mussolini once said: "Fascism isn't for export." Premier Stalin had a policy of "socialism in one country." Justicialism in reality has international aspects that General Perón himself enunciated but it has not yet caught on outside of Argentina.

The attack on La Prensa has to be fitted into this pattern and into the whole atmosphere of internal struggle for power and for a completely totalitarian state.

CHAPTER 3

Post-War Populism Lives on the Fringes

For several decades after the end of World War II, populism in Europe and the United States was treated with suspicion. Many public intellectuals warned about populism's proximity to fascist politics, and populists were mostly confined to fringe parties. Though figures like George Wallace and Ross Perot ran significant presidential campaigns, they were unsuccessful in their efforts. However, by the 1980s right-wing populism began to gain influence in Europe, while a populist version of political Islam emerged in the Middle East.

Poujadistes Pitch Fruit at French Candidates

BY HENRY GINIGER | DEC. 17, 1955

PARIS, DEC. 16 — François Mitterrand, who was Minister of the Interior under Premier Pierres Mendès-France, was hit on the nose by a pear the other night. The pear was preceded and followed by ripe tomatoes.

M. Mitterrand therefore was forced to halt an election speech in his home department, the Nièvre, south of Paris. Since he began his campaign for re-election as a Deputy next Jan. 2, he has had little respite from such attacks, for the Poujadistes are out to get him.

The Poujadistes are the followers of Pierre Poujade, a 35-year-old bookseller from a small southern town who by shirt-sleeve oratory and indefatigable organizing has worked what was a small-scale tax revolt into a nation-wide assemblage of the "discontented."

M. Mitterrand recently termed M. Poujade and his followers "back-of-the-store Fascists." The former minster's expression alludes to the kind of behind-the-scenes political scheming associated with "the boys in the back room" in United States politics.

M. Poujade has denied that his organization is a political one. But, having scored impressive victories last week in partial elections for municipal chambers of commerce, it now has 150 electoral lists entered in the ninety departments of Metropolitan France. This large-scale political act has the more conventional parties engaged in worried speculation as to both the strength and aims of the movement.

Up to now the movement's aims have been somewhat negative. M. Poujade formed his Union for the Defense of Tradesmen and Artisans in 1953 to protest against "ruinous" taxation of small business men in the poor and backward areas of south-central France.

Because they are inefficiently organized and uncompetitive, a large percentage of small businesses throughout France had resorted to tax fraud to stay alive. When the Government has attempted to crack down by on-the-spot inspection of books, the Poujadiste protest has taken the forms of physical violence against the inspectors and tax "strikes."

At the beginning of this year the movement was solidly implanted in all parts of France, including Paris. M. Poujade claimed 850,000 dues-paying members. The movement's attempts to put pressure on individual Deputies to call off the drive on tax delinquents were so successful that it came close to causing the overthrow of the Government of Premier Edgar Faure in March.

This petit bourgeois movement has been violently critical of Parliament, and in France anti-parliamentarianism is always equated with reactionary anti-democratic tendencies. Therefore, despite M. Poujade's protests, his organization has been almost automatically classified on the extreme Right.

It has naturally come into conflict with the extreme Left represented by the Communists, who once made overtures to it. It is also competing for votes with the non-Communist Left organized around M. Mendès-France, with whom M. Mitterrand is associated.

But M. Poujade is also attacking the center-conservative forces under M. Faure and Foreign Minister Antoine Pinay, for he has declared a plague on all parliamentary houses that he holds responsible for making life miserable for his followers.

In the campaign the movement has tried to branch out to get agricultural and working class elements behind it. Three kinds of lists have been formed, which in many departments are allied among themselves for voting purposes.

The lists have such titles as List for Civic Action and for the Defense of Consumers and Family Interests, List for French Union and Fraternity and List for the Defense of Agricultural and Wine-Growing Interests.

At the very least M. Poujade, not a candidate himself, can bank on a hard core of small tradesmen, who have changed from apathy to aggressiveness. M. Mitterrand has not been the only one to feel their wrath at election rallies.

The Ghost of Populism Walks Again

BY C. VANN WOODWARD | JUNE 4, 1972

AMERICAN POLITICAL CULTURE encourages the periodic revival of ghosts. The practice has become traditional. Revivals and celebrations of the past are national rituals. Before fully recovering from a Civil War Centennial, we gird ourselves for a Revolutionary Bicentennial. We have had two Whig parties and two Republican parties, and now we appear to be pregnant with a second Populist party. There is already a populist movement, some would have it a populist fad or myth. Populist slogans and populist candidates abound.

Some politicians proclaim themselves populists and even more are rather indiscriminately labeled populists. The term crops up everywhere — in book titles, manifestoes, speeches, editorials. It is used, as it always has been, both a term of abuse and a term of praise, depending on the ax the user has to grind or the history he has read and how he understands it. Increasingly it turns up in improbable and unaccustomed quarters and more and more as a term of approbation rather than opprobrium.

After a Rip Van Winkle sleep of 80 years, an old Populist of 1892 would awake in a bewildering world of 1972. He would not blink twice at a populist Senator from Oklahoma and one from South Dakota, or be startled by a Governor of Alabama in populist clothing, a Lieutenant Governor of Virginia who calls himself a populist, or assorted populist types in the Lower South. Those were all old Populist territories in the nineties with authentic traditions and precedents. What would give our old Populist a turn would be the sight of a populist from Maine or one from Park Avenue. What he would make of a self-proclaimed populist from West Virginia who bore the name John D. Rockefeller 4th, or the Presidential candidacy of Dr. Benjamin Spock on a populist ticket, or references to the "populist style" of Spiro Agnew — is beyond imagining.

Any resemblance between late 19th-century Populism and the movement now struggling to be born would at first appear entirely superficial. The world of Tom Watson, Cyclone Davis, Stump Ashby, Sockless Jerry Simpson, James B. Weaver and Mary E. Lease was a remote, intensely provincial, horse-and-buggy America of a forgotten long ago. Their world was rural, their values agrarian, their problems largely agricultural, their movement bred of prolonged depression. To many Americans today their language would seem quaint, their temper overwrought and some of their ideas cranky.

On the other hand, when one takes account of their grievances, their political and economic plight, their enemies, the coalitions they formed, the issues they raised, the platforms they wrote and the strategies they used, the remoteness and irrelevance of the old Populists diminishes and they begin to come into focus. They spoke for the little man against the establishment, the provinces against the metropolis, the poor and deprived against the rich and privileged. The issues they addressed centered on the unequal distribution of wealth and income, and the unjust distribution of power. These issues included prices, wages, money, taxes, unemployment, monopoly, consumers' rights, big-business corruption of government and government selling out to business.

IN A MOMENT of exasperation, the economist Henry Demarest Lloyd once called his fellow Populists "a fortuitous collection of the dissatisfied." And so they were. The mass of them were farmers, however, and their dissatisfactions were bred of three decades of agricultural depression, the last of which coincided with the worst industrial depression up to that time. Debt-ridden, mortgage-ladened, impoverished and helpless, millions of farmers saw themselves slipping from landowning to tenant status. Bitter and desperate, they undertook for a time to speak for and lead the oppressed of all classes.

Back of the Populist revolt were many organizations, unions and cooperatives, such as the Grangers and the Knights of Labor, but

LIBRARY OF CONGRESS PRINTS AND PHOTOGRAPHS DIVISION

A promotional print for the Grangers, a farmers' advocacy organization associated with the first populists.

none was as powerful as the Farmers' Alliance. Founded about 1875 in Texas, it exploded with new ideas and militant zeal in 1886, and swept through the whole South, establishing thousands of suballiances at the community level. In three years the Alliance claimed four and a quarter million members. Semisecret, highly centralized, with its own press and official corps of "lecturers" or propagandists, the Farmers' Alliance radicalized and disciplined the future Populist cohorts. The larger part of a similar but much smaller Northwestern Alliance merged with the dominant Southern organization as a National Alliance in 1889 and the Knights of Labor affiliated with it.

The "demands" of the Alliance evolved into the Populist platform. They focused on issues of money and credit, land and industrial monopoly, and transportation. They called for the abolition of national banks, Government control of credit and money and a substantial increase of the money in circulation by several means, including free coinage of silver. They also wanted the break-up of trusts and monopolies; an eight-hour law for labor; Government ownership of railroad and telegraph lines; a Federal income tax; initiative and referendum; and direct election of Senators.

Feeling strong enough to take over the Democratic party in the South in 1890, Alliance men did in fact elect 45 Congressmen and three Senators pledged to support their demands, and secured control of eight state legislatures. In the West, Alliance men set up several independent third parties of different names that elected eight Congressmen and two Senators. When most of the Alliance-elected Congressmen from the South lined up behind a conservative Democratic candidate for Speaker, Tom Watson of Georgia left his party and became the "People's party" or Populist candidate for Speaker, with support of the Western third-party men. Thus the new party had a Congressional delegation before it had national organization.

At a national convention the Populists welcomed alliance with the Knights of Labor, the Single-Taxers, the utopian Nationalists, Greenbackers and Prohibitionists, and attracted several Socialists. Their main problem lay in bridging the cleavages between the disconnected sections, parties, races and classes they sought to unite. They revived the old agrarian alliance between South and West, divided since the Civil War by the bloody-shirt issue. They struggled hard to unite black and white voters in the South against the racist propaganda of the old party. They appealed to labor and won over the declining Knights of Labor, but not the growing American Federation of Labor.

William Allen White of Kansas called Populist leaders of his state "wild-eyed, rattle-brained fanatics," and the very nicknames of such leaders as "Calamity" Weller of Iowa, "Bloody Bridles" Wait of Colorado and "Cyclone" Davis of Texas, lent themselves to the stereotype. But the variety of leaders defied generalization. They ranged from Virginia aristocrats with the oldest and most distinguished names to Texas evangelists and ex-cowpunchers. More typical was the middle range that included Tom Watson, twice the party's Presidential nominee and once the nominee for Vice President. A successful lawyer and editor, and a prolific author of history books, the red-headed Georgian was, before his party's collapse and his personal deterioration, utterly fearless and a formidable orator.

Leonidas L. Polk, a distinguished North Carolinian who was president of the National Alliance, was assumed to be the Populist choice for the 1892 nomination, but on his death James B. Weaver, the old Greenbacker from Iowa, was put forward. In spite of handicaps, the new party cast more than a million votes for their Presidential candidate, and elected 10 Congressmen, five Senators, three Governors, and some 1,500 members of state legislatures. In the elections of 1894 the third party increased the vote it polled in 1892 by 42 per cent, mainly in the South, and badly frightened the Democrats.

Democratic insurgents took over their own party in 1896, unseated the conservatives, and invited the Populists to put aside their more radical demands and support William Jennings Bryan on the silver issue. In spite of resistance by radicals, the silverites had their way. The Populists ran an independent ticket in two more Presidential elections, but the fight over fusion with Democrats in 1896 tore them apart and they never succeeded in reuniting.

The Old Populists left a vital heritage of protest and precipitated a historic realignment of American politics. It is far-fetched, however, to picture them as a model for modern radical reform. They lacked a firm grip on the problems even of their own time. Their parochial idiom, their evangelical style and their pentecostal politics are about as far removed from the present as anything in our history.

BUT TO CATCH the echo of the past in the present, to capture the appeal the Old Populism has for the New, one has to listen closely to the rhetoric of 19th-century Populism in old manifestoes, platforms and speeches. Here one senses the shared moods and common impulses of the two periods. They are moods of suspicion and resentment and a sense of betrayal, tones of frustration, disillusionment and alienation, disenchantment with the old parties, flashes of anger at injustice and neglect, disgust at private opulence and public squalor, indignation over fraud and bribery in government and corruption in high office, outrage over privilege of special interests and the arrogance of the rich.

As an example of the desperate tone and apocalyptic rhetoric of the Old Populists, the preamble of their platform of 1892 is often cited. It begins: "The conditions that surround us best justify our cooperation; we meet in the midst of a nation brought to the verge of moral, political and material ruin."

Yet neither the rhetoric of 1892 nor the bill of particulars that followed would seem especially out of date in any number of current-day speeches and editorials. The New York Times, for example, can ask rhetorically "whether a new rot has infected the American political-economic system" (April 2, 1972). According to a Harris Poll last September, a majority of Americans indicated distrust of every major institution in the country — business, the press, the media, the old parties and government in general, all the way up to and including the Presidency.

The New Populists on the whole enjoy advantages over the Old in their attack on common targets. They have more to shoot at, for one thing, and the targets are usually larger. The "bigness" that so disturbed the Populists of the nineties was minuscule compared with the bigness of the present. One has only to compare, for example, Standard Oil then with General Motors now. The old-fashioned Robber Barons were more conveniently personalized, but their corporate counterparts of today are more flagrant, as demonstrated by the recent histories of the nation's largest railroad, the nation's largest corporate conglomerate, or the nation's largest defense contractor.

The power of banks, which terrified the embattled farmers, was peanuts compared with the present-day concentration of bank power. In their wildest paranoid and conspiratorial dreams of interlocking directorates and financial monopolies, the Old Pops never imagined anything so extensive and elaborate as exists today among the largest commercial banks and the largest insurance companies.

There are certainly far more opportunities for contemporary scandal in view of the proliferation of Government contracts for national defense, highways, housing, airlines, health, education, welfare and agriculture. There are opportunities for Government subsidies, handouts and favoritism for business beyond anything dreamed of in the philosophy of the Old Pops. Besides a $4-billion annual subsidy to big corporate farmers, and fabulous subsidies to the largest defense contractors such as Lockheed, Boeing and General Dynamics, there are depletion allowances and import quotas for the powerful oil industry. Our Byzantine Federal tax structure has correctly been called "welfare for the rich and free enterprise for the poor," with built-in shelters, loopholes and exemptions that are closed to small incomes and wide open to the billions of the wealthy.

READY AND WAITING for the New Populism, therefore, are many of the issues that were exploited by its 19th-century predecessor plus a great many more concerns of the same character which have even greater popular appeal and explosive potential. The question remains, who will exploit them and to what ends? Will the resulting movement head to the right or the left? Is there any quality inherent in the nature of populism that dooms it to retrogressive and reactionary uses? Is there something about the ideology of populism, or about the type of leaders it produces or attracts, that justifies the rather sinister reputation it has among some intellectuals and more widely among the literate public?

To answer these questions, we must assess the findings of some scholars and look over the leaders populism has produced in the past as well as the potential leaders of the present in this country. But first a cursory glance at manifestations abroad might be instructive, for populism of one kind or another has found root lately in many parts of the world besides our own.

A conference of international scholars brought together in London five years ago to discuss world-wide manifestations of populism opened its summary report (a book entitled "Populism: Its Meaning and National Characteristics") with a phrase consciously lifted from the "Communist Manifesto" of 1848: "A specter is haunting the world — populism." Five years ago, the specter admittedly assumed a fantastic variety of forms. Among manifestations cited in the report were Poujade of France, Peron of Argentina, Vargas of Brazil, Zapata of Mexico and Belaunde of Peru. Populist leanings were found in Frantz Fanon's African following, in Gandhi's Indian movement, in the Sinn Fein of Ireland, in the Iron Guard of Romania, even in the doctrines of Tito, Mao and Castro.

A populist international has, of course, never developed, and to imagine a summit conference of world populists is to evoke comparison with the Tower of Babel. It would bring together left- and right-wingers; fascists and egalitarians; parliamentarians and totalitarians; the working class, middle class and peasants; movements that grew out of both rural and urban settings; and from developed and undeveloped countries (though predominantly the latter); upheavals bred of depression as well as booms; people with progressive as well as reactionary yearnings; and those with forward-looking as well as nostalgic impulses. It would also bring together movements that had never been conscious of one another, were unaware of a common denominator, and rarely adopted the name "populist."

Their grouping is not their own idea but that of theorists who impose on them the populist classification. Admitting the looseness and the contradictions inherent in the term, the theorists point to the looseness with which the terms "capitalism," "communism," and "democracy" are used, holding that "populism" is no more vague and that its use is equally unavoidable. When pressed for definitions of populism, political theorists say they are speaking more of a syndrome than an ideology, a situation rather than a theory, an emphasis, a dimension of political culture rather than a system. They speak of movements found "among those aware of belonging to the poor periphery of an industrial system," either in provinces or ex-colonies. Populism is a "tension between metropolis and province," an upheaval of the little man, the neglected many against an indifferent establishment. It proclaims the supremacy of the "will of the people," the common folk over the sophisticated, the wealthy, the powerful and the corrupt.

The two classic historical examples of populism, apparently the only two that embraced the name, occurred in the late 19th century in Russia and the United States. Mutually unaware of each other, they shared some characteristics, but their differences were more numerous. For one thing, Russian Populism was made up of intellectuals without a mass following, American Populism of a mass following with few intellectuals. Illuminating comparison is difficult, however. For example, there is the contrast between the figures of Czar Alexander II and President Grover Cleveland as national symbols of what populists of the two countries opposed; there is also the remarkable encounter between Count Leo Tolstoy and William Jennings Bryan — an interview without communication, as it turned out.

BEYOND THE OBVIOUS point that populism assumes many forms (as, indeed, do capitalism and Communism) and that comparisons are dangerous, this excursion abroad leaves us with the conclusion that for an understanding of the American heritage of populism we had best stick pretty closely to its domestic history. Even then we are confronted with sharp differences of opinion and interpretation among scholars. Populists and their forebears, and the populist tradition, have from the start had rough handling from conservative historians. But until the nineteen-fifties, historians of the progressive, liberal or radical tradition generally treated populists with respect as people with legitimate and serious grievances, striking at real economic and social evils, proposing rational and sometimes ingenious reforms, and working within the reform tradition toward humane ends.

A startling reversal of this picture took shape in the mid-nineteen-fifties at the hands of intellectuals caught in cross-currents of the cold war. Mainly social scientists rather than historians, these revisionists published numerous works, but most of their strictures on populism find expression in contributions to a book edited by Daniel Bell, "The New American Right" (1955). None of the writers repudiated democracy, but they fixed on populism or what they loosely and sometimes wrongly identified with it in all periods of American history — as embodying the seamy and sinister side of democracy, often referred to as "mobism" or "plebicitarism."

Few professed much knowledge of the historic party of Populism or historic Populists, but those who did joined in attributing to the 19th-century movement a basically irrational mentality that was expressed in paranoidal obsessions, conspiratorial delusions, nostalgic dreams of a golden age and hostility to industrial progress. Populists were described as opportunists given to demagogic exploitation of racism, anti-Semitism and the hatred of foreigners (xenophobia) and immigrants (nativism).

Most of the revisionists were more interested in the present than in the past, and were particularly concerned over the mass support

Senator Joseph McCarthy was then winning in his anti-Communist crusade of character assassination. They seized upon populism, in its newly conceived reactionary image, as proto-Fascism and the roots of authoritarianism — the "radical right" and all that was retrograde in the mid-nineteen-fifties and in the whole American political tradition. Thus Prof. Talcott Parsons of Harvard discovered "elements of continuity between Western agrarian populism and McCarthyism," and Prof. Edward A. Shils of Chicago thought them connected by "a straight line." An extreme statement by Peter Viereck declared that underneath the old populism "seethed a mania of xenophobia, Jew-baiting, intellectual-baiting and thought-controlling lynch spirit."

THIS INTERPRETATION OF historic American Populism, or one derived from it, is the one still fixed in the mind of the educated public. It has given the word the sinister connotation that it has for so many, and is responsible for the moral and political disreputability under which the New Populism suffers. Many informed people, even some who are — or otherwise would be — drawn to support the new movement, continue to renounce or apologize for the heritage of Populism and to disavow any connection with it.

Thus even Jack Newfield and Jeff Greenfield, authors of "A Populist Manifesto: The Making of a New Majority," a spirited platform for the New Populism, feel obliged to renounce the proper heritage of the movement in their book. And in a subsequent appeal they write: "We emphasize a 'new' populism because there was plenty wrong with the old Populism which flourished in the late 19th century: racism, paranoia, xenophobia. The movement we seek rejects these poisons."

If popular protest and radical reform movements of the present are obliged to cut their roots with the past, they will wither and die. If they, unlike those of the past, habitually regard political impulses in the mass of ordinary people as inherently irrational or poisonous, they cut off their source of support. If every mass protest against existing institutions is discredited as "populist," we are lost. If intellectuals and

LIBRARY OF CONGRESS PRINTS AND PHOTOGRAPHS DIVISION

Competing signs for prospective Democratic presidential candidates George Wallace and Shirley Chisholm. Wallace is a pro-segregation populist, while Chisholm is the first African-American woman to run for the Democratic nomination.

enlightened folk are alienated from the sources of revolt, mass dissent will be consigned to the demagogues, the racists and the unscrupulous. The very core of the democratic faith is at stake here.

Rarely have crises in public affairs so closely coincided with scholarly concerns. Yet the public has fallen behind the scholars. The sinister interpretations of populism, biased by the mood of the mid-fifties, have been since then subjected to searching criticism in monographs and articles of limited circulation, some yet to be published. These have effectively disproved the charge of xenophobia and nativism, discounted the evidence of anti-Semitism, and greatly diminished and brought into perspective of a racist society the charge of racism. They have stressed the reality of Populist grievances, the vital importance of Populists' issues, the rationality of their demands, and the courage of their leaders. If Populists were anti-intellectual, we are reminded that intellectuals of the time were hysterically anti-Populist. The late

Richard Hofstadter, whose "Age of Reform" (1955) shaped much of the earlier view but not its extreme form, conceded the validity of much of this criticism in later publications.

A curious twist of history, it can now be seen, fastened upon the Populists a reputation for the tactics, bigotries and policies of their enemies, their betrayers, or a few old Populists like Tom Watson who did not age gracefully. Only thus can a George Wallace be conceded the mantle of Populism. A Ben Tillman or a Jim Hogg, or their epigone, the Heflins, Bilbos and Cole Bleases, are now regularly labeled "Populists," yet they were the bitter enemies of Populism. It was they who disfranchised the Negro and used white-supremacy demagoguery to destroy Populism. It was the Populists who tried and often succeeded, at a time when Negrophobia was approaching a peak, in uniting black and white voters behind the party of reform.

As for the theory giving more recent right-wing demagogues populist roots and origins, it received a severe blow from a study by Michael P. Rogin, "The Intellectuals and McCarthy" (1967), which proved that the overwhelming majority of those who sent Joe McCarthy and his supporters to the Senate were antiprogressive regular Republicans and predominantly economic conservatives.

FEW SCHOLARS ARE SO naive as to believe that the mass of people who support any leftward movement are devoid of irrational and retrograde impulses. Nor for that matter are the masses who support rightist movements in the old parties. Certainly the populist masses had their share of such impulses, and it was always a struggle between leaders who appealed to the retrograde and those who addressed the better nature of the discontented. The same sort of struggle is raging today for leadership of the nascent New Populism.

As a matter of fact the New Left students were among the first to sense the rise of incipient populism in the nineteen-sixties and make ineffectual bids to organize and capture it. At one New England university a professor of history, known for his writing on populism, was repeatedly approached by student activists seeking his support for reviving the Populist party under New Left auspices. His advice was that nothing was better calculated to alienate the sort of people they sought to attract than certain "life-styles," class attitudes and varieties of arrogance. The New Left tried but failed. The later efforts of some chastened old New Lefters to organize populist sentiment at the community level through their New American Movement remain indeterminate.

The Nixon Republicans, with their appeal to "The Silent Majority" and "Middle America," were trying in their way to capture at least a share of the same constituency. It is not too fantastic to regard Vice President Agnew's assaults on the "effete East" and assorted sophisticates in this light. The Nixon-style populism, however, has already written off one element essential to any successful populist coalition — the black votes. The "Southern strategy" and the Presidential stand on busing and other race issues indicate that clearly enough.

Last September populist-watchers with strict standards believed they saw the genuine article emerging out of Oklahoma when Senator Fred Harris announced his Presidential candidacy. The son of a sharecropper from Mississippi, he spoke the true idiom in down-to-earth style. "No more hogwash" was the way he paraphrased his real slogan for the networks. "There simply cannot be a mass movement without the masses," he maintained, and he meant masses of all colors. He spoke, he said, "in the spirit of the old Populism," which he believed "contains lessons with modern applications." After six weeks he withdrew from the race, declaring simply, "I am broke."

George Wallace of Alabama, in spite of the crippling attempt on his life, continues to be a formidable contender in this field. The busing issue is the latest version of his original stand as defender of segregation and white supremacy. He knows that hard-line segregationists can have perfectly rational economic grievances and political demands, and makes his pitch accordingly. Any candidate for the Democratic nomination in 1972 who seriously addresses himself to the valid and rational issues of discontent, Senator George McGovern, for example, will have to contend with an opponent skilled at combining and confusing the irrational with the rational. The two candidates will be appealing to overlapping pads of the same constituency. After Senator Robert Kennedy was assassinated and Senator Eugene McCarthy was eliminated from the race in 1968, many of their supporters turned to Wallace in the general election. Four years later we seem faced with the possibility of a re-enactment of such a struggle.

BOTH SENATOR HUMPHREY and Senator McGovern are making bids for the neo-populist constituency, each in his own way. Humphrey has made more explicit concessions to the Wallace line on busing, and, like Wallace, relies less on economic issues than on folksy identification with the masses. McGovern, on the other hand, has drawn a rather strict line against racist appeals and in his dry, firm, sometimes angry voice, hammers home economic issues and his program of reforms. Acknowledging a kinship between his supporters and those of Wallace, and insisting that the latter be granted a hearing at Miami, McGovern goes so far as to say, "Governor Wallace and I have different solutions, but both of us are saying with a perfectly straight, clear conscience that we are fed up with conditions as they are."

An air of paradox hangs over the Humphrey-McGovern contest. While the former history professor, McGovern, apparently clings to the darker interpretation of historic Populism and disavows the Populist label, he is closer to the old Populist tradition in his economic reforms and his moral outrage than any of his opponents. Yet organized labor leans more to Humphrey than to McGovern and so do the black voters. Both of these Humphrey constituencies seem to be guided by historic allegiances and debts of the past rather than by concerns of the present. McGovern's advantage lies in his appeal to youth and in his anti-Establishment reputation. That reputation is indispensable to any Populist leader and Humphrey has not been able to acquire it.

It must be admitted that the New Populism is still a sentiment and not an organization: Candidates seeking to co-opt that sentiment for their national ambitions do have organizations, but not the sentiment itself. The new populists lack what the old Populists had painfully built up by the rank and file in their local and state organizations, founded on the discipline and radical education of the Farmers' Alliance, vital precursor of the party. Lacking such discipline and political education, the new populists are more susceptible to demagogic appeal. In dragging them into national politics prematurely, Presidential candidates act in a parasitic rather than a constructive role and may dissipate the sentiment before it achieves coherence.

Part of the anti-establishment tradition of both populist movements is a distrust of the two old parties. Then and now they are pictured as equally reactionary, corrupt and cynical — Tweedledee vs. Tweedledum. The obvious answer is a third party. Wallace may still be able to run a replay of his third-party adventure if he is not the choice at Miami. If the Democrats nominate an establishmentarian we may well have a second "third" party, dividing the populists into hostile right- and left-wing camps.

The chances of the Democrats co-opting the populists, a replay of the Bryan performance of 1896, are not to be dismissed out of hand. It is true, as Newfield and Greenfield point out, that the main current of Democratic thought has run counter to the party's populist tradition for a generation. Labor unions enlisted in the cold war and liberals grew conservative and elitist. The party rejected Estes Kefauver, who had the common touch and the true populist reform zeal, and fell under the charm of Adlai Stevenson and John Kennedy, bewitched by "style." What there was of the populist in Lyndon Johnson was quickly submerged under his Vietnam disaster and he was scorned as much for the one as for the other by liberal elitists.

Signs of a reversal of the elitist current in the Democratic party are not lacking. Bobby Kennedy's reception among South Bend blue collars and in Watts pointed the way in 1968, and George McGovern is claiming his mantle. The drastic reform of delegate elections for the Democratic National Convention now curbs the dominance of bosses and party establishmentarians and gives youth, blacks and women a striking prominence. The submerged populist tradition has a better opportunity of surfacing than it has had in many years. As in '96, of course, the populists may be joining a losing coalition.

It remains to see what part the New Populism might play in the major voting realignment that political scientists have been predicting, and whether 1972 may qualify as one of our historic "critical elections." These realignments and critical elections have periodically served to relieve the build-up of tension in our society and restore the health of the party system and the body politic. They have come in cycles of 28 to 36 years: 1800, 1828, 1860, 1896, 1932. Each one from Jefferson to Franklin Roosevelt was founded on a new coalition, represented major breaks in the voting habits of millions and reflected widely perceived national crises such as slavery, the Populist revolt or the Great Depression. Dominant sentiment on such polarizing issues either captures one of the major parties or forms a new one: Anti-Masons in the eighteen-twenties, Free Soilers in the eighteen-fifties, Populists in the eighteen-nineties, La Follette Progressives in the nineteen-twenties.

By almost every sign, we are already ripe for a new realignment, whether it comes now or later. More than the normal span between "critical elections" has elapsed. Huge blocs of voters have cut loose from traditional moorings: the South growing more Republican, New England more Democratic, blacks and other ethnic groups more independent and politically conscious. Ticket-splitters multiply, and between a fourth and a third of all voters now classify themselves as independents. Some 25 million persons between the ages of 18 and 25 will be eligible to cast their first votes for President in 1972, and almost half of them refuse to profess affiliation with either of the old parties. The aimless drift and confusion of the old parties that has always preceded a major realignment has long prevailed.

THE GREAT UNKNOWN is which of several possible issues or combinations of them will polarize the voters, be captured by the winning candidate, precipitate the new realignment and shape the dominant coalition. "Rational" or "irrational" issues? Is race "the one question in American life today that seems to pack the emotional punch necessary for a party realignment" as David S. Broder, author of "The Party's Over," fears? Fred Harris would seem to agree. "Race is the central fact in American politics today," he writes, "because it is the deepest and most dangerous problem of American life." If so, the new realignment could be an ugly one. Ominous questions of this sort lend an urgency and a poignancy to the questions we have been raising about the new and old populism.

Few who write about or instruct or govern ordinary Americans have kept in very close touch with them in recent years of crisis. One who has both kept in touch and kept his faith in them is Dr. Robert Coles of Harvard, author of many fine books about them. "In my experience," he writes, "if ordinary 'average' Americans are anything, they by and large are loyal to this nation's populist tradition. It is a tradition that goes back into the 19th century, when farmers and factory workers railed in down-to-earth language against 'big-money boys' and 'the crooked politicians.' It is a tradition that includes white Southerners, among them avowed segregationists, Midwestern small-town people, miners and blue-collar workers. And it is a tradition that is by no means dead."

History would appear to be forcing a new test on that tradition. On the outcome of that test — and on the frustrations and fears, the real problems and grievances, the good sense and good faith of the people who submit to it — hangs the shape, of our future.

C. VANN WOODWARD, Sterling Professor of History at Yale, is the author of several works on Populism. His most recent book is "American Counterpoint: Slavery and Racism in the North-South Dialogue."

Religious Revival Is Sweeping Across the World of Islam

BY JONATHAN KANDELL | NOV. 23, 1978

TEHERAN, IRAN, NOV. 22 — In Iran, a 2,500-year-old monarchy, backed by the most powerful military force in Central Asia and a surfeit of oil riches, is staggered by a loosely organized, unarmed opposition led by conservative Islamic clergymen.

In neighboring Afghanistan, the pro-Soviet regime installed by a military coup earlier this year lashes out at its opponents as "foreign agents covering their faces with an Islamic mask" — and hastens to strengthen its own legitimacy by publicly embracing the teachings of the Koran.

In Egypt, Moslem fundamentalists last year assassinated a Cabinet minister who opposed their program. And in Malaysia, university students are putting pressure on the Government to adopt a Sharia legal code, aligning civil, criminal and commercial laws with Islamic doctrine.

From North Africa and the Middle East to Central and Southeast Asia, the winds of a religious revival are sweeping with various degrees of force through the world's 600 million Moslem faithful.

LEFT AND RIGHT SEEM VULNERABLE

Both conservative and radical regimes appear vulnerable. Even though a resurgent Moslem movement has taken special aim at the alleged excesses of Western influence, it is hostile to Marxist ideals as well.

For the United States, Europe and Japan, the primary concern over the Moslem revival focuses on how its success would affect the supply of oil and the status of billions of dollars of investments in the area. The reduction of petroleum exports and calls for the expulsion of foreigners during the current unrest in Iran have already created apprehension in the West.

The Russians, who also saw part of their natural gas supply cut off by striking Iranian workers, appear uneasy over the Islamic revivalist movement's potential influence on the Soviet Union's own millions of Moslems. Recently the Russians asked for an additional consulate in Libya, but quickly withdrew the request when the Libyan leader, Muammar el-Qaddafi, an Islamic activist, demanded in return a Libyan consulate in Tashkent, the major city in the heavily Moslem region of the Soviet Union.

Within Islamic countries, the Moslem revival has rattled minorities fearful of religious or ethnic intolerance, businessmen concerned that a return to religious legal codes will hamper economic activity, planners eager to modernize their countries, and middle-class people comfortable with Western mores and materialism.

INGREDIENTS OF IRAN'S BACKLASH

In Iran, now the center of Moslem unrest, the ingredients for an explosive revivalist backlash have been growing for years. Beginning in the early 1960's, Shah Mohammed Riza Pahlevi strongly antagonized the religious establishment of the majority Shiite Moslem sect by stripping away its large landholdings as part of an agrarian reform program, and ending its dominant voice in education, marriage and divorce. The Shah has also ignored a 1906 Constitution that divided political power among the monarchy, Parliament and the religious leaders, who were supposed to determine whether legislation was in keeping with Islamic laws.

An industrialization program started 15 years ago has cut the proportion of Iranians living in rural areas from 75 percent to 52 percent of the population. But the Shah's vision of transforming his country into a global power has proved a good deal less inspiring than the conservative social and religious values that were left behind in the rural villages.

These traditional values have been sorely challenged by the accelerating Westernization that followed a 1973 oil price boom. The arrival

KEYSTONE/HULTON ARCHIVE/GETTY IMAGES

The Ayatollah Khomeini sitting in a garden in Pontchartrain, on the outskirts of Paris, earlier this month.

of 100,000 more Western businessmen, technicians and their families; the pursuit of Western-style affluence by the growing middle and upper classes; the alleged moral laxity of the wealthy; the evident pervasiveness of government and business corruption; the films, nightclubs, liquor stores and other symbols of Western "decadence" — all of this helps to swell the ranks of the religious backlash.

A NEED TO SAVE OIL

The Ayatollah Khomeini, the most powerful religious opposition leader despite his 15 years in exile, has spoken of the need to "save petroleum reserves for future generations."

Another religious revivalist, Libya's Colonel Qaddafi, has limited oil production and sought to screen out Western influence in his country. Even in Saudi Arabia, whose conservative leaders are seemingly beyond reproach from Moslem fundamentalists, a vocal minority has argued that petroleum output should be slashed to hold back the influx of Western goods and mores.

Xenophobia has played a major role in the Moslem opposition movement shaping Iran, despite assertions by religious leaders that incidents have been the work of small groups of irresponsible fanatics.

A major reason behind the oil strike was the demand by Iranian employees that foreigners be excluded from petroleum operations. Similar demands have disrupted air transportation and the country's communications system, and even a steel factory complex being directed by the Russians.

Non-Western minorities, including Kurds, Jews and Armenians, have also been shaken by the Moslem opposition movement.

Intolerance by Moslem fundamentalists has occasionally erupted in other countries as well recently. In Egypt, President Anwar el-Sadat's last-minute intervention foiled a legislative attempt to declare the death penalty for anyone seeking to convert a Moslem to another faith — a move aimed at the Coptic Christian minority. In Malaysia, a fundamentalist Islamic organization, known as the Army of Allah, has called for the expulsion of non-Moslems and has been accused of desecrating more than 20 Hindu temples.

In Afghanistan, the pro-Moscow regime of President Nur Mohammed Taraki has been troubled by a fundamentalist Moslem guerrilla movement, based in Pakistan. Apparently fearful of the possibility of a larger Moslem opposition, President Taraki has paid visits to mosques and made certain that Koranic teachings are more widely disseminated than Marxist literature.

BHUTTO DENOUNCED AS IMPIOUS

In Pakistan, conservative Moslems played a role in the military overthrow of Prime Minister Zulfikar Ali Bhutto, who was not only convicted of murder but also of failing to live according to the teachings of the Koran.

His successor, Gen. Mohammed Zia ul-Haq has fought hard to promote Moslem orthodoxy as a unifying force for the country, and has promised to align the legal system with the requirements of Islamic law. One such reform now under way would gradually eliminate interest charges from the banking and financial system.

In Iran, Islamic leaders have also raised the possibility of removing interest from financial transactions. Hostility to the modern banking system was evident in recent violent demonstrations that destroyed scores of banks in Teheran and other cities. At the same time, however, the bazaar merchants, who have been an important element in the Moslem opposition, have long made a practice of charging even higher interest rates than the banks in their money-lending operations.

‘A Man of the Right’ Is Rousing Passions in France

BY JOHN VINOCUR | MAY 29, 1984

PARIS, MAY 28 — Almost every night last week, there was a campaign rally, and almost every night there was a fight to go with it, a scenario of sirens and blood: Jean-Marie Le Pen speaks, the crowd shouts “Fascist! Racist!” and politics turns into clubs and fists and the gyre of lights from tens of police cars.

It is “the foreigners,” Arab and African immigrants, and the Commies — “les cocos” in French slang — who have been trying to break up his meetings, Mr. Le Pen says.

The explanation he offers for the violence is essentially the same one he provides for most of France’s problems, and its apparent simplistic appeal has turned Mr. Le Pen into a discomforting political phenomenon.

If the current polls are correct, Mr. Le Pen and his rightist National Front party should easily win seats for the first time in the European Parliament in voting taking place June 14 and 17 in the 10 members countries of the Common Market. Perhaps more than elsewhere, the vote in France is pure domestic politics, a quasiplebiscite on the Socialist-Communist Government; following Mr. Le Pen’s description, the balloting is historic in France because it will permit “the eruption of the National Front into what you could call the classic political scene.”

PARTY’S QUICK RISE

Eighteen months ago, Mr. Le Pen’s party barely existed. In the intervening period, a time of growing unemployment and economic frustration in France, the National Front did well in a number of municipal elections, insisting that it is not fascist or extremist, but shouting that France is being “colonized by an Islamic-Arabic wave,” stealing jobs, bringing crime and drugs, and turning the French into second-class citizens in their own country.

Now, with the prospect of winning four or five seats among the 81 French representatives to the Parliament in Strasbourg, the party believes it is on the edge of respectability. Of all the elements that distress the French political establishment about Mr. Le Pen's rise, perhaps the strongest is what many politicians say is his success in rendering himself relatively innocuous, in making his vocabulary — more one of verbal winks and nudges than outright demagoguery — part of the acceptable political dialogue.

For Mr. Le Pen, the classic spectrum of French politics, including the traditional moderate and conservative parties, holds responsibility for what he calls the country's misery. Weak, soft, corrupt, sentimental, lying: France's political leaders of the past 30 years, he insists, have tricked and manipulated the French. Minus any grand philosophical pretentions, Mr. Le Pen's summary vision, defined by Rene Rémond, an historian of the French right, "is that of a poor man's Vichy" — a society of order and authority as characterized by Marshal Philippe Pétain's collaborationist Government in World War II.

"I'm not a religious democrat," Mr. Le Pen says, trying to offer his own definition of himself. "That means that once you've installed democracy you just don't let it run and everyone turns out happy and prosperous. No, I'm a man of the right."

MASTER OF DOUBLE MEANINGS

At 56 years of age, he is blond and beefy, a near caricature of the Foreign Legion officer he once was. A substantial inheritance gave him a large house on the bluffs of St. Cloud, overlooking Paris. Behind its gates are two Doberman pinschers; inside, two life-size wooden blackamoors stand guard, holding candelabra alongside the fireplace.

When he talks, it is softly at first. But the volume comes soon, particularly to express "what a horrible lie" the idea is that because he wants to send immigrants home he might be a manipulator of violence and hatred. Mr. Le Pen's strongest skill would seem to be his mastery of double meanings and contradictions, his ability to offer denials of accusations against him, and then, almost in the same breath, modify them so that his audience senses where his heart is.

For example, Mr. Le Pen says it is absurd to suggest that he or his party is anti-Semitic, although one of his running mates has written that "the Jews have a tendency to occupy all the key posts in the Western countries." French Jews are like all other French citizens, according to Mr. Le Pen. But using his voice as an elbow to nudge his audience, he adds, "On the other hand, I don't consider myself obliged to like Mme. Veil's policies, or Chagall's painting, or Mahler's music."

MAIN TARGET OF CAMPAIGN

Mme. Veil is Simone Veil, the former president of the European Parliament, who heads the unified ticket of the main moderate and conservative parties in next month's elections here. As a former Minister of Health under President Valery Giscard d'Estaing, she played an important role in the relaxation of French abortion laws and has become a main target of Mr. Le Pen's campaign.

Mrs. Veil is Jewish and a survivor of Auschwitz. When Mr. Le Pen was asked if he had described her law on abortion as being "responsible for the genocide of thousands of French babies," the answer was no, but that the remark, "seen personally, of course, seems to correspond to reality."

When the question is whether his party stands to the left or right of the Italian neo-Fascists, who hold four seats in the European Parliament, the reply is a question, "They voted for Mme. Veil as President of the Parliament, didn't they?"

Mr. Le Pen's skill is that he mixes this kind of remark with statements like: "I defy anyone to show that we are extremists. Our ideas are constitutionalist and in favor of the republic. We participate in all the elections. We've never been accused of operating against the external or internal security of the state."

"Extremist in our actions?" All the violence, he says, is directed against the National Front.

CALLED AN ADVENTURER

For Mr. Rémond, the National Front calls neither for violence nor for the destruction of French political institutions. But he insists that "an extremism remains in the sense that it proposes simplistic solutions for complex problems."

Curiously, the political scientist is less hard on Mr. Le Pen than Pierre Poujade, the old right-wing politician who once regarded Mr. Le Pen as a protege during his brief period of success in the middle 50's. Mr. Poujade described him as "an adventurer," a man ready "to say absolutely anything, dance any pirouette to grab a couple of votes."

Mr. Le Pen's vote-getting techniques these days include publishing a book that features grip-and-grin pictures of himself with two Republican members of the United States Senate, Paul Laxalt of Nevada and Paula Hawkins of Florida, taken at a fund-raising event for President Reagan in Miami this year.

The politicians are in evening clothes, and it is this kind of badge of respectability that seems so attractive to Mr. Le Pen. When he talks about the meaning of the probable entry of his party into the European Parliament, he says it is basically that people with political opinions like his own will stop being treated "like untermenschen" — subhumans.

There is the quick smile of a man who is convinced he has just said something witty.

"Anybody can hang a swastika around my neck and put a helmet on my head," Mr. Le Pen goes on. "That's easy. You can do it to President Mitterrand too. I just want to talk the way I am, and if they let me talk, I dare say, they'll know I've been passing through."

The Politics of Frustration

BY KEVIN PHILLIPS | APRIL 12, 1992

In the 1890's and 1930's, like today, boom turned to bust and left a bitter and radicalized electorate.

AS THE 1992 PRESIDENTIAL CAMPAIGN unfolds, it is increasingly evident that the United States has entered a period of political alienation and turmoil the likes of which we have experienced only a few times in our history. Frustrated voters have embraced one angry "outsider" candidate after another: David Duke, Patrick Buchanan, Jerry Brown and perhaps H. Ross Perot. Their unrest reflects deep worries about the economy, Washington, foreigners and job security unseen since the 1890's and 1930's, the last two occasions when Americans experienced deep economic pain from global upheavals and great debt bubbles imploding after speculative booms. The end of the cold war has only added to the popular focus on domestic troubles.

As in the 1890's and 1930's, today's politics of frustration is not confined to the United States. Neo-Nazism is stirring in the mountains and valleys of Austria, Bavaria and Lombardy, as well as in the hills of Louisiana. The rout of the Socialists in France's recent regional elections showed that the anti-immigrant far right of Jean-Marie Le Pen is an increasingly serious electoral force. Benito Mussolini's reasonably glamorous granddaughter — her aunt happens to be Sophia Loren — announced earlier this year that she found Italy's changing political climate favorable enough to stand for Parliament this month as a neo-Fascist. And Ehud Sprinzak's new book, "The Ascendance of Israel's Radical Right," ponders the collapse of the center and the rise of ultranationalist extremism there, too.

In the 1890's and 1930's, American politics succeeded in capturing and separating out the legitimate ingredients of voter anger, suppressing the extremism and creating a new vital center. Only in the

1850's did the process fail, and we fought the Civil War. While no one is suggesting that we are heading for another cataclysm, we should not underestimate the seriousness of the current voter unrest. Historically, subduing frustration politics has been a stressful process. Moreover, there are reasons to believe that today's entrenched parties, with their crippling array of interest groups, may have more trouble responding to the aroused electorate than did their predecessors in the 1890's and 1930's.

WHILE THE SPOTLIGHT of early 1992, quite logically, has been on Presidential politicking, the current mix of middle-class populism, frustration and fringe politics has been evident for at least a year and a half. Last year's precursor phenomena included David Duke, the former Klansman and American Nazi, edging out Louisiana's sitting G.O.P. governor in an open primary, and then, while losing November's gubernatorial run-off, still managing to draw 55 percent of the white vote. Another message-bearer was the Pennsylvania Democrat Harris Wofford, a mild-mannered former civil rights activist and college president. Wofford turned himself into a fierce middle-class populist and came from more than 40 points behind to defeat Richard Thornburgh, a cocksure Republican fresh from George Bush's Cabinet.

Wofford stunned the White House and lured Patrick Buchanan into the G.O.P. primaries. But the basic drumbeat actually went back to 1990 — to unexpected populist successes that superficially made no ideological sense. Besides Duke's first strong statewide race in Louisiana, Bernard Sanders had ridden soak-the-rich rhetoric to become the first Socialist elected to Congress from Vermont, and Paul Wellstone, a former Jesse Jackson state co-chairman, gained a Minnesota Senate seat for the Democrats by mocking the incumbent Republican Senator as a voice only for his financial contributors.

While voter outrage ignored philosophic and ideological boundaries, the core insurgency was obviously on the populist right, where Buchanan and the faded Duke struck at George Bush and his increasingly shaky Republican national coalition. Buchanan astonished the news media and the White House in February when his "Middle Class Revolution" won 37 percent of the vote in the New Hampshire primary. For a month thereafter, in state after state, 30 percent to 40 percent of Republican voters refused to support George Bush's renomination. It was the most serious challenge to an elected G.O.P. President since 1912; even Herbert Hoover, in the Great Depression year of 1932, had not had to seriously campaign for renomination.

By mid-March, Buchanan stopped attacking Bush, and the wind went out of his sails. In the Michigan primary, therefore, independent voters flocked to the Democratic race to vote for the new emerging voice of hostility to Washington and the nation's "corrupt" economic elites, Jerry Brown, the former Governor of California. Brown then went on to win in Connecticut with the same percentage that Buchanan had commanded in New Hampshire.

But even as Brown displaced Buchanan in the spotlight of populist insurgency, yet another Republican-led insurgency was taking shape — the billionaire businessman Ross Perot outlined a plan to put a new third party on all 50 state ballots. It would be a populist campaign to clean up Washington, Perot said last month, and as he weighed his final decision, volunteers reported more than a million telephone calls of support in the first three weeks.

THE SOURCES OF the repeated, unexpected successes of outsider and frustration politics are familiar ones in American history: economic trauma and disillusionment. An early example occurred in the 1840's and early 1850's, when drawn-out hard times following the Panic of 1837 and the huge surge of Catholic Irish and German immigrants in the 1840's produced the anti-Catholic splinter politics of the American, or "Know-Nothing," Party. Yet the two most recent examples of frustration politics provide a better backdrop for today's outburst. The populist surge of the 1890's and the "Share Our Wealth" movement of Huey Long and the National Union for Social Justice of the

Rev. Charles Coughlin, which grew out of the Great Depression of the 1930's.

Populism was provoked when Washington's tight money policies from the 1870's through the 1890's put American farmers through a wringer of rising costs and declining receipts that makes the current middle-class squeeze look like a church picnic. When the Panic of 1893 intensified a deflation into a depression, manufacturing and service workers also grew fearful about their jobs and declining incomes. With a new wave of immigrants pouring in, frustration politics hit a pitch not seen since the Civil War. Anti-immigrant, anti-Catholic feeling soared, and within a year the American Protective Association, tapping anti-immigration sentiments akin to those surging today, claimed 2.5 million members and played a prominent role in the 1894 Congressional elections.

In 1896, the insurgent Populist Party fused with the Democrats to nominate William Jennings Bryan for President. In the subsequent strong but losing campaign, Bryan attacked Wall Street and blamed British bankers for United States economic problems, much as populism's Republican and Democratic heirs a century later would bash Japan.

Bryan, not surprisingly, was also more or less an isolationist, and a few populists like the Kansas firebrand Mary Elizabeth Lease also attacked Jews and linked the Rothschilds and Jewish bankers to an international capitalist conspiracy. Yet despite these and other fringe positions, many of populism's legitimate demands — from trustbusting to a progressive income tax and direct popular election of United States Senators — wound up becoming law within 20 years. That was part of how the system defused frustration.

Over the next 30 years or so, splinter-party politics ebbed and flowed, without greatly affecting the national landscape, except for Teddy Roosevelt's Bull Moose effort. Then in 1934 and 1935, as it became clear that the new Democratic Administration of Franklin D. Roosevelt was making little progress against the Depression, the country produced still another round of radicalism, again reflecting fear for the American Dream. This movement blended the rhetoric and attributes of late-19th-century populism with elements of the new Fascism that was exploding in Italy, Germany and other parts of Europe.

The Long and Coughlin movements represented a modern evolution from populism, a label they rejected as hopelessly tainted with bumpkinism. Huey P. Long, as Governor and then Senator from Louisiana, was virtually as corrupt and as contemptuous of the law as any European or Latin American strongman of the time. Yet his pretensions of acting in the name of ordinary citizens and against Wall Street, millionaires and big business did have an element of the old populism. By 1934, Long was breaking with Franklin Roosevelt and the New Deal, accusing F.D.R. of being a captive of economic special interests.

After organizing his revolutionary "Share the Wealth" clubs, which claimed seven million members, Long laid plans to run as a third-party candidate for President in 1936. Opinion polls soon convinced Roosevelt to steal Long's populist thunder by proposing the "Wealth Tax Act of 1935" and declaring that "our revenue laws have operated in many ways to the unfair advantage of the few and they have done little to prevent an unjust concentration of wealth and economic power." Revealingly, much the same issue is gathering force again in the 1990's.

After Long was assassinated in 1935, Father Coughlin, the "radio priest" who ran the National Union for Social Justice, tried and failed to step into the Louisiana Senator's shoes. Within a few years, his attacks on British bankers and internationalists turned into advocacy of isolationist and America First policies (with currents of anti-Semitism) aimed at keeping the United States out of World War II. Similar themes are visible in the rhetoric of Duke and Buchanan.

Like today's apostles of frustration — and in contrast to the populists of the 1890's — Long and Coughlin had no quarrel with small-town merchants, bankers, businessmen and other paragons of the middle class. If anything, they upheld them as real Americans fighting a losing battle with the distant, alien forces of big business, Wall Street, big labor and big government. Today, once again, insurgents are directing their appeals to middle-income voters fearful that their homes, jobs and modest successes will be swept away by economic change.

Which brings us to the alienation of 1992. All the ingredients of the past surges are present again: economic anguish and populist resentment; mild-to-serious class rhetoric aimed at the rich and fashionable; exaltation of the ordinary American against abusive, affluent and educated elites; contempt for Washington; rising ethnic, racial and religious animosities; fear of immigrants and foreigners, and a desire to turn away from internationalism and concentrate on rebuilding America and American lives.

During the last two years, the surprise populist-surge candidacies have pursued at least two or three of these themes and psychologies, and not merely with a wide range of ideology but with a bewildering confusion of it. Buchanan is a conservative Republican and Senator Tom Harkin of Iowa is a liberal Democrat. But both are the sons of Irish-Catholic fathers who listened to Father Coughlin in the 1930's, and both are economic nationalists, America First quasi-isolationists, class warfare practitioners — and, not coincidentally, also the only two Presidential candidates to attack George Bush as an American King George III.

The breakdown of old ideological lines is a particularly important signal of frustration politics. In New Hampshire, Buchanan drew almost as well among self-identified liberals and moderates as among self-identified conservatives. His economic nationalism, neo-isolationism and doubts about the gulf war had Republicans from John Sununu to Dan Quayle complaining that the right-wing firebrand was really a liberal. Meanwhile, in the most uplifting hour of his insurgency, Buchanan's concern about the unemployed, the voiceless and the homeless earned favorable attention from several major liberal newspapers. Even Duke has styled himself a liberal on a number of economic and environmental issues.

Jerry Brown, too, mixed ideologies as he emerged in the Michigan and Connecticut primaries. His environmental and pro-labor positions, along with his musings about having Jesse Jackson as his running mate, speak to the left. His open contempt for Washington is a universal language, but his controversial support for a 13 percent flat tax on all income draws on right-wing, "supply side" thinking. Ross Perot's putative third party would also be a hybrid — fiercely populist in its proposed crackdown on Congress and Washington lobbyists, progressive in its endorsement of gun control, abortion rights and higher taxes on the rich, but conservative in the sense of Perot's image as a Sun Belt Republican, self-made billionaire businessman, Naval Academy graduate and hip-hip-hooray patriot.

Political scientists have described what we've been seeing recently as "center extremism" — the radicalization of the usually nonideological midsection of the population because of cultural and economic trauma. This can lead to dangerous politics, the most terrible example being Germany in the 1920's and early 1930's, when hard times and a collapsing center produced Adolf Hitler.

One measure of the depth of the current frustration in America is that Duke could win the support of a majority of white Louisiana voters in two straight statewide elections, notwithstanding television advertisements showing him in Ku Klux Klan robes and swastika armbands. Buchanan took many of the same positions as Duke on immigration, race, welfare, trade and nationalism, albeit more moderately. And the charges of nativism, fascism, xenophobia and anti-Semitism inspired by his statements had little effect on his support. When a radicalizing middle class regards the establishment as bankrupt and the status quo as intolerable, normal standards fall quite easily.

Although Buchanan and Duke have pursued class warfare against country-clubbers, Wall Street speculators and "vulture capitalists," both have declined to attack the unfairness to the middle class of Reagan-Bush economic policies that redistributed income upward and helped inflate the debt-driven speculative bubble of the 1980's, despite polls showing that majorities of Republican voters favor a surtax on millionaires as well as an increase in Federal income tax rates on the rich. This is a central dishonesty of right-wing populism.

And it is where Democratic populism enthusiastically leaps in. The left-leaning populists who became surprise winners — Sanders, Wellstone and Wofford — took strong positions against 1980's favoritism to the rich and for higher taxes on the top 1 percent of Americans. Of course, there are other aspects of ordinary Americans' frustration — from crime and pornography to racial quotas and welfare — that liberals and Democrats ignore or sidestep. This is the frequent dishonesty of left-wing populism. However, some of the Democrats' new frustration strategists, like Bill Clinton's adviser James Carville, understand that this neglect must be corrected.

FRUSTRATION POLITICS, even in its more extreme forms, represents a sort of primal scream by the electorate that major party politics must heed if the center is to hold. Indeed, this has been a reliable strength of America's political realignment process. From 1968 to 1972, the Republicans absorbed the valid elements of popular anger to capture and defuse the George Wallace vote; the Democrats of a generation earlier managed to surround and absorb the worried Americans for whom Huey Long and other radicals had become a fairness symbol.

But the precedents of previous watershed eras do not exactly apply. Economics are only part of today's equation; the 1990's are much less brutal than the 1930's, and public concern about jobs, living standards and foreign commercial advantages will persist even in a mild 1992 recovery. Race, too, is only part of the equation, for the 1990's are much less incendiary than the 1960's.

What's new is that two historic downturns may be underway simultaneously: the slow decline of the United States as the world's leading economic power and the related erosion of the middle class. Voters are justifiably nervous, and Japan is already replacing the Soviet Union as America's primary enemy in public opinion polls.

What's also new is the failure of America's parties and political leaders either to fathom the depth of the problems or to present a coherent set of policies capable of attracting angry voters and welding them into a new centrist governing coalition. Our political leaders understandably are having a difficult time grasping the possibility that they have mishandled the fortunes and future of the United States for the last quarter century.

The sad truth is that frustration politics has built to a possibly scary level precisely because of the unnerving weakness of the major parties and their prevailing philosophies. Too much attention has been paid to the hints of extremism and fascism in frustration candidates' politics and too little to the role of Reagan-Bush conservatism and fashionable liberalism in jointly re-enacting some of the ineptness and miscalculation of Germany's Weimar Republic that helped turn people toward extremism.

Three straight G.O.P. Administrations have mismanaged the economy into a cumulative straitjacket of debt and a slough of voter despond — finally sending the President of the United States to Tokyo in January as beggar in chief. Beyond that, they have periodically unleashed the anti-black and anti-Israel messages they now complain about in more blunt politicians as "bigotry." Conservatives and nationalists in Germany in the late 1920's and early 1930's behaved somewhat similarly.

Such politics, in turn, could not have succeeded if liberalism — first in Weimar, then in the United States since the late 1960's — had not in some respects been a politics of avant-garde cabaret values, mockery of patriotism and enthusiastic trespass on bourgeois culture. If Patrick Buchanan is to be put in a 1930-something context, so should the second-rate conservatives and liberals responsible for the economic and social failures from which he and other outsiders have drawn so many angry votes.

Two centuries of history, luckily, suggest that no such limited analogy should stop Americans from piecing together a new "vital center," and there are already faint signs of that in the rhetoric of Bill Clinton and elsewhere. But before that can happen, this country's political leadership will have to pay more attention to frustration politics, its legitimate complaints and its remedies. The democracy on which American politics fundamentally rests cannot work if the electorate's primal screams go unheeded.

KEVIN PHILLIPS is the author most recently of "The Politics of Rich and Poor."

CHAPTER 4

Attitudes of Anti-Globalization Spark a New Populism

The turn of the 21st century sparked a process of globalization, during which the United States embraced free trade and the European Union took shape as a transnational diplomatic entity. Many who felt left out of this period of economic growth pushed back. On the left were populist leaders in Latin America, the Occupy Movement and protests against fiscal austerity in the European Union. On the right, populist movements resisted multiculturalism and immigration in Europe and the Obama administration in the United States.

Rebels in Search of Rules

OPINION | BY NAOMI KLEIN | DEC. 2, 1999

IT IS ALL TOO EASY to dismiss the protesters at the World Trade Organization meeting in Seattle as radicals with 60's envy. A seemingly more trenchant criticism is that they are simply behind the curve, fighting against a tide of globalization that has already swamped them. Mike Moore, the director of the W.T.O., describes his opponents as nothing more than protectionists launching an assault on internationalism.

The truth, however, is that the protesters in Seattle have been bitten by the globalization bug as surely as the trade lawyers inside the Seattle hotels — though by globalization of a different sort — and they know it. The confusion about the protesters' political goals is understandable: this is the first movement born of the anarchic pathways of the Internet. There is no top-down hierarchy, no universally recognized leaders, and nobody knows what is going to happen next.

This protest movement is really anti-corporate rather than anti-globalist, and its roots are in the anti-sweatshop campaigns taking aim at Nike, the human rights campaign focusing on Royal Dutch/Shell in Nigeria and the backlash against Monsanto's genetically engineered foods in Europe.

At any time, one huge multinational company may be involved in several disputes — on labor, human rights and environmental issues, for example. Activists learn of one another as they aim at the same corporate target. Inadvertently, individual corporations have become symbols of the global economy in miniature, ultimately providing activists with name-brand entry points to the arcane world of the W.T.O.

This is the most internationally minded, globally linked movement the world has ever seen. There are no more faceless Mexicans or Chinese workers stealing our jobs, in part because those workers' representatives are now on the same e-mail lists and at the same conferences as the Western activists. When protesters shout about the evils of globalization, most are not calling for a return to narrow nationalism, but for the borders of globalization to be expanded, for trade to be linked to democratic reform, higher wages, labor rights and environmental protections.

This is what sets the young protesters in Seattle apart from their 60's predecessors. In the age of Woodstock, refusing to play by state and school rules was regarded as a political act in itself. Now, opponents of the W.T.O. — even those who call themselves anarchists — are outraged about a lack of rules and authority. They are demanding that national governments be free to exercise their authority without interference from the W.T.O. and asking for stricter international rules governing labor standards, environmental protection and scientific research.

Everyone, of course, claims to be all for rules, from President Clinton to Microsoft's chairman, Bill Gates. In an odd turn of events, the need

CHRISTOPHER MORRIS/CORBIS HISTORICAL/GETTY IMAGES

Seattle Police contain demonstrators against the World Trade Organization with tear gas.

for "rules-based trade" has become the mantra of the era of deregulation. But deregulation is by definition about the removal of rules. The W.T.O., charged with defining and enforcing deregulation, is only concerned with rules that regulate the removal of rules.

The W.T.O. has consistently sought to sever trade, quite unnaturally, from everything and everyone affected by it: workers, the environment, culture. This is why President Clinton's suggestion yesterday that the rift between the protesters and the delegates can be smoothed over with small compromises and consultation is so misguided.

The face-off is not between globalizers and protectionists, but between two radically different visions of globalization. One has had a monopoly for the last 10 years. The other just had its coming-out party.

NAOMI KLEIN is the author of the forthcoming "No Logo: Taking Aim at the Brand Bullies."

In the Time of Hugo Chávez

BY DEBORAH SONTAG | JUNE 2, 2002

EARLY ONE SUNDAY, when morning mist still shrouded the Avila Mountains encircling Caracas, I arrived at the Venezuelan leader's hacienda-style residence for a live broadcast of his weekly program, "Hello, President!" Sixties-era revolutionary ballads wafted from a crackling speaker as I made my way inside, past soldiers standing sentry in red-laced boots and a grandfather clock that no longer keeps time.

Some Venezuelans faithfully tune in to Hugo Chávez Frías's radio and television program; others shun it because their ex-paratrooper president, like his avuncular ally, Fidel Castro, rambles self-indulgently for hours. That day, however, the whole country would be watching to see how Chávez handled the first program since he was toppled by a coup and then quickly restored to power. Would he preach reconciliation or launch into one of his infamous tirades against "squalid oligarchs" (the elite), "devils in vestments" (the church hierarchy) or "counterrevolutionaries" (those who disagree with him)?

It was late April, and two weeks had passed since the three days so bloody and tumultuous that they seemed likely to change Venezuela forever. On the surface, everything was restored. Chávez had disappeared and then reappeared — resurrected," as he put it again and again, before the "third cock had a chance to crow." His proclaimed revolution of the people was back on track; his presidential term was still due to expire in 2007. Yet the veneer of normalcy — complete with postcoup analyses on talk shows featuring ads for sushi bars — was disorienting for most Venezuelans. And Chávez himself seemed dazed as he silently waited at his desk for the program to start.

A broad-shouldered man with militarily erect posture, Chávez, 47, was dressed casually in a cranberry sweater vest, as if just two weeks earlier he hadn't been a prisoner, certain that he was about to be assassinated yet so determined to retain his presidential dignity that he gave a thumbs up — captured on videotape — to the helicopter pilot who ferried him into captivity. But his mood never quite matched his attire; his grip on power was still far too tenuous for that.

A superb manipulator of icons who is believed to have something of a martyr complex, Chávez asked the TV cameras to pull back to show the two large portraits flanking him. To his right was Jesus Christ, "my commanding officer." To his left was Simón Bolívar, the 19th-century liberator of South America and Chávez's hero. Missing from the scene, however, was Chávez's dogeared copy of the new constitution, written in 1999 to his specifications. As Chávez groped for it, Col. Oswaldo Gutiérrez, a loyal aide, jumped to his feet. Gutiérrez happened to know that I had a pocket-size edition of the charter with me. "Give me your constitution!" the colonel demanded, and he ran with it from my purse onto the president's set.

For three transfixing hours, Chávez disgorged a seamless address to the nation, without teleprompter or notes. It was a torrential outpouring that flowed from public announcements about hydroelectric plants to chatty revelations about his captivity — he had requested a priest in order to make a final confession and a cellphone to ask his wife, Marisabel, to tell the world that Hugo Chávez had not resigned.

Chávez made his point by repetition, accumulation, exaggeration. The presidential patio contained not just trees but mango trees, guava trees, plum trees, pomegranate trees, palms; recent events in Venezuela were unparalleled in history or at least in the last five centuries on any of the five continents or for that matter on Mars. At one point, overcome by emotion, Chávez squeezed shut his eyes and inhaled audibly through his nose; offstage, his vice minister of information clasped her hands, sighing, "Qué bueno!"

A man who usually talks in exclamations, Chávez strained to come across as modulated, as a democrat and a cheek-turning Christian who had no desire for vengeance. "Those who don't want Hugo Chávez to be the president of the republic," he shrugged, "fine, go organize yourself." The constitution allows for a referendum to be called in 2003, he noted, and he would take his chances at the polls. "I'm not wed to power in an unhealthy way," he said. "I'm not Yo el Supremo. I'm just Hugo, a regular guy."

"I the Supreme," the classic novel by Paraguayan writer Augusto Roa Bastos to which Chávez referred, is a brilliant portrait of a president-for-life, one in a subgenre of dictator literature that flourished in Latin America before multiparty democracies began taking root. Whether Chávez is indeed a latter-day caudillo or simply a charismatic populist with authoritarian tendencies or actually a genuine leftist revolutionary is a matter of fierce debate in Venezuela. But many believe that he is so gifted and yet so flawed a leader that he almost seems to be the fictional creation of a Bastos or a Gabriel García Márquez.

In Venezuela, almost everyone is either passionately for Chávez or against him, a Chavista or an anti-Chavista. The poor who feel embraced by Chávez worship the Venezuelan president as their redeemer: "Hugo the Messiah!" His equally zealous foes see him as Hurricane Hugo, with the power to transform Venezuela into a Communist backwater like Cuba or, alternatively, a violent, riven republic like Colombia.

Whether they love him or loathe him, Venezuelans say that Chávez, who took office in early 1999, has awakened Venezuela from its political somnolence, empowered the poor and stirred the elite to re-engage after years of inactivity. He has been like a shock therapist, exposing and exploiting the profound class divisions in Venezuelan society that can never be ignored again.

"There is no going back to the way things were B.C.," before Chávez, said Nelson Ortiz, president of the Caracas Stock Exchange and a self-proclaimed "anti-Chavista light." "In the passions that he arouses, Chávez is one in a million. For many generations to come, people will be talking about him and about this very surreal, probably defining, moment in our history."

For decades, Venezuela had plodded along as perhaps the dullest and least fantastic country in the region. An oil nation with the largest reserves outside the Middle East, it has boasted a relatively dependable, although flawed, democratic system since 1958. Then just as Latin America began stabilizing, democratizing and catching up to staid Venezuela, along came Chávez with his camouflage pants and his talk of revolution. Finally this spring, the Venezuelan president, a throwback in so many ways, provoked an equally retrograde reaction: a coup. And the events in Venezuela raised unsettling questions in the region as a whole: Could epaulets come back in style? Was democracy securely anchored? Could Latin America slide backward into old, familiar patterns?

Listening to the revolutionary ballads at the president's home, I felt a keen sense of time warp, as I did at a pro-Chávez march in which every other man seemed to be wearing a Che T-shirt. I also felt transported back in time when I arrived in the stuffy Caracas apartment where Pedro Carmona Estanga, 60, was under house arrest, surrounded by relatives and porcelain figurines. The elevator opened into his fourth-floor home in a gated, guarded, Florida-style condo tower where Carmona's wife greeted me, wringing her hands. "My husband didn't do anything against the law!" she said.

Carmona, mild-mannered leader of a business association, had stunned Venezuela by defying his nebbishy character to become dictator for a day. At the behest of right-wing generals who hijacked a massive civic uprising against Chávez on April 11, Carmona agreed to become provisional president after the generals announced Chávez's resignation. But soon Marisabel Chávez was getting out the word that her husband had not resigned, and Chávez's supporters were advancing on the presidential palace, where Carmona was busy dissolving the National Assembly and dismissing the Supreme Court. Amid national and regional outcry, forces loyal to Chávez took advantage of the pandemonium to recapture the palace, Chávez was flown back from the island of Orchila and Carmona was arrested. A month later, he would escape from his house and seek political asylum from Colombia.

Yet Carmona said that day that he had been terribly misunderstood, and his words echoed Chávez and generations of Latin leaders who believed themselves to be fulfilling a historical imperative. "I have no special taste for power," Carmona told me, clasping his hands atop a crocheted tablecloth. "After decades of an impeccable trajectory, I didn't suddenly become a dictator overnight, an apprentice of Pinochet, for goodness' sake. There simply was a vacuum of power, and somebody had to fill it."

I repeated that remark to Teodoro Petkoff, an influential newspaper editor who was a leftist guerrilla in the 1960's. "Ah, the famous vacuum of power; what century are we in again?" Petkoff said, glancing out at a lively modern newsroom. "Fidel Castro was supposed to be the last Latin American caudillo. And as for ultraright juntas. ... "

At an anti-Chávez rally, a young, American-educated dentist expressed the same sentiment more colloquially. "Revolutions and coup d'états are so yesterday," she said in English. "It's really embarrassing for Venezuela."

A mestizo like most Venezuelans, Chávez is dark-skinned and grew up in a provincial family of limited means. Poor Venezuelans — 80 percent of the country's population of 24 million — see him as one of them. "Chávez has changed our self-image," Oscar Rodríguez, a 29-year-old hardware-store clerk, told me. "Now poor Venezuelans look in the mirror and see a future president. That is what makes the elite feel threatened."

Indeed, many in the elite do feel threatened, not by the awakening of the poor per se but by the vengeful mood in which they have woken up. Some affluent Venezuelans believe that Chávez has polarized a country that never knew the intense class divisions of most others in Latin America. Granted, they acknowledge, the underclass has long been resentful that the wealth of their oil-rich nation has not trickled down to them. But Chávez has nurtured and fetishized that resentment.

"If you are Venezuelan, you are told from the day that you are born that you are wealthy," said Moisés Naím, editor of Foreign Policy magazine and a former trade and industry minister of Venezuela. "But the daily reality is that you are very poor. So that means someone is stealing what's yours. That sentiment is what Chávez is exploiting."

Chávez's parents were elementary-school teachers who imbued in him a love of Venezuelan history. After high school, he enrolled in a military academy with the principal aspiration of making the army baseball team. Injuries detoured him into a more conventional soldier's life, but he was not destined to be a conventional soldier. Chávez had discovered that his own ancestors played key roles in 19th- and early-20th-century rebel struggles against landowners. It seemed as if destiny was calling.

So as a young lieutenant, Chávez began conspiring against the status quo. He formed a semiclandestine group within the army called the Bolivarian Revolutionary Movement. Its members, not without reason, saw a corrupt "cupola" at the top of every institution in Venezuela. In 1992 the movement attempted a coup. The military leadership didn't see it coming, according to Fernándo Ochoa Antich, an ex-general who was then the defense minister. "We had some information, but we didn't take it seriously," he said. "Until the coup. Then we realized that Chávez had created an ideologized sector that was more loyal to him than to the institution of the military."

Although Chávez's men did manage to take control of key garrisons in the winter of 1992, they failed to seize the presidential palace during a showdown with loyalist troops. Chávez surrendered, and he was allowed just over a minute on national television to persuade his comrades around the country to lay down their arms. In that time, Chávez, who was unknown, communicated such calm, charisma and authority that he became an overnight star. After several years in prison, he remarkably translated a failed coup into a stunning success at the polls.

As Ochoa's maid served coffee, Ochoa told me that he had glimpsed Chávez's unique charisma when they both taught military history at the same academy. "He was an unusually good motivator," he said. But the former general said that he also detected in Chávez then a softness, a kind of cowardice. "He didn't put up much of a fight when push came to shove in 1992," Ochoa said. "Just as he didn't when the generals demanded his resignation on April 11." Ochoa leaned forward, offering up a rumor that I had heard from others who want to portray Chávez as psychologically unstable. "Perhaps you've heard that Chávez broke down and cried that night?"

It is hard to imagine that Ochoa would have hailed Chávez for resolute courage if more blood had been spilled either in 1992 or in April. Dozens of Venezuelans lost their lives during those three days in April, not a lot by the standard of world conflicts. But many Venezuelans fear that April was just a prelude to future unrest. And they are haunted by it. They can still hear the screaming after sharpshooters fired into a huge pro-Chávez march, the deathly silence in the hours right after the coup, the smashing of storefronts, the wailing of sirens and the furious banging of pots and pans as the barrios celebrated Chávez's return.

Soon afterward, they say, everything appeared to be falling back into place. In the shantytown known as the Great Power of God, where cardboard houses cling to the hillside above Caracas, the residents returned to their work as roadside mechanics or vendors of life's inessentials. "I was so relieved when Chávez returned," Zenaida Martínez told me, straddling the sewer pipe that transects her makeshift home, "because I felt sure the dictator Carmona would have thrown us in the street."

Across the valley, in penthouse apartments with commanding views of the "Arabian Nights"-style brothel that is a centerpiece of the capital's skyline, the elegant dinner parties recommenced. "On the Sunday after Chávez returned, people could barely get out of bed, they were so depressed," Ortiz, the stock exchange president, said. "It was like the boogeyman had come back. People were crying in church. But life goes on."

Still, everyone knew that the passions released in April had only been sublimated; they were lurking barely beneath the surface. A wealthy couple told me a remarkable story of an experience right after the coup, when pro-Chávez supporters overtook the streets to demand his restoration.

The woman, a petite, stylish blonde, was returning from Paris; her husband, a leading industrialist, went to pick her up at the airport. The road home runs past the pro-Chávez barrio of Catia, and it was blocked by the crowds. The couple had to abandon their car and proceed on foot. The woman darkened her fair face with makeup, hid her tresses under a cap and pulled her blouse out over her slacks. Still, the couple did not succeed in blending in, and before long, as they described it calmly and sadly, a mob was descending on them, screaming, "Murderers!" and "Oligarchs!"

The couple darted through the alleyways of the poor neighborhood until a 70-year-old woman stopped the businessman, calling out his name, a very well known name in Venezuela, a rich man's name. It was a tense moment until the woman identified herself; her father, she said, had been his father's barber for decades. "You'd better come with me," she said, ushering the couple into her modest home. "I am a Chavista," she said, but she kept them safe. The pair spent the night there; imagine a couple of Rockefellers seeking overnight refuge in a Bedford-Stuyvesant apartment in the middle of a riot. Poignantly, the couple discovered that the barber's relatives, of whose existence they were barely aware, had scrapbooks documenting the industrialist's family's history.

Early the next morning, the couple made their way by taxi back up into the elegant hillside neighborhood where they live, passing by the sobering aftermath of a night of rage. As they arrived in their quarter, they saw neighbors out jogging in short shorts, shutting out the world with headphones on their ears. The woman, startled, wanted to shout out the window, "Don't you know we're in a civil war?"

In that very barrio, Catia, Conchita Mata, a retired government worker, gathered friends and relatives in her small, simple house to drink beer, eat arepas and praise the revolution. Recalling the coup, her sister, Miriam, took my hand as tears welled in her eyes: "The idea that they could try to destroy in 48 hours all the dreams of the people! I fear an international conspiracy. To the world, we're not Venezuela. We're just oil."

After hearing the new constitution extolled many times, I asked if anyone had a copy. Hands dug into pockets and purses and turned up a dozen copies of what has become the new bible. One older man gave me his as a present, a palm-size edition covered in powder blue vinyl; he was tickled to learn later that it had traveled "via gringa" to President Chávez himself.

Mata's guests thought that Chávez was being too conciliatory toward the coup plotters. Carmona should be in prison, they said, not in his condominium. There is rage in the pro-Chávez neighborhoods. "The people are not subtle," Juan O'Connor, Mata's boyfriend, said. "They want justice."

On May Day, when hundreds of thousands of Venezuelans poured into the streets blowing whistles for and against Chávez, I ducked into a psychiatrist's office and resisted stretching out on his black leather couch. Dr. Pedro Delgado, an expert on the appeal of Chávez, says that Venezuela is in such a state of traumatized confusion right now that business couldn't be better. "Anxiety, depression, uncertainty, rage — I thank Chávez," he said, "although I lament that it is at the expense of the mental health of the nation."

Delgado considers Venezuela to be a country in the throes of adolescence that made an immature decision to elect Chávez but a decision that was part of its identity-formation process, like trying drugs.

"Chávez was an experiment for a society looking for a way out of the old, corrupt order of things," Delgado said. "He is a great seducer, and he bewitched the electorate. I didn't vote for him because I know what placing a military man in a leadership position implies in Latin America. We have a hard time resisting strongmen who say they will solve all our problems. We want to believe in them passionately, blindly."

When Chávez was elected president by the biggest margin of victory in the country's electoral history, his ambitions were grandiose. He wanted to remake Venezuela, starting with its very name, which was changed to the Bolivarian Republic of Venezuela. He wanted to refashion Latin America into a more integrated region less dependent on the United States. And he ultimately wanted no less than to reshape the world order so that the balance of power was "multipolar."

But Chávez, politically inexperienced, thin-skinned and confrontational by nature, didn't have the diplomatic skills or management ability to fulfill his ambitions. "He has poor impulse control," Delgado said.

Chávez's greatest success has been in consolidating his own power in the face of a flaccid opposition. He easily eviscerated the two political parties that for four decades had traded the reins of power. At the polls, he won overwhelming support for a new constitution that strengthened the executive, weakened the Legislature and judiciary and expanded government control of the economy. The constitution also lengthened his term from five to six years and awarded him the right to succeed himself.

In a creeping militarization of the government, Chávez enlisted the armed forces in a utopian "Bolívar Plan" to rebuild the country's infrastructure and named generals to head both the state oil company and its American subsidiary, Citgo. Chávez also used the military to help him open hundreds of schools; alarming conservatives and economists alike, he has staffed some of those schools with Cuban teachers borrowed from Castro in exchange for oil at bargain-basement prices.

But Chávez's policies have yet to produce the promised social revolution. There have been few tangible dividends for his poor supporters as the economy has contracted; unemployment and underemployment have swelled as capital flight has accelerated. Many of his followers, however, are still willing to give him the benefit of the doubt because his intentions, they say, are good and it is not all his fault: the elite is withdrawing its resources.

In the eyes of the elite, Chávez grew more antagonistic and radical as the rapid transformation of Venezuela eluded him: he proposed land expropriations, he visited Saddam Hussein on OPEC business, he praised the Cuban "sea of happiness" as a model for Venezuela and he warned that the Bolivarian revolution was literally armed. Chávez had made an enemy of the leading labor union federation by trying and failing to eliminate it. In so doing, he fostered an unlikely collaboration between union leaders and industrialists who opposed him. In the months before the coup, the country was seriously disrupted by work stoppages and protest marches that brought together hard-hatted construction workers and Prada-wearing housewives.

On April 11, the fateful day, an anti-Chávez demonstration swelled as a result of what was perceived to be Chávez's ham-handed takeover of the state oil company. Most of the president's critics, including the powerful media, wanted to pressure him to resign or to face another referendum.

"What we didn't want was a coup," a leading businessman insisted. "We are a modern nation." The man added: "Believe me, if the key businessmen in this country had backed the coup, it would have succeeded! It wouldn't have been this farce. Do you think we would have entrusted this Carmona — he's not a businessman, he's an employee of businessmen — with our future? This Carmona and these generals took advantage of a civic revolt. Good heavens. They blew it for all of us!"

The industrialist was chatting with me at a dinner party on the open-air terrace of a Caracas penthouse. We were sipping wine and nibbling on tequeños, Venezuelan cheese sticks; in the background, the Berlin Philharmonic played on a large-screen TV.

At the party, I did not hear the usual Chávez bashing and mocking that had become sport before April 11. True, there was a moment when a grande dame wrapped in a pashmina shawl remarked to me, "On a superficial note, have you noticed that Chávez surrounds himself with the ugliest women?" But most of what I was hearing I hadn't anticipated — sober-minded self-chastisement on the part of the elite.

"In the early days of our democracy, well-off Venezuelans considered it their work and their hobby to build our nation," said Eugenio Mendoza, a wealthy businessman. His wife, Maria Luisa, continued: "In the last 20 to 30 years, the private leadership of this country fell in love with the ease of accumulating wealth and concentrated on getting richer. We have neglected our society's institutions and let them get corrupt. I know I sound like Chávez, but his arguments about what is wrong with our country are the same as mine. His solutions are back to the Stone Age. He doesn't have management ability, thank God. But his diagnosis is correct."

Sauntering over, Maria Luisa's brother, Oscar Guruceaga, joined in. "Chávez did something important for this country," said Guruceaga, a rancher who spends a lot of time in Tibet. "He woke us up. After years and years. We have no choice now but to embrace our responsibility."

"Pardon me," their elegant mother threw in, sniffing, "but did he have to use such vulgar language?"

Colonel Gutiérrez, deputy chief of the presidential honor guard that retook the palace in the countercoup, took me for a walk near the president's house, passing by soldiers who clicked their heels and saluted.

Gutiérrez unfolded a copy of El Nacional. He was furious because it included a how-to story about investing in Florida. "They're encouraging people to withdraw their money from Venezuela and invest it in Orlando!" he fumed. "The media in this country make me nauseous. Let's get a café con leche."

Outside a bakery, a middle-aged woman with a long ponytail stopped Gutiérrez. "My colonel," she said. "How do I get to see the president? I think we are at the most divided point in our nation's history. I wasn't a Chavista before the coup, but when I contemplated a dictatorship of the oligarchy, I remembered why we elected Chávez in the first place."

Gutiérrez suggested that she write Chávez a detailed letter, and he elbowed me in the ribs. "You see," he told me, "the coup will end up strengthening my president. It failed because those behind it didn't take four factors into consideration: God, the people, the grass roots of the armed forces and the ineradicable nature of democracy in this country. I'm 45 years old, and I never lived under a dictator until April 11. And I never plan to again."

On that "hello, president!" in late April, Chávez described a tumultuous baseball game in which a pitcher hit two batters with his tosses, the second batter threw his bat at the pitcher and then the players emptied out of the dugouts and duked it out on the field. "Thus is Venezuela in this moment!" he said, thrusting a finger into the air and then calling for everyone to return to his position so that the "national game" could go on.

But it is hard to imagine how it can. Chávez can soften his rhetoric and shake up his cabinet and preach reconciliation. He can buy some time while Venezuela recovers from the shock of what transpired in April. But his many and diverse opponents are not prepared to back down, and the country is probably too fractured to heal naturally.

When Chávez left Venezuela in mid-May to attend a meeting in Spain, I received an e-mail message reporting that he had taken along 40 suitcases and suggesting wishfully that this chapter of Venezuelan history might end with the leader disappearing into the night with his luggage. It is far more likely, however, that there will be a bitter fight over the future of Chávez. What form that fight takes remains to be seen. Ochoa, the ex-general, told me that he believes more bloodshed is inevitable; the armed forces are divided, there are weapons on both sides and the political opposition to Chávez is leaderless. But he may well be wrong. It may turn out that April taught Venezuela a sobering lesson: that the future does not lie in repeating the mistakes of the past.

Bolivia's Newly Elected Leader Maps His Socialist Agenda

BY JUAN FORERO | DEC. 20, 2005

LA PAZ, BOLIVIA, DEC. 19 — After his decisive win in the election for president on Sunday, the Socialist indigenous leader, Evo Morales, vowed Monday to respect private property but repeated his pledge to increase state control over the energy industry and reverse an American-backed crusade against coca, the plant used to make cocaine.

Wearing his trademark black jeans and tennis shoes, Mr. Morales arrived in La Paz to begin laying the groundwork for an economic and political transformation that he says will give voice to the poor, indigenous majority that fueled his campaign. "The voice of the people is the voice of God," he said late Sunday.

Mr. Morales, 46, a former small-town trumpeter and soccer player who turned a movement of coca farmers into the country's most potent political force, stunned his countrymen on Sunday by burying seven challengers in the most important election since Bolivia's transition from dictatorship to democracy a generation ago.

Unofficial results showed that Mr. Morales won up to 52 percent of the vote to become the first Indian president in Bolivia's 180-year history, a victory that solidifies a continent-wide shift of governments to the left.

"For the first time a candidate wins with 50 percent plus 1, and it's the biggest margin between the first two finishers," said Gonzalo Chávez, an economist and political analyst at Catholic University in La Paz. "This is a democratic revolution. The voting was tremendously strong, and signifies a tremendous demand for change in Bolivia."

President Hugo Chávez of Venezuela and President Néstor Kirchner of Argentina, two of the continent's leading left-leaning leaders, quickly offered their congratulations, as did Chile, Spain and the European Union.

The United States tried to discredit Mr. Morales in the past by alleging ties to drug trafficking, and ended up increasing his popularity. The administration offered cautious congratulations to Mr. Morales and to the Bolivian people "for carrying out a successful election."

But American officials acknowledged that they viewed his presidency with serious concern, while insisting that they would wait to see how he actually governed.

A State Department official noted that Bolivia had experienced several years of chaos in government, "and now they have chosen a leader and still have a constitutional process," adding, "We have to respect that, whatever else Morales has said." He declined to be identified, citing department policy.

Mr. Morales's party, the Movement Toward Socialism, won nearly half the 27 seats in the Senate and up to half the 130 seats in the lower house. Unofficial figures showed the MAS, as the party is known, also won at least two of nine governorships.

Podemos, the party of Jorge Quiroga, a former president, finished a distant second. Three other traditional parties practically disappeared from the national scene.

The MAS is now poised to push through legislation tightening the terms on British Gas, Repsol YPF of Spain, Petrobras of Brazil and other foreign energy companies operating here. Mr. Morales has promised to "nationalize" the lucrative natural gas industry, not by expropriating it, but rather by expanding state control over operations, policy and the commercialization of gas.

"The government will exercise its right to state ownership of Bolivia's hydrocarbons," he said Monday.

Foreign oil companies have in the past said that financially onerous terms could prompt them to cut back on investments, which have fallen from $608 million in 1998 to $200 million last year. But on Monday, Ronald Fessy, spokesman for the Bolivian Hydrocarbon Chamber, said it was too soon to predict.

"Governments have to be seen in action, not in times of campaigning," he said. "We hope that this government will work to achieve scenarios that would lead to policies that are good for investments that this industry and Bolivia urgently need."

Mr. Morales has also pledged to reverse Bolivia's longstanding alliance with the United States in the generation-long fight against drugs, which has greatly curtailed the coca planting but has set off politically volatile uprisings by coca farmers. Mr. Morales and his followers say much of Bolivia's coca goes for traditional uses, to be chewed or used in tea, while Washington says most of it becomes cocaine.

"The fight against drug trafficking is a false pretext for the United States to install military bases," Mr. Morales told reporters on Monday.

Even with the mandate from voters, Mr. Morales is not expected to have an easy time in a country rocked by years of social protests fueled by inequality and poverty.

He will be under pressure to ensure that the country's budding exports of textiles and furniture continue, while answering to indigenous leaders who seek radical change. Some social movements have vowed to apply pressure. The Bolivian Workers Central, the country's largest labor confederation, said the government would have to expropriate private energy installations from private companies, or face the kind of protests that forced out two presidents since 2003.

"He has to make changes or he falls," Jaime Solares, the head of the confederation, said in an interview.

In the main square of La Paz, where one president was lynched on a lamppost in 1946, most people seemed tired of protests and wanted to give Mr. Morales a chance.

"We have to give him some time," said Martín Bautista, 35, a truck driver. "I feel happy because here a lot of things are about to change."

Thousands Rally in Capital to Protest Big Government

BY JEFF ZELENY | SEPT. 12, 2009

WASHINGTON — A sea of protesters filled the west lawn of the Capitol and spilled onto the National Mall on Saturday in the largest rally against President Obama since he took office, a culmination of a summer-long season of protests that began with opposition to a health care overhaul and grew into a broader dissatisfaction with government.

On a cloudy and cool day, the demonstrators came from all corners of the country, waving American flags and handwritten signs explaining the root of their frustrations. Their anger stretched well beyond the health care legislation moving through Congress, with shouts of support for gun rights, lower taxes and a smaller government.

But as they sang verse after verse of patriotic hymns like "God Bless America," sharp words of profane and political criticism were aimed at Mr. Obama and Congress.

Dick Armey, a former House Republican leader whose group Freedomworks helped organize the protest, stood before the crowd and led the rallying cries in nearly the same spot where Mr. Obama took his oath of office eight months ago.

"He pledged a commitment of fidelity to the United States Constitution," Mr. Armey said, suggesting that Mr. Obama was in violation of what the founding fathers intended the size and scope of the government to be.

"Liar! Liar! Liar! Liar!" the crowd shouted back, echoing the accusation that Representative Joe Wilson, Republican of South Carolina, hurled at the president three days earlier during his address to Congress.

The demonstrators numbered well into the tens of thousands, though the police declined to estimate the size of the crowd. Many came on their own and were not part of an organization or group.

AMANDA LUCIDON FOR THE NEW YORK TIMES

A crowd marched toward the Capitol as people from around the country gathered to express their discontent with the government.

But the magnitude of the rally took the authorities by surprise, with throngs of people streaming from the White House to Capitol Hill for more than three hours.

The atmosphere was rowdy at times, with signs and images casting Mr. Obama in a demeaning light. One sign called him the "parasite in chief." Others likened him to Hitler. Several people held up preprinted signs saying, "Bury Obama Care with Kennedy," a reference to the Massachusetts senator whose body passed by the Capitol two weeks earlier to be memorialized.

Other signs did not focus on Mr. Obama, but rather on the government at large, promoting gun rights, tallying the national deficit and deploring illegal immigrants living in the United States.

Still, many demonstrators expressed their views without a hint of rage. They said the size of the crowd illustrated that their views were shared by a broader audience.

AMANDA LUCIDON FOR THE NEW YORK TIMES

Protesters in Washington, D.C., during a rally on Sunday.

"I want Congress to be afraid," said Keldon Clapp, 45, an unemployed marketing representative who recently moved to Tennessee from Connecticut after losing his job. "Like everyone else here, I want them to know that we're watching what they're doing. And they do work for us."

As Mr. Obama traveled to Minnesota on Saturday to rally support for his health care plan, he flew over the assembling crowd in Marine One. The helicopter could be seen flying overhead as the demonstrators marched down Pennsylvania Avenue.

"This is not some kind of radical right-wing group," Senator Jim DeMint, Republican of South Carolina, said in an interview as dozens of people streamed by him. "I just hope the Congress, the Senate and the president recognize that people are afraid of what's going on."

Mr. DeMint and a few Republican legislators were the only party leaders on hand for the demonstration. Republican officials said privately that they were pleased by the turnout but wary of the anger directed at all politicians. And most of those who turned out were not likely to have been Obama voters anyway.

Protesters came by bus, car and airplane, arriving here from Texas and Tennessee, New Mexico and New Hampshire, Ohio and Oregon. The messages on their signs told of an intense distrust of the government, which several people said began long before Mr. Obama took office.

For the most part, Democrats stayed silent on Saturday, with the exception of a small group of counterdemonstrators who gathered behind a roadblock to protest what they called a "right-wing rally." Many were members of the clergy, who said they were concerned about misinformation propagated by opponents of health care legislation.

"We'd like to have an honest debate," said Chris Korzen, director of the nonprofit Catholics United. "I don't see a lot of substance here."

While there was no shortage of vitriol among protesters, there was also an air of festivity. A band of protesters in colonial gear wended through the crowd, led by a bell ringer in a tricorn hat calling for revolution. A folk singer belting out a protest ballad on a guitar brought cheers.

In conversations with demonstrators, people identified themselves as Republicans, libertarians, independents and former Democrats. Several speakers denounced the Obama administration's health care plan as "socialism." A few Confederate flags waved in the air, but there were hundreds of American flags and chants of, "U.S.A.! U.S.A.! U.S.A.!" A young girl held a sign saying, "Don't redistribute the wealth of my Barbies."

Ruth Lobbs, 57, a schoolteacher from Jacksonville, Fla., said she flew to Washington on Saturday to protest how she believes the government has violated the Constitution. She said she did not vote for the president, adding that her anger has been building for years.

"It's more than Obama — this isn't a Republican or a Democratic issue," Ms. Lobbs said as she held a yellow flag that declared, "Don't Tread on Me."

"I don't know if anything will come of this or not," she said, "but this is a peaceful way of showing our frustration."

THEO EMERY and **ASHLEY SOUTHALL** contributed reporting.

The Left Declares Its Independence

OPINION | BY TODD GITLIN | OCT. 8, 2011

IF SOME ASPECTS of the Occupy Wall Street protest feel predictable — the drum circles, the signs, including "Tax Wall Street Transactions" and "End the FED" — so does the right-wing response. Is it any surprise that Fox News and its allied bloggers consider the protesters "deluded" and "dirty smelly hippies"?

Then again, maybe it is surprising. As more than a few observers have noted, the Occupy Wall Street chant, "We Are the 99 Percent" — a shot across the bow of the wealthiest 1 percent of the country, which includes the financial predators and confidence gamers who crashed the global economy with impunity — seems synonymous with the Tea Party's "Take Back America" ethos.

Those similarities, though, mask profound differences. The two movements both loathe the elite, but their goals, and the passions that drive them forward, could not be more at odds.

The Tea Party, for all its apparent populism, revolves around a vision of power and how to attain it. Tea Partiers tend to be white, male, Republican, graying, married and comfortable; the political system once worked for them, and they think it can be made to do so again. They revile government, but they adore hierarchy and order. Not for them the tents and untucked shirts, the tattoos, piercings and dreadlocks that are eye candy for lazy journalists. ("Am I dressed too nice so the media doesn't interview me?" read one Occupy Wall Street demonstrator's sign.)

In contrast, what should we make of Occupy Wall Street? The movement is, of course, nascent, and growing: on Oct. 5, it picked up thousands of marching supporters of all ages, many from unions, professions and universities, and crowded Foley Square. Its equivalents rallied in 50 cities. Deep anger at grotesque inequities extends far beyond this one encampment; after all, a few handfuls of young activists do not have a monopoly on the fight against plutocracy. Revulsion in the face of a perverse economy is felt by many respectable people: unemployed, not yet unemployed, shakily employed and plain disgusted. A month from now, this movement, still busy being born, could look quite different.

And yet it remains true that the core of the movement, the (mostly young and white, skilled but jobless) people who started the "occupation" three weeks ago, consists of what right-wing critics call anarchists. Indeed, some occupiers take the point as a compliment — because that is precisely the quality that sets them apart from the Tea Party. Anarchism has been the reigning spirit of left-wing protest movements for nearly the past half century, as it is in Zuccotti Park.

In this recent incarnation, anarchism, for the most part, is not so much a theory of the absence of government, but a theory of self-organization, or direct democracy, as government. The idea is that you do not need institutions because the people, properly assembled, properly deliberating, even in one square block of Lower Manhattan, can regulate themselves. Those with the time and patience can frolic and practice direct democracy at the same time — at least until the first frost.

The anarchist impulse is nothing new in America. There were strong anarchist streaks in the New Left of the 1960s — stronger than the socialist streak, in fact, despite all the work Marxists did to define proper class categories for the student movement. "Let the people decide," one of the early rallying cries of Students for a Democratic Society (of which I was president from 1963 to 1964), meant, in practice, "Let's have long meetings where everyone gets to talk." De facto, this meant that politics was for people who, in a sense, talked for a living — in other words, college types.

It was a revolutionary idea, at least for its time and in certain places: in the Deep South, for civil rights workers and black farm workers just to meet and talk was a dangerously radical, and radically dangerous, proposition.

But the left's distrust of outside authority reached, and still reaches, much further. The bumper sticker of the 1960s New Left could have been Bob Dylan's lyric "Don't follow leaders, watch the parkin' meters," cheekily pairing hierarchy with overregulation. By 1967, its membership soaring, the S.D.S. was so suspicious of leadership, so disdainful of the formal structures of its first five years, as to abolish its own presidential and vice-presidential offices.

As the S.D.S. discovered in 1969, when quarreling Maoist-Guevarist and Stalinist factions tore it apart, chaotic meetings and suspicion of formal procedures didn't keep tiny hierarchies from exercising decisive control. Radical feminists came to similar conclusions. Nevertheless, hostility to elitism remained all the rage. From the early '70s on, activists went into revolt against just about anybody's authority, even their own. Vertical authority had a foul odor: it smacked of colonialism, patriarchy, bad white men lording themselves over voiceless minions. In left-wing activist circles, establishments of all sorts were the immoral equivalents of The Establishment.

Disgruntled by big-talking leaders, turned off by celebrity media, the left of the '70s developed a horizontal style, according limited authority to their own leaders, who were frequently at pains to deny that they were leaders at all. "Affinity groups" and "working groups" replaced organized factions and parties. Even movements that seemed to require some level of verticality — those with concrete goals, like banning nuclear power and weapons, or opposing apartheid — were mostly leaderless.

That explains why, to the bafflement of their ideological opponents, such movements barely paused at the fall of Communism. When Leninist regimes collapsed, and their self-confident social democratic rivals crumpled as well, anarchism's major competitors for a theory of organization imploded.

This new protest style is more Rousseau than Marx. What the Zuccotti Park encampment calls horizontal democracy is spunky, polymorphic, energetic, theatrical, scattered and droll. An early poster showed a ballerina poised gingerly on the back of Wall Street's bull sculpture, bearing the words: "Occupy Wall Street. September 17th. Bring Tent." It likes government more than corporations, but its own style is hardly governmental. It tends to care about process more than results.

And oh, how it loves to talk. It is no surprise that it makes fervent use of the technologies of horizontal communication, of Facebook and Twitter, though the instinct predated — perhaps prefigured — those tools. Not coincidentally, this was also the spirit of the more or less leaderless, partyless revolutions of Tunisia and Egypt that are claimed as inspiration in Lower Manhattan. An "American Autumn" is their shot at an echo of the "Arab Spring."

Occupy Wall Street, then, emanates from a culture — strictly speaking, a counterculture — that is diametrically opposed to Tea Party discipline.

So where do these romantics go from here? The Zuccotti Park core doesn't seem to have a plan, or even to take kindly to the idea of consolidating a list of demands. And yet, by taking the initiative, they have aroused, as with the Oct. 5 march, less romantic and more conventionally organized allies who do not disdain political demands. Such is the cunning of political history. Having set out to be expressive, the anarchists have found themselves playing, willy-nilly, a most strategic role.

Such movements hope to remain forever under construction, fluid, unfixed. They slip laughingly through the nets of journalism, which prefers hard-and-fast answers to the question "What do you people want?"

But the interesting, difficult, even decisive moment in the career of such a movement comes when allies arrive, especially allies not so enamored of horizontal democracy and more taken by the idea of getting results. These forces showed up on Oct. 5. De facto, there is an alliance in the cards.

It makes sense. Here, finally, is what labor and the activist left have been waiting for. For two years, Barack Obama got the benefit of the

OZIER MUHAMMAD/THE NEW YORK TIMES

The Wall Street protest on its 14th day. Many demonstrators are jobless; a few are self-described anarchists.

doubt from fervent supporters — I'd bet that many of those in Lower Manhattan during these weeks went door-to-door for him in 2008 — and that support explains why no one occupied Wall Street in 2009. Now, as Jeremy Varon, a historian at the New School, said of Zuccotti Park: "This is the Obama generation declaring their independence from his administration."

By allying itself with the protest, the left at large is telling the president that a campaign slogan that essentially says "We're better than Eric Cantor" won't cut it in 2012. "We are the 99 percent" would be more like it. If President Obama takes this direction, the movement's energy may be able to power a motor of significant reform.

That raises the question, though, of whether the inchoate quality of the Occupy Wall Street movement can continue. Probably not, since an evolving alliance demands concrete goals, strategies and compromises. But perhaps something of the initial free spirit can flourish.

There is plenty of public sentiment to nourish it. It doesn't take public opinion polls to detect American anger at the plutocracy and the impunity with which it lords it over the country.

The culture of anarchy is right about this: The corporate rich — those ostensible "job creators" who somehow haven't gotten around to creating jobs — rule the Republican Party and much of the Democratic Party as well, having artfully arranged a mutual back-scratching society to enrich themselves. A refusal to compromise with this system, defined by its hierarchies of power and money, would be the current moment of anarchy's great, lasting contribution.

Until now, fury at the plutocracy and the political class had found no channel to run in but the antigovernment fantasies of the Tea Party. Now it has dug a new channel. Anger does not move countries, but it moves movements — and movements, in turn, can move countries. To do that, movements need leverage. Even Archimedes needed a lever and a place to stand to move the world. When Zuccotti Park meets an aroused liberalism, the odd couple may not live happily ever after. But they can make a serious run at American dreams of "liberty and justice for all."

TODD GITLIN is a professor of journalism and communications at Columbia and co-author of "The Chosen Peoples: America, Israel, and the Ordeals of Divine Election."

Who Speaks for the Silent Majority?

OPINION | BY MATTHEW D. LASSITER | NOV. 2, 2011

ANN ARBOR, MICH. — American politics might appear polarized along a red-blue divide, but the Tea Party and Occupy Wall Street movements are claiming to do the same thing: defend the real majority against the powerful elites and vocal interest groups that control the political system. Conservatives in the Tea Party attack big government and rally behind the slogan "Silent Majority No More!" Progressives in Occupy Wall Street denounce big business and embrace the manifesto "We Are the 99 Percent."

On both the right and the left, strategists want to mobilize the elusive group of voters that Richard M. Nixon first labeled the "great silent majority" during a speech about the Vietnam War on Nov. 3, 1969. With one rhetorical stroke, Nixon identified a new populist category that redefined how political groups strive for influence.

At the time, polls revealed that two-thirds of Americans hoped the conflict would end quickly but simultaneously opposed antiwar demonstrations. Nixon called for unity on the home front and asked patriotic Americans to speak out against efforts by a "vocal minority" to defeat the United States. Tens of thousands of letters from self-identified members of the silent majority poured into the White House.

Nixon's conservative populism attempted to obscure the differences between working-class and affluent voters by portraying the silent majority as both heroes and victims of this tumultuous period. In the 1968 campaign, Nixon praised the "forgotten Americans, the nonshouters, the nondemonstrators" — hard-working, tax-paying Americans whose values were under siege by antiwar protesters, urban rioters, criminals and antipoverty liberals.

In 1970, Nixon's chief of staff, H. R. Haldeman, asked the president's political team to develop "a plan to mobilize the Silent Majority." The White House operative Charles Colson incorporated "Silent

Majority Inc." in all 50 states and organized rallies through fake grassroots organizations like Americans for Winning the Peace and the Honor America Committee. The administration worked on an internal "blue-collar strategy" to finesse the economic liberalism and cultural conservatism of white working-class Democrats viewed as potential Republican voters. The White House even orchestrated the formation of a National Black Silent Majority Committee to represent African-Americans being "shouted down by a handful of militants."

Nixon was always careful to say that black Americans were part of the silent majority, but his populist agenda targeted white voters who believed that the civil rights and antiwar movements had gone too far. "Enough Is Enough," a manifesto circulated by conservative groups in the late 1960s, spoke for the Americans who "pay taxes to provide schools for sit-ins, books for burning, rallying points for off-campus riots and study courses in anarchism." During the 1972 campaign, Nixon invited "those millions who have been driven out of their home in the Democratic party … to join us as members of a new American majority."

Nixon's landslide reelection obscured the class and ideological divisions within his fabled silent majority. Faced with a weakening economy, Nixon portrayed Democrats as the party of racial quotas, busing, urban welfare and weakness on foreign policy. After the election, internal memos circulated by Nixon's political team acknowledged that he had won by mobilizing a "nonpartisan" majority against liberalism rather than by creating a cohesive Republican coalition. The point person for the blue-collar strategy even warned of a fierce reaction if the administration betrayed middle-income voters by returning to "big-business-dominated Republicanism."

The legacies of Nixon's pursuit of the silent majority can be found across the political spectrum. In 1972, the community organizer Saul Alinsky portrayed the silent majority as "up for grabs" and promised to "show the middle class their real enemies: the corporate power elite that runs and ruins the country." In 1980, the Religious Right televangelist Jerry Falwell proclaimed that "God is calling millions of Americans in the so-often silent majority to join in the moral-majority crusade to turn America around." In his 1981 inaugural, Ronald Reagan updated Nixon's formula by informing the "heroes" of America — an allegedly classless majority made up of factory workers and entrepreneurs — that "government is not the solution to our problem; government is the problem."

The Democrats regained the White House only by combining Nixon's populist outreach to the silent majority with assurances that government intervention could address economic malaise. Bill Clinton promised to listen to the "quiet, troubled voice of the forgotten middle class," while Barack Obama said that they had "a right to be frustrated because they've been ignored."

Mr. Obama's challenge in 2012 is not the ideological fervor of Tea Party conservatives, but rather the recognition by many working-class and middle-class voters that both parties favor Wall Street over Main Street. While activist groups on the right and left compete to portray big government or big business as the enemy, the silent majority is still out there in the volatile political center, up for grabs.

MATTHEW D. LASSITER, an associate professor of history at the University of Michigan, is the author of "The Silent Majority: Suburban Politics in the Sunbelt South."

Europe's Right and Left on March to Populism

BY JIM YARDLEY | MAY 23, 2014

ROME — For weeks, Beppe Grillo, the Italian political insurgent, has crisscrossed the nation in what might be called his vitriol tour. He has let loose zesty, bellowing insults against journalists, businessmen, Italian politicians and Angela Merkel, the German chancellor and avatar of European austerity. He has even taken a swipe at Dudu, the fluffy white poodle belonging to former Prime Minister Silvio Berlusconi.

"I come across as a guy who yells," Mr. Grillo admitted recently on a television talk show, "Porta a Porta." "It's true. I am angry and sometimes I exaggerate, but it's an anger that has united the dreams of 10 million Italians."

Or so Mr. Grillo hopes. With voting for the European Parliament to conclude on Sunday, the elections will provide the best indicator yet of the depth of disillusionment and anger in southern Europe. The belt of Mediterranean countries has borne the worst of the five-year economic crisis and churned with seething resentment and outright fury over the austerity policies imposed by the elites perceived as running Europe.

For months, media attention has primarily focused on far-right, euro-skeptic parties making gains in northern Europe, including the National Front in France and the United Kingdom Independence Party, which showed strongly in local elections Friday and now seems poised to shake up the politics of Britain.

Even so, the stakes are arguably higher in the south. Especially in Italy and Greece, poor showings by the governing parties could increase pressure for early national elections, and make it more difficult for the fragile coalition governments to carry through on political and economic reforms. This type of instability worries European leaders and could also rattle financial markets.

"We are exporting instability," cautioned a political commentator, Antonio Polito, in a front-page editorial this week in Corriere della Sera, a leading Italian newspaper. "What is abnormal — because it does not happen elsewhere — is that such a result might blow up the entire, very fragile balance upon which acrobats like the government and Parliament are hanging on."

Europe's parliamentary elections are still a relative novelty, with a low turnout expected, which is why many analysts warn that voters might use the races to send a protest message that they have had enough.

In Italy and Greece, voters have a pick of choices to express their anger: from the left, there is Syriza in Greece; from the right, there is the neo-fascist Golden Dawn in Greece or the anti-immigrant Northern League in Italy; and there is the pox-on-all-their houses ethos of Mr. Grillo, an anti-establishment wrecking ball.

In Spain, the two dominant parties, the Popular Party and the Socialists, are expected to lose seats to smaller parties, some with anti-Europe positions but most to the political left of the Socialists.

"There is no one populism in Europe," said Brigid Laffan, an expert on European politics at the European University Institute. "Populism and the neo-right predated the crisis. But the crisis gave a new opening."

At a "State of the Union" conference this month in Florence, European leaders convened to discuss the coming elections and the recurrent theme of voter anger. In a midday speech, Prime Minister Matteo Renzi of Italy warned that only a few years ago, during the height of the financial crisis, Italy's problems centered on lending rates — known as "the spread." Now, he said, the problem was the spread of angry, political populism.

Mario Monti, the professorial technocrat who served as Italy's prime minister at the height of the crisis, said Mr. Grillo's rise had also pushed mainstream, center-right parties such as Mr. Berlusconi's Forza Italia and the New Center Right to become more anti-Europe, anti-Germany and anti-European Central Bank.

He said that nationalist parties in northern Europe wanted to reclaim sovereignty from Brussels, but Mr. Grillo wanted to destroy the status quo.

"Grillo's movement came up essentially as a challenge to the establishment, to traditional politicians and political parties," Mr. Monti said. "The real enemy for him is the politician."

Mr. Grillo's political organization, the Five Star Movement, unexpectedly finished a strong third in last year's inconclusive national elections, with 25 percent of the total vote. His momentum then seemed to stall as lawmakers from his party began to bicker, with some complaining that Mr. Grillo was acting like an autocrat.

The infighting also coincided with the emergence of the charismatic Mr. Renzi, who wrested control of his Democratic Party and became prime minister in February on promises of sweeping reforms.

But now Mr. Grillo is reinvigorated, traveling the country and posting tirades on his blog. The most recent polls have shown the Democratic Party with a lead, but Mr. Grillo has been drawing large crowds as he vows to finish first, gleefully lashing out at the establishment and promoting a vaguely defined system of direct representation through online referendums. Those, he says, will also allow voters to punish what he calls the three "destroyers:" journalists, industrialists and politicians.

"This horrendous trio has to be judged via a popular media trial that will start after the European elections," he wrote on his blog. "It'll take place on the Internet, where there'll be a reconstruction of a virtual castle, with prison cells."

A surge by the Five Star Movement could undermine Mr. Renzi, who is trying to push an economic and electoral reform package through Italy's Parliament as European officials are increasing pressure on the government to move faster to reduce the country's massive public debt and reduce its fiscal deficit.

In Greece, Prime Minister Antonis Samaras is trying to rally support for his coalition government, arguing that a victory by the left-wing Syriza, which is narrowly leading in polls, could threaten the country's slightly improving economy — a charge Syriza dismisses as a desperate scare tactic. He has stepped up his attacks in recent days, even as Syriza's leader, Alexis Tsipras, has continued to challenge the terms of the financial bailout that saved Greece from bankruptcy but inflicted punishing austerity.

Two years ago, Mr. Samaras's New Democracy pulled out a slim victory in national elections, as the rest of Europe was fraught with concern that a Syriza victory might threaten the stability of the euro.

Now, Mr. Samaras must contend with Syriza on the left as well as Golden Dawn on the far right. Last year, the government declared Golden Dawn a criminal organization, not a political party, and arrested several party leaders, including some elected officials.

The party's electoral status was unclear until this month, when Greece's Supreme Court ruled that Golden Dawn could participate in the European elections. Now many analysts predict that the party could finish third, or better. At a rally this month, about 300 flag-waving supporters gathered in an outdoor basketball court in a leafy, middle-class neighborhood of Athens. Golden Dawn's local candidates stood together on a platform — mostly heavily muscled men with close haircuts, wearing black shirts and pants.

"Positive, extremely positive," answered Ilias Panagiotaros, a Golden Dawn leader watching the rally, when asked about his party's electoral prospects. "We are going for second place, if not first."

"Two years ago, we had a debt that was 129 percent of gross domestic product," he added. "We were dying. That's what they were saying. Now we have a debt that is 170 percent of G.D.P. And they say we are going well. That is unexplainable."

He relished the thought of not only destabilizing Greek politics but sending his party's candidates to Brussels.

"For the first time, the next European Parliament will have something different to deal with," he predicted. "There will be 10 or 15 nationalist parties, plus euro-skeptic parties. And they will change the agenda."

DIMITRIS BOUNIAS contributed reporting from Athens, and **GAIA PIANIGIANI** and **ELISABETTA POVOLEDO** from Rome.

The South's Lesson for the Tea Party

OPINION | BY CURTIS WILKIE | AUG. 12, 2014

OXFORD, MISS. — Last week's Republican primary in Tennessee resulted in a comfortable win for Senator Lamar Alexander over his Tea Party-backed challenger, State Assembly Representative Joe Carr. But make no mistake: The Tea Party is on a roll across the South, having mounted major primary challenges in Texas, Mississippi and South Carolina, and knocked out Representative Eric Cantor of Virginia.

The movement's success, with its dangerous froth of anti-Washington posturing and barely concealed racial animus, raises an important question for Southern voters: Will they remember their history well enough to reject the siren song of nativism and populism that has won over the region so often before?

We often think of the typical segregationist politician of yore as a genteel member of the white upper crust. But the more common mode was the fiery populist. Names like Thomas E. Watson of Georgia, "Pitchfork" Ben Tillman of South Carolina and James K. Vardaman and Theodore G. Bilbo of Mississippi may be obscure outside the South, but for most anyone brought up here, they loom large.

In the early 20th century, these men rose on an agrarian revolt against Big Business and government corruption. They used that energy, in turn, to disenfranchise and segregate blacks, whose loyalty to the pro-business Republican Party made them targets of these racist reformers.

Their activities spawned a second wave of Southern Democratic populists, who defied federal court orders and civil rights legislation during the 1960s, even as more moderate politicians were moving on. Gov. George C. Wallace of Alabama, among others, portrayed himself as a tribune of the working class while championing segregation.

It's hard not to hear echoes of those eras today. Tea Party candidates have targeted federal taxes and spending, while attacking

Chamber of Commerce interests and the leadership of the Republican Party. Racism has been replaced with nativism in their demands for immigration restrictions, but the animosity toward the "other" is the same. And there remains a whiff of the ancient fumes of bitter-end resistance: Chris McDaniel, a state senator who took Senator Thad Cochran into a runoff in Mississippi, still refuses to accept the validity of the election.

Mr. McDaniel had all the bona fides of an old-time demagogue. He was once a conservative radio talk show host who dabbled in ethnic innuendo. He made appearances before neo-Confederate organizations. When Mr. Cochran solicited votes in the runoff from black Mississippians, Mr. McDaniel's supporters vowed to monitor polling places in black-majority precincts, a move reminiscent of old-fashioned Election Day intimidation.

Tea Party spokesmen, as well as the Republican establishment, complain that the movement was unfairly trumped by a race card. Whit Ayres, a Republican pollster working for Mr. Alexander, says the movement isn't racist, but rather it represents people "who are economically pressed, who feel betrayed, who feel leaders in Washington caused their housing values to decline, for their retirement accounts to plummet."

But that's precisely the point, and the hope, for those worried about the Tea Party insurgency. What looks like a mounting wave may have reached its crest this year, running up against the many Southerners — white and black, liberal and conservative — who know well how such passions were once perverted by demagogues.

It's trite to recall William Faulkner's line about the past not being the past, but Southerners do remember their history: A considerable body of literature about the populist rebellion was once required reading in college for a generation of Mississippians old enough to remember the second reactionary period 50 years ago.

In "The Mind of the South," still in print seven decades after it was published, W. J. Cash wrote that populist forces in the region were

LEIGH GULDIG

driven by "the rage and frustration of men intolerably oppressed by conditions which they did not understand and which they could not control." And A. D. Kirwan's 1951 history, "Revolt of the Rednecks," traced the political rise of the Mississippi racists Vardaman and Bilbo to the disillusionment of white farmers who felt "forgotten" and singled out by "an enemy class" of Wall Street speculators and railroad owners backed by big government. The economic struggle, Kirwan wrote, was "complicated by the Negro," who became a victim of the politicians' zeal to prevent blacks from holding any power.

Education became their whipping boy. A century ago, the first wave of populist demagogues withheld funds for poor, segregated schools and tried to purge college faculties of nonbelievers. The second wave, citing "states' rights," threatened to shut schools rather than integrate and denounced federal aid to education as a sinister investment. In the Cochran-McDaniel race, you could hear that same strain in Tea Party criticisms of the federal government, of federal aid to education and of the "establishment."

Over a century ago, demagogues did more than anyone to impose the system of strict segregation that lasted until the 1960s. The second wave, though successful in some places, was turned back in others, by moderate, middle-class Southern whites who were tired of seeing their region isolated and stigmatized. With Mr. Cantor's loss, Mr. Cochran's narrow survival and Mr. Alexander's clear victory, we are faced with an open, and very unsettling question: Which way will the South go this time?

CURTIS WILKIE is a fellow at the Overby Center for Southern Journalism and Politics at the University of Mississippi.

CHAPTER 5

Global Right-Wing Populism Overtakes the Establishment

In the last decade, populism drifted rightward. European fringe parties grew due to anti-immigration and law and order rhetoric. In the United States, these tendencies were epitomized by the unlikely success of Donald Trump's presidential campaign. His defeat of Hillary Clinton (who herself faced a primary challenge by left populist Bernie Sanders) was seen by many as a vote against the establishment. Subsequently, left and centrist candidates have emerged, checking the right's gains with an alternative populist appeal on economic and social justice grounds.

Voter Insecurities Feed Rise of Right-Leaning Populist Politicians

BY DAVID D. KIRKPATRICK | DEC. 10, 2015

LONDON — Mass shootings by Islamist militants. Migrants crashing borders. International competition punishing workers but enriching elites.

Across the Western world, a new breed of right-leaning populists like Donald J. Trump, Marine Le Pen in France and Viktor Orban in Hungary are surging in popularity by capitalizing on a climate of insecurity rivaling the period after the First World War.

Many of them — as Mr. Trump did this week — have made headlines by railing against Muslim immigrants, calling them a threat to public safety and cultural identity. Left-leaning critics have compared the populists to the fascists of the early 20th century. Some riding the wave, like the Freedom Party in Austria or Golden Dawn in Greece, have specific neo-Nazi roots.

Unlike earlier right-wing movements, this generation of populists disavows the overt racism, militaristic rhetoric and associations with fascism that until recently scared away many mainstream voters.

Before the recent terrorist attacks or the European migrant crisis cast a spotlight on Muslim immigration, the populists had built support as trade protectionists or economic nationalists appealing to working-class voters who felt disaffected from established parties and political elites. And, for the first time in nearly a century, established parties across Europe and the United States are struggling to fend off or counter the populist insurgents as their competition pulls the mainstream to the right.

STEPHEN CROWLEY/THE NEW YORK TIMES

Donald J. Trump has railed against Muslim immigration, claiming it threatens public safety.

"What you are seeing here is quite a radical shift," said Roger Eatwell, a political scientist at the University of Bath who studies right-wing parties.

Ms. Le Pen is the best-known figure from more than a dozen right-leaning populist parties across Europe that have scored big gains over the last two years. This week, her National Front party won the largest share of the vote in the first round of regional elections in France, with 30 percent, making her a contender for the presidency in 2017. She campaigns against what she calls the Islamization of France and has compared Muslims praying in French streets to the Nazi occupation.

But Ms. Le Pen fuses her cultural chauvinism with appeals to the economic anxieties of working or lower-middle class voters who — like their counterparts across Europe — have suffered from high unemployment, stagnant wages and growing income inequality, especially since the financial crisis of 2008.

"They are pulling out all the stops for the migrants, the illegals, but who is looking out for our retirees?" Ms. Le Pen asked in a recent campaign appearance. "They are stealing from the poor to give to foreigners who did not even ask our permission to come here."

Mr. Trump on Monday evoked comparisons to Ms. Le Pen and her European counterparts with his call to close American borders to all Muslims "until our country's representatives can figure out what the hell is going on."

Ms. Le Pen said that was too much for her, perhaps in part because she feared jeopardizing the progress she had made in shedding her party's previous image as racist and anti-Semitic.

"Seriously, have you ever heard me say something like that?" she asked on Thursday when questioned about Mr. Trump's comments during a television interview. "I defend all the French people in France, regardless of their origin, regardless of their religion."

Others in Europe's right-leaning populist parties, though, are applauding Mr. Trump for breaking with what they call the multiculturalist orthodoxy of dominant political elites.

"He is a phenomenon," said Gawain Towler, a spokesman for the U.K. Independence Party, a right-leaning populist party here.

"They are glad that somebody is saying things along these lines, and that is the same reason why you are now seeing significant support for political groups on the continent of Europe — whether in France, or Denmark or Finland or the others — who do not just repeat the shibboleths of the old establishment," Mr. Towler said. In all the countries, he said, "the same people have been governing for a long time, and they have completely let down the indigenous inhabitants, particularly at the lower end of the economic spectrum."

Streaks of nativism have surfaced in Western Europe since it first welcomed waves of immigrants from former colonies in the middle of the last century, with thousands of Indians, Jamaicans and others arriving in Britain.

But only in the last two decades — with the growing numbers of people arriving from Asia, the Middle East and Africa — has nativist sentiment in Europe approached its prominence in the United States, where immigration is central to the national experience.

In another change, the voices that have taken up the cause of defending national borders and cultures against immigration and other perceived threats are now coming for the first time from populist voices outside the political establishment. (One exception is Hungary, where Mr. Orban, the prime minister, is a right-leaning populist who leads an establishment party, pulled further rightward by competition from a more extreme rival, the Jobbik party.)

Links that once tied parties to their constituencies — Christian Democrats to Roman Catholic churches, for example, or Social Democrats to labor unions — have frayed. Changes in mass media have made celebrities of some political leaders while devaluing some traditional party organizations.

But at the same time, establishment parties on the left and right alike have also largely failed to provide solutions to the problems that most vex working-class voters: income stagnation, insecurity and inequality in an age of technological change and global competition.

A poll conducted in Europe last spring by the Pew Research Center found extraordinary gloom about the state of their economies: Sizable majorities in a half-dozen countries expected children to be worse off than their parents. That pessimistic view was held by 58 percent of the German respondents, 68 percent of the British, and 85 percent of the French.

A Pew poll in the United States around the same time found that two-thirds of respondents believed government polices since the 2008 financial crisis had primarily benefited the wealthy instead of the middle class or the poor — a view held by 70 percent of those making less than $75,000 a year and by 55 percent of Republicans.

Until this year, economic anxieties appeared to be the main fuel propelling the growth of upstart populist parties across Europe, including a few on the left as well as the right. They campaigned as Euroskeptics, assailing the transfer of decision-making to the distant European Union authorities in Brussels and denouncing the cost of bailouts or the pain of austerity measures.

Even before the migrant crisis and the recent terrorist attacks, the populists scored big gains in a dozen countries during the European parliamentary elections in the spring of 2014 and led the polling in Britain and France.

"The financial crisis and the eurozone crisis and all the problems the E.U. was having — they all created fears that these parties were able to channel very well," said Ruth Wodak, a professor at Lancaster University in England and the author of "The Politics of Fear: What Right-Wing Populist Discourses Mean."

In each case, the core constituencies of the new right-wing parties were working-class men. "These are voters who feel economically left behind, under threat from immigration and rapid social change, and cut adrift from established politics," said Matthew J. Goodwin, a political scientist at the University of Kent who studies the right.

Mr. Trump, similarly, draws much of his support primarily among voters without a college education. The latest nationwide New York Times/CBS News poll showed that Mr. Trump had the support of 40 percent of Republican primary voters without a college degree, but 26 percent of those who had a degree. No other candidate's support was related so closely to level of education. The poll was largely taken before his statement on Monday afternoon proposing to temporarily bar Muslims from entering the United States.

Unlike his populist counterparts in Europe, Mr. Trump does not come out of any movement or ideology, nor does he have much history in the Republican Party.

But like Ms. Le Pen and others on the right, he has combined his signature themes about the perils of immigration with stances that speak to the economic anxieties of working people as well. He has accused hedge funds of "getting away with murder," calling them "guys that shift paper around and get lucky." And he has denounced free-trade deals, vowed to put tariffs on imports and to stop immigrants or foreign workers from competing for jobs.

Pat Buchanan, who ran his own right-leaning populist presidential campaigns in the United States for three elections beginning in 1992, said in an interview that he recognized many of his own cultural and economic themes in the speeches of Mr. Trump, Ms. Le Pen and the others around Europe. Their movements were manifestations of the same global forces, he argued.

"Nationalism and tribalism and faith — these are the driving forces now, and they are tearing apart transnational institutions all over the world," he said.

It all reminded him, he wrote in a follow-up email, of a line from the "The Second Coming," by W.B. Yeats: "Things fall apart; the center cannot hold."

AURELIEN BREEDEN contributed reporting from Paris.

How Can Donald Trump and Bernie Sanders Both Be 'Populist'?

ESSAY | BY MICHAEL KAZIN | MARCH 22, 2016

DONALD TRUMP AND Bernie Sanders share an upbringing in New York's outer boroughs and a repugnance for trade deals, but the similarities pretty much end there. Sanders routinely inveighs against "corporate America"; Trump is an executive of almost 500 business entities, more than 200 of which are named after himself. Trump lends his name to a line of power ties and cuff links; the adjective most often applied to Sanders's wardrobe is "rumpled." Yet journalists routinely refer to both men as "populists." How can a word that purports to describe both a proud socialist and an arrogant billionaire have any meaning?

For half a century, most presidential campaigns have featured one or more "populists" from the right, the left or somewhere in between. In 1968, reporters and academics pasted the label on George Wallace, whose campaign literature asked, "Can a former truck driver married to a dime-store clerk and son of a dirt farmer be elected president?" In 1972, Time dubbed George McGovern a "prairie populist" because he had a modest plan to redistribute wealth and hailed from the rural heartland. In 1996, The Atlantic observed that Pat Buchanan's "hard-right-wing populism ... may be the shape of politics to come." In 2012, The Hill announced, "Obama cranks up populist pitch" after the president, who previously shied away from us-versus-them talk, called for higher taxes on the rich.

There was a time when "populist" meant something more specific. The word originated with the decidedly left-wing People's Party that emerged in the Midwest and the South amid the economic turmoil and rampant inequality of the 1890s. Journalists who knew some Latin started calling them "Populists" as a shorthand, and the name stuck. Those uppercase Populists championed small farmers and wage-earners who thought "the money power" — banks and industrial corporations — had seized control of both America's economy and its government. The party called for nationalizing the railroads, breaking up the trusts and strengthening labor unions. At times, their leftism toppled over into paranoia; to explain society's ills, they invoked "a vast conspiracy against mankind," engineered by a plutocratic cabal.

The Populists joined forces with the Democrats for the 1896 election and collapsed soon afterward. The word "populist" mostly disappeared into academic studies until the 1950s, when Joseph McCarthy, a previously obscure Republican senator from Wisconsin, rose to prominence with his claims that Communists had infiltrated positions of power in the American government and military. Many targets of his rants were members of the East Coast liberal intelligentsia.

Millions of Americans cheered on McCarthy's crusade — horrifying liberal intellectuals like the historian Richard Hofstadter and the sociologist Daniel Bell, who reached back to the precedent of the Populists to understand the roots of the new anti-elitist fervor. In McCarthy, they heard echoes of the original Populists' conspiracy theorizing — only this time, the perpetrators were well-born "pinkos" or "reds."

Other scholars dismissed the comparison as deeply unfair, but Hofstadter's effort to link the Populists to what he called "the paranoid style" of the new right resonated. And so "populism" began to morph into a handy tool of journalistic discourse.

In the 1960s, the streets and airwaves were crowded with protesters of all ideological persuasions who claimed to be fighting for the interests and values of a virtuous, exploited people against an immoral, grasping elite. "Populist" became a handle applied to anyone who fought the powers that be, however they were defined. Wallace protested a federal order to integrate the University of Alabama by stating, "There can be no submission to the theory that the central government is anything but a servant of the people." On the left, young radicals vowed that with "participatory democracy," they could topple racists like Wallace, along with the rest of "the power elite." Ralph Nader, then a liberal lawyer, stoked a revolt by consumers enraged at auto companies that increased their profits by concealing design flaws in their vehicles.

Like Trump and Sanders today, '60s "populists" chose to blame elites for what ailed the nation. For Nader, it was greedy corporations and enabling politicians. For Wallace and Ronald Reagan, it was the federal state. These habits live on today. From the Tea Party to the fight for a $15-an-hour minimum wage, Americans keep turning their ire against institutions that appear to betray the promise of fair and equitable treatment of ordinary workers, homeowners or taxpayers. Sometimes, it seems, "populism" is just a synonym for widespread unhappiness with the status quo.

Yet differences of language matter; they suggest what a candidate will seek to accomplish if he or she takes power. The 19th-century antecedent that Trump evokes in his nativist appeals to white working- and middle-class Americans is not the populism of the People's Party but rather that of the Know-Nothing Party of the 1850s, which similarly argued that immigrants were taking Americans' jobs and breaking the nation's laws. Trump's "populism" is a brilliant specimen of performance art but one that bears little resemblance, even in style, to the capital-P kind. The earnest activists from the People's Party of old brandished a lengthy blueprint for reform; Trump's personality overshadows his program. His canny lack of finesse finesses us all.

The original Populists would probably warm up to Sanders, even if their constituents in places like rural Kansas and Georgia might be puzzled to hear familiar rhetoric spoken by an elderly Jew with a Brooklyn accent. The Populists' 1892 platform thundered: "The fruits of the toil of millions are boldly stolen to build up colossal fortunes for a few." Sanders similarly attacks "the billionaire class," whose supposed grip on the state has led to "an enormous transfer of wealth from the middle class and the poor to the wealthiest people in this country."

Critics of Sanders and Trump often condemn them with the same pejorative. The conservative National Review, for instance, recently scorned both as "demagogues" who exploit public alarm and peddle impossible solutions to difficult problems. But as that word has been applied to everyone from Andrew Jackson to Joe McCarthy to President Obama, it has lost much of its sting. The "populist" whose politics you abhor is always a demagogue disguised as a hero of the masses.

And those who disparage "populism" in general neglect its salutary function. When populist talkers direct their outrage at elites, in government or business, who neglect the needs and betray the trust of ordinary citizens, they can perform a service to the nation. They train their language of discontent on those accused of betraying the core ideal of American democracy — one that is no less powerful because it can never be fully realized.

In their own fashion, Sanders and Trump are protesting inequalities and the corruption of public life without calling the entire system into question. (Sanders may speak of "revolution," but he still chose to run for president within the two-party system.) You may love such upheavals or loathe them. Trump's hostility toward undocumented immigrants and Muslims is certainly reprehensible. But every major "populist" insurgency is a warning about serious problems festering in our politics. To simply blame the messenger is an exercise in denial.

MICHAEL KAZIN teaches history at Georgetown University and is co-editor of Dissent. He is the author of "War Against War: The American Fight for Peace, 1914-1918," which will be published in January 2017 by Simon & Schuster.

Donald Trump Is Elected President in Stunning Repudiation of the Establishment

BY MATT FLEGENHEIMER AND MICHAEL BARBARO | NOV. 9, 2016

DONALD JOHN TRUMP was elected the 45th president of the United States on Tuesday in a stunning culmination of an explosive, populist and polarizing campaign that took relentless aim at the institutions and long-held ideals of American democracy.

The surprise outcome, defying late polls that showed Hillary Clinton with a modest but persistent edge, threatened convulsions throughout the country and the world, where skeptics had watched with alarm as Mr. Trump's unvarnished overtures to disillusioned voters took hold.

The triumph for Mr. Trump, 70, a real estate developer-turned-reality television star with no government experience, was a powerful rejection of the establishment forces that had assembled against him, from the world of business to government, and the consensus they had forged on everything from trade to immigration.

The results amounted to a repudiation, not only of Mrs. Clinton, but of President Obama, whose legacy is suddenly imperiled. And it was a decisive demonstration of power by a largely overlooked coalition of mostly blue-collar white and working-class voters who felt that the promise of the United States had slipped their grasp amid decades of globalization and multiculturalism.

In Mr. Trump, a thrice-married Manhattanite who lives in a marble-wrapped three-story penthouse apartment on Fifth Avenue, they found an improbable champion.

"The forgotten men and women of our country will be forgotten no longer," Mr. Trump told supporters around 3 a.m. on Wednesday at a rally in New York City, just after Mrs. Clinton called to concede.

In a departure from a blistering campaign in which he repeatedly stoked division, Mr. Trump sought to do something he had conspicuously avoided as a candidate: Appeal for unity.

"Now it's time for America to bind the wounds of division," he said. "It is time for us to come together as one united people. It's time."

That, he added, "is so important to me."

He offered unusually warm words for Mrs. Clinton, who he has suggested should be in jail, saying she was owed "a major debt of gratitude for her service to our country."

Bolstered by Mr. Trump's strong showing, Republicans retained control of the Senate. Only one Republican-controlled seat, in Illinois, fell to Democrats early in the evening. And Senator Richard Burr of North Carolina, a Republican, easily won re-election in a race that had been among the country's most competitive. A handful of other Republican incumbents facing difficult races were running better than expected.

Mr. Trump's win — stretching across the battleground states of Florida, North Carolina, Ohio and Pennsylvania — seemed likely to set off financial jitters and immediate unease among international allies, many of which were startled when Mr. Trump in his campaign cast doubt on the necessity of America's military commitments abroad and its allegiance to international economic partnerships.

From the moment he entered the campaign, with a shocking set of claims that Mexican immigrants were rapists and criminals, Mr. Trump was widely underestimated as a candidate, first by his opponents for the Republican nomination and later by Mrs. Clinton, his Democratic rival. His rise was largely missed by polling organizations and data analysts. And an air of improbability trailed his campaign, to the detriment of those who dismissed his angry message, his improvisational style and his appeal to disillusioned voters.

He suggested remedies that raised questions of constitutionality, like a ban on Muslims entering the United States.

He threatened opponents, promising lawsuits against news organizations that covered him critically and women who accused him of sexual assault. At times, he simply lied.

But Mr. Trump's unfiltered rallies and unshakable self-regard attracted a zealous following, fusing unsubtle identity politics with an economic populism that often defied party doctrine.

His rallies — furious, entertaining, heavy on name-calling and nationalist overtones — became the nexus of a political movement, with daily promises of sweeping victory, in the election and otherwise, and an insistence that the country's political machinery was "rigged" against Mr. Trump and those who admired him.

He seemed to embody the success and grandeur that so many of his followers felt was missing from their own lives — and from the country itself. And he scoffed at the poll-driven word-parsing ways of modern politics, calling them a waste of time and money. Instead, he relied on his gut.

At his victory party at the New York Hilton Midtown, where a raucous crowd indulged in a cash bar and wore hats bearing his ubiquitous campaign slogan "Make America Great Again," voters expressed gratification that their voices had, at last, been heard.

"He was talking to people who weren't being spoken to," said Joseph Gravagna, 37, a marketing company owner from Rockland County, N.Y. "That's how I knew he was going to win."

For Mrs. Clinton, the defeat signaled an astonishing end to a political dynasty that has colored Democratic politics for a generation. Eight years after losing to President Obama in the Democratic primary — and 16 years after leaving the White House for the United States Senate, as President Bill Clinton exited office — she had seemed positioned to carry on two legacies: her husband's and the president's.

Her shocking loss was a devastating turn for the sprawling world of Clinton aides and strategists who believed they had built an electoral machine that would swamp Mr. Trump's ragtag band of loyal

DAMON WINTER/THE NEW YORK TIMES

Donald Trump at a campaign event in Long Beach, Calif., in September 2015.

operatives and family members, many of whom had no experience running a national campaign.

On Tuesday night, stricken Clinton aides who believed that Mr. Trump had no mathematical path to victory, anxiously paced the Jacob K. Javits Convention Center as states in which they were confident of victory, like Florida and North Carolina, either fell to Mr. Trump or seemed in danger of tipping his way.

Mrs. Clinton watched the grim results roll in from a suite at the nearby Peninsula Hotel, surrounded by her family, friends and advisers who had the day before celebrated her candidacy with a champagne toast on her campaign plane.

But over and over, Mrs. Clinton's weaknesses as a candidate were exposed. She failed to excite voters hungry for change. She struggled to build trust with Americans who were baffled by her decision to use a private email server as secretary of state. And she strained to make a persuasive case for herself as a champion of the economically downtrodden after delivering perfunctory paid speeches that earned her millions of dollars.

The returns Tuesday also amounted to a historic rebuke of the Democratic Party from the white blue-collar voters who had formed the party base from the presidency of Franklin D. Roosevelt to Mr. Clinton's. Yet Mrs. Clinton and her advisers had taken for granted that states like Michigan and Wisconsin would stick with a Democratic nominee, and that she could repeat Mr. Obama's strategy of mobilizing the party's ascendant liberal coalition rather than pursuing a more moderate course like her husband did 24 years ago.

But not until these voters were offered a Republican who ran as an unapologetic populist, railing against foreign trade deals and illegal immigration, did they move so drastically away from their ancestral political home.

To the surprise of many on the left, white voters who had helped elect the nation's first black president, appeared more reluctant to line up behind a white woman.

From Pennsylvania to Wisconsin, industrial towns once full of union voters who for decades offered their votes to Democratic presidential candidates, even in the party's lean years, shifted to Mr. Trump's Republican Party. One county in the Mahoning Valley of Ohio, Trumbull, went to Mr. Trump by a six-point margin. Four years ago, Mr. Obama won there by 22 points.

Mrs. Clinton's loss was especially crushing to millions who had cheered her march toward history as, they hoped, the nation's first female president. For supporters, the election often felt like a referendum on gender progress: an opportunity to elevate a woman to the nation's top job and to repudiate a man whose remarkably boorish behavior toward women had assumed center stage during much of the campaign.

Mr. Trump boasted, in a 2005 video released last month, about using his public profile to commit sexual assault. He suggested that female political rivals lacked a presidential "look." He ranked women on a scale of one to 10, even holding forth on the desirability of his own daughter — the kind of throwback male behavior that many in the country assumed would disqualify a candidate for high office.

On Tuesday, the public's verdict was rendered.

Uncertainty abounds as Mr. Trump prepares to take office. His campaign featured a shape-shifting list of policy proposals, often seeming to change hour to hour. His staff was in constant turmoil, with Mr. Trump's children serving critical campaign roles and a rotating cast of advisers alternately seeking access to Mr. Trump's ear, losing it and, often, regaining it, depending on the day.

Even Mr. Trump's full embrace of the Republican Party came exceedingly late in life, leaving members of both parties unsure about what he truly believes. He has donated heavily to both parties and has long described his politics as the transactional reality of a businessman.

Mr. Trump's dozens of business entanglements — many of them in foreign countries — will follow him into the Oval Office, raising questions about potential conflicts of interest. His refusal to release his tax returns, and his acknowledgment that he did not pay federal income taxes for years, has left the American people with considerable gaps in their understanding of the financial dealings.

But this they do know: Mr. Trump will thoroughly reimagine the tone, standards and expectations of the presidency, molding it in his own self-aggrandizing image.

He is set to take the oath of office on Jan. 20.

AMY CHOZICK, **ASHLEY PARKER**, **PATRICK HEALY** and **JONATHAN MARTIN** contributed reporting.

Brexit's Bitter Winners

OPINION | BY OWEN JONES | NOV. 30, 2016

LONDON — David Bowie died, and it was all downhill from there. That's how 2016 felt if you were on the losing side of Britain's referendum on membership in the European Union.

Post-Brexit Britain is now mired in crisis. The ruling Conservative government, lacking any coherent plan for leaving the union, is embroiled in a bitter legal fight over the process, while a divided opposition contemplates the disintegration of its electoral coalition. In a country polarized and paralyzed, an unchecked authoritarian right-wing populism — Trumpism without Trump — is coming to define the political culture.

The latest convulsion was caused by a lawsuit brought by a London-based investment manager, Gina Miller, to force the government to hold a debate and vote in Parliament before activating Article 50, the treaty provision that begins the process of leaving the bloc. Ms. Miller, who was born in Guyana, has been advised by the police to avoid public spaces for fear of attack. But it was the judges of the High Court who came in for abuse when, earlier this month, they ruled in Ms. Miller's favor.

"Enemies of the People," bellowed the front page of The Daily Mail, the country's second-most-read newspaper, below images of the three judges who had made the decision. One was denounced as "an openly gay ex-Olympic fencer."

"Loaded foreign elite defy will of Brit voters" was the verdict of The Sun, a newspaper owned by the press tycoon Rupert Murdoch. The Brexiteers are bitter winners.

The referendum itself was easily framed as the establishment versus the people. An Eton-educated prime minister warned that a vote for Brexit would "put a bomb under our economy" and risked Europe's descending into war, and he assembled corporate titans to issue ominous warnings; the Leavers promised an independent, sovereign Britain that would "take back control." One demanded support for the status quo, or else; the other promised change, and a punch in the face to a detested establishment as a bonus. A YouGov survey before the referendum found that more than a quarter of likely Leave voters believed that the Security Service was working to undermine the result.

The High Court did not overturn the referendum result; it merely obliged the government to hold a parliamentary debate and vote before invoking Article 50. (Paradoxically, one plank of the Leave platform was a call to restore sovereignty to Britain's Parliament.) The government's appeal will go to the Supreme Court, but it seems unlikely to succeed — and some Conservative members of Parliament are calling for it to be dropped rather than provide another "opportunity for ill-motivated people to attack the judiciary."

In post-Brexit Britain, the rule of law has become just another liberal elite institution designed to thwart the popular will. At her party's annual conference in October, the new prime minister, Theresa May, caught the mood.

"They find your patriotism distasteful, your concerns about immigration parochial," she said. "If you're a citizen of the world, you're a citizen of nowhere."

Why such antagonism over a referendum about membership of a trading bloc? The vote exposed and widened divisions familiar also in America: metropolitan, university-educated people against working-class people; big cities versus small towns; young versus old. The Leave campaign appealed to communities battered by deindustrialization and working-class people whose lives are defined by insecurity.

Take the former industrial town in Northern England where I grew up: Stockport. The people there are seeing the longest squeeze in wages since the 19th century; a housing crisis caused by the lowest level of homebuilding since the 1920s; and public services under strain because of the worst budget cuts in generations. Many of the town's residents view all these problems through the prism of immigration.

This highlights a dilemma for the opposition Labour Party on how to position itself. A chaotic Brexit beckons, which the Conservative chancellor, Philip Hammond, concedes will mean two years of "fiscal uncertainty," and which is likely to conclude in an unfavorable deal for Britain. So should Labour use the court judgment to try to block Brexit in Parliament, hoping that enough Leave voters will feel buyer's remorse over the referendum result and return to the Labour fold?

Labour's own woes amply match the government's problems. Although a fragile internal cease-fire currently holds, the party is chronically divided. Its left-wing leader, Jeremy Corbyn, has the enthusiastic support of grass-roots members, hundreds of thousands of whom have joined over the last year and a half. About three-quarters of the party's members of Parliament, however, rebelled but failed to oust him in a leadership election following the referendum debacle.

A greater problem looms over both Corbyn supporters and opponents: Labour's virtual annihilation in the next general election. According to one projection, if the votes in the referendum were applied to a hypothetical general election, Leave would win 421 parliamentary seats against 229 for Remain (which the Labour Party backed).

Labour's electoral coalition is unwieldy, to say the least, with fractures of class and region exposed by the Brexit referendum. Despite the party line, more than a third of Labour's supporters voted Leave, especially in northern heartlands. Party leaders privately believe that the greatest threat to Labour is losing this segment of electoral support.

A further wrinkle is that if Labour attempts to use parliamentary process to disrupt the government's plans, the government could respond by calling a snap election. All the polling suggests that the Conservatives would bury Labour in a landslide.

So despite internal divisions over Brexit — with many supporters favoring a second referendum in hopes of overturning the first — Labour has rather desperately changed tack, emphasizing its commitment to Brexit, rather than offering opposition. The party's economic spokesman, John McDonnell, has praised "the enormous opportunities" offered by Brexit, and suggested that those seeking to frustrate the triggering of Article 50 are "on the side of certain corporate elites."

How should Labour navigate this politically perilous path? Polling suggests that British voters are evenly split between cutting immigration and retaining access to the single market as the key objective of Brexit negotiations. Labour surely must emphasize that it would put the economy first, meaning maximum access to the single market, while addressing concerns caused by freedom of movement in the European Union by clamping down on the undercutting of wages and compelling multinational companies to train local workers. If the economy does indeed suffer, then Labour can pin it on the government's failed strategy.

There are other possible openings. Britain's national debt has been a key bone of political contention, used to clobber Labour in the 2015 general election as a spendthrift party in denial of economic realities. But when the Tories' "austerity chancellor," as George Osborne was called by one financial journalist, was ousted after Brexit, the Conservatives' credibility as the party of fiscal discipline went with him. The referendum showed that voters wanted economic regeneration, and Mr. Corbyn won the leadership election largely because of his clear opposition to austerity, but Labour has yet to lay out a clear alternative — and risks being defined by its opponents instead.

Labour must redefine patriotism, too, despite the left's traditional discomfort with such ideas. With Scottish nationalism dominant north of the border, national identity increasingly matters to English voters. Defending great British institutions like the National Health Service and the welfare state can be patriotic; corporate elites who put profit before people could be called unpatriotic.

The government may lose its Supreme Court appeal, but Parliament is sure to vote to activate Article 50. Even so, Nigel Farage, the then interim leader of the U.K. Independence Party (often known as "UKIP"), has — Trump-like — warned of riots if the referendum outcome is undermined, calling for a march on the court. One

Conservative member, himself a Leave campaigner, has resigned from Parliament in protest at the government's handling of the Brexit process, telling friends the party was now "UKIP-lite."

An extremism that was once consigned to the fringes is now center stage in British politics. Right-wing populism may remake Britain in its own image. It may only be Labour that can stand in its way, but the party faces an immense challenge if it is not to be steamrolled by the forces that gave us Brexit.

OWEN JONES is a columnist for The Guardian and the author of "The Establishment: And How They Get Away With It."

How a Liberal Dissident Became a Far-Right Hero, in Hungary and Beyond

BY PATRICK KINGSLEY | APRIL 6, 2018

BUDAPEST — During the final days of communism in Hungary, a young, liberal dissident wrote to a foundation run by the Hungarian-American philanthropist George Soros, asking for a grant to finance his research into grass-roots democracy.

Hungary would soon "transition from dictatorship to democracy," the student wrote in 1988. "One of the main elements of this transition can be the rebirth of civil society."

The student was Viktor Orban. Now the prime minister, Mr. Orban is expected to lead his party to victory in parliamentary elections on Sunday — not as the pro-Western statesman he once promised to be, but as a hero to the far-right, a scourge of civil society (and of Mr. Soros), and the embodiment of the failed promise of liberalism in post-Cold War Eastern Europe.

Each country has its own story. But societies across Central and Eastern Europe are dominated by similar figures — some by politicians who, like Mr. Orban, have lost interest in the liberal democratic project that followed the crumbling of communism in 1989, and others by those with different motivations who have exploited voters' growing disaffection with liberalism.

"It's a regionwide phenomenon," said Jiri Pehe, a former senior aide to Vaclav Havel, the first Czech president. "Democracy proved to be a very difficult project for this generation of politicians to master."

In the early 90s, as prominent dissidents such as Mr. Havel and Lech Walesa in Poland entered office, it was widely assumed that the region would transition naturally into democratic states and market economies. Voters expected that living standards would soon match those in Western Europe — especially as many former communist countries moved to join the European Union.

Personal freedoms and wealth did increase, but the chaotic nature of the process, compounded by the global financial crisis in 2008, meant that expectations often outpaced progress. In some countries, the privatization of state assets was perceived as benefiting foreign investors and corrupt politicians more often than it did ordinary citizens.

Politicians sensed the mood, and shifted rightward. The current Czech president, Milos Zeman, was a liberal-minded dissident in the dying years of communism but now courts the far right. His prime minister, Andrej Babis, was never a freedom fighter but was elected last year on a populist platform attacking the perceived failings of the post-1989 political elite.

In Poland, the leader of the governing party, Jaroslaw Kaczynski, is a conservative who was once ostracized by the early leaders of post-communist Poland. But his nativist, autocratic ideas have gained currency as resentment over aspects of the transition set in when voters' aspirations exceeded the pace of social and economic change.

"Kaczynski is a master of playing on bad emotions," said Radoslaw Sikorski, who was foreign minister and speaker of the Polish Parliament during the government that preceded Mr. Kaczynski's.

But no one exemplifies the angry direction of post-communist Eastern Europe more than Viktor Orban, whose journey from liberal academic to illiberal populist is starker than any of his regional contemporaries. He used the Soros grant to study the history of civil society at Oxford University, fought communism as a dissident from behind the Iron Curtain and then, as a center-right politician, helped to steer Hungary into the European Union and NATO.

Now Mr. Orban is a populist hero to Stephen K. Bannon, President Trump's former strategist, and the self-declared leader of a "cultural counterrevolution" that is dividing the European bloc he once fought to join.

"The worst nightmare, in terms of Orban-ism spreading, has come true," said Gerald Knaus, the director of the European Stability Initiative, a Berlin-based research group.

MAURICIO LIMA FOR THE NEW YORK TIMES

An Afghan family held by police officers in Asotthalom, Hungary, in 2015. By that year, Mr. Orban had cajoled several Central and East European countries to block the European Union response to the migration crisis.

The young Mr. Orban was a passionate dissident, famous for a 1988 speech in which he demanded that Soviet troops leave Hungarian soil. At another rally, Mr. Orban risked his life to protect another opposition leader, Gaspar Miklos Tamas, taking several blows to his head as he thrust himself between the police and Mr. Tamas.

He gave little hint of his future trajectory — save a cameo role in a student production of the German Absurdist drama “How Mr. Mockinpott Was Cured of His Sufferings”, in which he played a demagogue.

“It was not his aim to be a politician,” said Gabor Fodor, Mr. Orban’s former roommate and best friend. “He wanted to be an intellectual and to be a member of Hungarian intellectual circles.”

That all began to shift in 1990, with the approach of Hungary’s first democratic elections in half a century. Mr. Orban had co-founded a liberal youth group, Fidesz, that was reconstituted as a political party and won 22 seats in the new Parliament.

Appointed as the party's leader, Mr. Orban spoke out against nationalism, defended civil society and opposed clerical influence in politics. But behind the scenes, his political ideology was beginning to morph — and he was beginning to exert greater control on the management of Fidesz.

By 1993, Mr. Orban had assumed overall leadership of Fidesz, redefined it as a more nationalist and centrist party and ruthlessly sidelined its liberal faction, headed by his now former friend, Gabor Fodor.

Quite why Mr. Orban changed is a matter of debate. Some contemporaries believe it was the genuine ideological shift of a young man whose politics were a work in progress. Others argue he grew resentful of cosmopolitan liberals.

But most feel that Mr. Orban's transition was a pragmatic response to the landscape of Hungarian politics. Overshadowed by other left-of-center parties, Fidesz lacked a clear brand. By tacking toward the political center, Mr. Orban reckoned that his party could stand out.

Unlike most other Hungarian politicians of the time, Mr. Orban "thought about politics in a more professional way," said Zsuzsanna Szelenyi, one of the Fidesz lawmakers sidelined by Mr. Orban in 1993. "He realized it was about power."

Despite Mr. Orban's machinations, Fidesz did poorly in the 1994 elections. He responded by shifting further to the right, turning Fidesz into a center-right Christian democratic party — one still open to Western and American ideals.

"The 1990s were wonderful for American diplomats," said Donald Blinken, who, as the American ambassador to Hungary from 1994 to 1997, lunched annually with Mr. Orban. "Everyone loved us, the Cold War was won, and we thought it was this great period of peace and prosperity."

But Mr. Orban kept growing more nationalistic — and, apparently, more religious.

Married in a civil wedding a decade earlier, Mr. Orban and his wife, Aniko Levai, renewed their vows in a religious ceremony in 1996.

Gabor Ivanyi, the pastor who performed that second ceremony, has since become skeptical of Mr. Orban's motivations. "He had to convince people, to win over the conservative right," Mr. Ivanyi said. "He is an unscrupulous person."

Mr. Orban finally assumed power in 1998, becoming prime minister for the first time at the head of a conservative coalition. (Voters were angered by the Socialist-led government's handling of the struggling economy.)

For the next four years, Mr. Orban operated as a relatively orthodox center-right politician. His administration was tainted by minor corruption scandals, but his performance was mostly praised.

He brought Hungary to the brink of European Union membership and shepherded the country into NATO, an event he celebrated with a private dinner in Brussels attended by several of his mentors, including Zbigniew Pelczynski, his politics professor at Oxford.

It was his defeat in the 2002 elections that accelerated his pivot to the far right.

"They say that power spoils good politicians," said Jozsef Debreczeni, an adviser to Mr. Orban after his first rightward turn — and later his biographer. "With Orban that wasn't the case. It was the loss of power that did that."

During an intense one-and-a-half days after the election, Mr. Debreczeni listened as Mr. Orban blamed his political demise on a partisan news media that needed to be reined in.

Mr. Debreczeni said that Mr. Orban had drawn one conclusion: "This democracy thing, where power can slip so quickly from you, was no good."

"And from that point on," Mr. Debreczeni added, "he spent his time preparing so that if he ever won power again, he wouldn't lose it."

The global financial crisis of 2008, coupled with increasing resentment of the Socialist-led government, eventually gave Mr. Orban that chance. The Socialists, who were also in power during the economic turmoil of the 1990s, were accused of squandering the political and economic potential of the transition from communism.

Mr. Orban reinvented himself as an outsider who promised to restore Hungarian control to an economy buffeted by external forces — a popular policy among Hungarians rankled by how privatization efforts after 1989 had allowed foreigners to take over parts of Hungarian industry.

"To understand the Orban phenomenon, you have to go back to 1989," said Laszlo Andor, who was once Hungary's most senior representative at the European Commission, the European Union's executive arm. "People's ambitions were not fulfilled."

Elected by a landslide in 2010, Mr. Orban has steadily weakened Hungary's democratic institutions while invoking the self-contradictory concept of "illiberal democracy" and hailing the autocratic governments of Vladimir V. Putin of Russia and Recep Tayyip Erdogan of Turkey.

To outflank a major far-right opposition party, Jobbik, he tacked further to the right on immigration. By 2015, Mr. Orban had cajoled several Central and East European countries to block the European Union's efforts to resettle thousands of migrants fleeing violence elsewhere — and provided a template for a democratic backslide in Poland.

His influence then crept further west. He forged an alliance with Horst Seehofer, the new German interior minister; appeared with Geert Wilders, the Dutch nationalist politician; and became a frequent subject of praise during recent election campaigns in Austria that ended with a far-right party joining a coalition government.

Mr. Orban sees all this as nothing less than the march of history.

"What we are experiencing now is the end of an era: a conceptual-ideological era," he said in a major speech in 2015, as he began to expand his international profile. "Putting pretension aside, we can simply call this the era of liberal babble."

BENJAMIN NOVAK contributed reporting from Budapest, and **PALKO KARASZ** from London.

Jair Bolsonaro Wins Brazil's Presidency, in a Shift to the Far Right

BY ERNESTO LONDOÑO AND SHASTA DARLINGTON | OCT. 28, 2018

RIO DE JANEIRO — Brazil on Sunday became the latest country to drift toward the far right, electing a strident populist as president in the nation's most radical political change since democracy was restored more than 30 years ago.

The president-elect, Jair Bolsonaro, has exalted the country's military dictatorship, advocated torture and threatened to destroy, jail or drive into exile his political opponents.

He won by tapping into a deep well of resentment at the status quo in Brazil — a country whiplashed by rising crime and two years of political and economic turmoil — and by presenting himself as the alternative.

"We have everything we need to become a great nation," Mr. Bolsonaro said Sunday night shortly after the race was called in a video broadcast on his Facebook account. "Together we will change the destiny of Brazil."

He appeared eager to dispel concerns that he would govern despotically, saying his government would be a "defender of the Constitution, democracy and liberty."

Mr. Bolsonaro, who will take the helm of Latin America's biggest nation, is further to the right than any president in the region, where voters have recently embraced more conservative leaders in Argentina, Chile, Peru, Paraguay and Colombia. He joins a number of far-right politicians who have risen to power around the world, including Italy's deputy prime minister, Matteo Salvini, and Prime Minister Viktor Orban of Hungary.

"This is a really radical shift," said Scott Mainwaring, a professor at Harvard University's Kennedy School of Government who specializes in Brazil. "I can't think of a more extremist leader in the history of democratic elections in Latin America who has been elected."

With 98 percent of votes counted, Mr. Bolsonaro was ahead with 55 percent, guaranteeing him a win over Fernando Haddad of the leftist Workers' Party, who had 45 percent.

Hundreds of supporters gathered outside Mr. Bolsonaro's seaside home in Rio de Janeiro, jumping and hugging one another when the results were announced. As golden fireworks lit up the sky, they chanted "mito," or legend, paying homage to their president-elect.

Reeling from the deepest recession in the country's history, a corruption scandal that tarnished politicians across the ideological spectrum, and a record-high number of homicides last year, Brazilians picked a candidate who not only rejected the political establishment but at times also seemed to reject the most basic democratic tenets.

Mr. Bolsonaro's victory caps a bitter contest that divided families, tore friendships apart and ignited concerns about the resilience of Brazil's young democracy.

Many Brazilians see authoritarian tendencies in Mr. Bolsonaro, who plans to appoint military leaders to top posts and said he would not accept the result if he were to lose. He has threatened to stack the Supreme Court by increasing the number of judges to 21 from 11 and to deal with political foes by giving them the choice of extermination or exile.

Mr. Bolsonaro, 63, a former army captain who has been a member of Congress for nearly three decades, beat a crowded field of presidential contenders, several of whom entered the race with bigger war chests, less baggage and the backing of powerful political parties.

Mr. Bolsonaro said that President Trump called to congratulate him, calling it "obviously a very friendly contact."

Part of the reason for Mr. Bolsonaro's victory was the collapse of the left. Many cried foul after former President Luiz Inácio Lula da Silva, the longtime front-runner in the race, was ruled ineligible to run after he was imprisoned in April to start serving a 12-year sentence for corruption and money laundering.

His Workers' Party had won the last four presidential elections, and Mr. da Silva, a former metalworker, retained a devoted following among poor and working-class Brazilians who felt represented by him personally and had benefited from his party's social inclusion policies.

But many more Brazilians showed through their votes that they had had enough of the Workers' Party, which steered the country from 2003 to 2016 through a boom-and-bust cycle that ended in an economic morass and the impeachment of his successor, President Dilma Rousseff.

Despite his influence, Mr. da Silva was not able to pull off the last-minute transfer of votes to the candidate chosen to replace him on the ballot, the bookish and urbane — but less charismatic — Mr. Haddad.

And for those Brazilians who saw the political establishment they inherited from the Workers' Party as venal, Mr. Bolsonaro was an enthralling candidate.

He accomplished little in his long legislative career, but his roster of offensive remarks — he said that he'd rather his son die than be gay and that women don't deserve the same pay as men — was interpreted by many as bracing honesty and evidence of his willingness to shatter the status quo.

"The way he's run his campaign is very clever," said Matias Spektor, a professor of international relations at Fundação Getulio Vargas University. "He has managed to align himself with the institutions that Brazilians still believe in: religion, family and armed forces."

Mr. Bolsonaro, the patriarch of a family from Rio de Janeiro that includes three sons who are also lawmakers, ran an insurgent campaign that defied the political playbook that brought his predecessors to power.

A year ago, Mr. Bolsonaro's bid was widely regarded by political veterans in Brasília as fanciful in a nation renowned for the cordiality and warmth of its people. Some of the candidate's remarks were so offensive the country's attorney general earlier this year charged him with inciting hatred toward black, gay and indigenous people. In a country where most of the population is not white, this alone might have seemed to disqualify him.

Yet, the vitriol and outrage Mr. Bolsonaro brought to the campaign trail as he traveled around the country largely mirrored Brazilians' dystopian mood.

Nearly 13 million people are unemployed. The homicide rate is among the highest in the world — last year, 63,880 people were killed. And Mr. da Silva, the former president many had idolized, had left office with an approval rating of 87 percent only to become the most prominent scalp taken by a corruption scandal that has ensnared dozens of the country's political and business leaders.

Part of Mr. Bolsonaro's appeal lay in the extreme solutions he proposed to assuage the population's anger and fear of violence.

He vowed to give the police forces in Brazil — some of the most lethal in the world — expanded authority to kill suspects, saying with trademark bluntness that a "good criminal is a dead criminal." He also promised to lower the age of criminal responsibility, impose stiffer sentences for violent crimes and ease Brazil's gun ownership restrictions so civilians could better protect themselves.

"Violence must be reduced because otherwise we are headed toward total chaos," said Roberto Levi, 36, a police officer in Rio de Janeiro who voted for Mr. Bolsonaro.

Over the past two years, while many of Brazil's traditional political parties and powerful kingmakers were busy defending themselves against corruption allegations stemming from the investigation known as Lava Jato, Mr. Bolsonaro flew around the country, drumming up support, particularly among young men, and in comparatively wealthier and whiter areas.

While rivals spent small fortunes on marketing firms, video editors and consultants, Mr. Bolsonaro relied primarily on Facebook, Twitter,

YouTube and the instant messaging service WhatsApp to communicate with voters and expand his base.

Opponents enjoyed far more advertising time on television and radio — which is allotted by party size — and rolled out slickly edited campaign materials. But Mr. Bolsonaro's campaign drowned them out with a bare-bones, scrappy communications strategy. He and his sons broadcast shaky, poorly lit videos on Facebook and Instagram in which Mr. Bolsonaro cracked jokes, took aim at adversaries and bemoaned the state of Brazil.

On WhatsApp, supporters created hundreds of groups to share memes, videos and messages that often contained falsehoods and misleading content that cast Mr. Bolsonaro in a positive light and disparaged his rivals.

One dominant message, spread widely via WhatsApp, asserted with no evidence that Mr. Bolsonaro's opponents encouraged schoolchildren to become gay or reconsider their gender identity by employing sex education materials referred to as "gay kits."

"I like what Bolsonaro stands for," said Cintia Puerta, 55, an architect in São Paulo, said Sunday after voting. "My sister works in a school so I know they are teaching 'gay kits' to children, teaching them about sexuality at age 5 and 6. They're indoctrinating children in the school."

Mr. Bolsonaro's presidential ambition nearly ended on Sept. 6 when a man sliced a knife into his stomach during a campaign rally, slashing his intestines and several other organs.

After that, Mr. Bolsonaro declined to participate in debates and did few probing interviews, leaving significant gaps in the electorate's understanding of his position on pivotal issues, including pension reform and the privatization of state enterprises.

In the wake of the attack, Mr. Bolsonaro's standing in the polls rose steadily after languishing in the low 20-percent range for weeks. Last-minute endorsements from the influential evangelical lobby and agribusiness leaders gave him a boost.

After the first round of voting, in which Mr. Bolsonaro received just shy of the 50 percent required to win outright, some political analysts expected him to moderate his rhetoric in order to appeal to centrist or undecided voters.

They were wrong.

Last Sunday, he issued a threat to members of the Workers' Party that critics called downright fascist.

"Those red good-for-nothings will be banished from the homeland," he said during an address, delivered via a video linkup, to thousands of supporters gathered in São Paulo. "It will be a cleanup the likes of which has never been seen in Brazilian history."

For the Workers' Party, Sunday's presidential defeat leaves a political movement that won accolades from much of the population for affirmative action and inequality-reducing policies significantly weakened and effectively leaderless.

Party luminaries hoped that Mr. da Silva, a lion of Latin America's left known as Lula, would return to the presidential palace. Even after Mr. da Silva was jailed, party leaders said that "an election without Lula is fraud."

When courts made clear Mr. da Silva would not be allowed to run, and the Workers' Party nominated Mr. Haddad, a former education minister and mayor of São Paulo, the campaign's slogan was "Haddad is Lula."

During his campaign, Mr. Haddad visited Mr. da Silva in prison multiple times, and did little to take responsibility for the party's mistakes. This lack of atonement pushed many hesitant Brazilians toward Mr. Bolsonaro, said Mr. Mainwaring, the Harvard professor.

"The Workers' Party strategy was centered too much around Lula and too little around thinking about the future of the country and about winning this election," he said. "An important part of the Brazilian electorate would have voted for the P.T. if it had drawn a line in the sand and renounced the corruption of the past."

MARIANA SIMÕES and **MANUELA ANDREONI** contributed reporting.

Alexandria Ocasio-Cortez Is Leading and Following at the Same Time

OPINION | BY THOMAS B. EDSALL | JAN. 23, 2019

The Democratic electorate has shifted sharply to the left, taking many politicians along with it — willingly and unwillingly.

THE MOST ACTIVE WING of the Democratic Party — the roughly 20 percent of the party's electorate that votes in primaries and wields disproportionate influence over which issues get prioritized — has moved decisively to the left. With all the attention that is being paid to Alexandria Ocasio-Cortez, Ayanna Pressley, Rashida Tlaib and other new progressive voices in Congress, this may not seem like news, but we are only just beginning to realize the full significance of this shift.

The Primaries Project at the Brookings Institution conducted extensive polling of 7,198 Democratic voters in the 2018 primaries and found that 60.4 percent described themselves as liberal, including 26.4 percent who said they were "very liberal."

In its most recent analysis, Gallup found that from 1994 to 2018, the percentage of all Democrats who call themselves liberal more than doubled from 25 percent to 51 percent.

Over the same period, the percentage of Democratic moderates and conservatives fell steadily, with the share of moderates dropping from 48 to 34 percent, and of conservatives dropping from 25 to 13 percent. These trends began to accelerate during the administration of George W. Bush and have continued unabated during the Obama and Trump presidencies.

In recent years, the internal pressures to hew to the left, driven largely by Democratic primary voters, have steadily gained strength.

They include the determination to oppose all things Trump, especially his anti-immigrant policies, his racism and his religious bigotry; the rise of outspoken, well-educated liberals, many of them young; the #MeToo movement and Trump's disrespect for women; the Occupy movement; the mobilization of anti-establishment voters by Bernie Sanders during the 2016 primaries; and the consistent exodus of more conservative white voters from the Democratic Party, supplanted by more politically liberal minority voters.

The anti-establishment faction contributed significantly to the large turnout increases in Democratic primaries last year. Pew found that from 2014 to 2018, turnout in House primaries rose from 13.7 to 19.6 percent of all registered Democrats, in Senate primaries from 16.6 to 22.2 percent and in governor primaries from 17.1 to 24.5 percent.

Isabel Sawhill, a senior fellow at Brookings, agrees with the analysis that core voters and activist leaders within the party are "moving leftward":

> *Medicare for All, free college, a universal jobs guarantee, a $15 minimum wage, an expansion of the EITC to the entire bottom half, workers on boards of directors, ending ICE, raising marginal tax rates to 70 percent are all big, bold leftist ideas and appear to be gaining currency.*

These "big, bold leftist ideas" pose a strategic problem for liberals and the Democratic Party, Sawhill, who published "The Forgotten Americans: An Economic Agenda for a Divided Nation" last year, wrote in an email:

> *In my view, it's a trade-off between exciting the base thereby insuring higher turnout vs. broadening the base to include independents and Republicans that don't like Trump.*

Sawhill argues that if the goal of Democrats is victory, as opposed to ideological purity, they must focus on general election swing voters who are not die-hard Democrats.

One key Democratic target, Sawhill observes, is the "well-educated, suburban women, many of them Republican, who voted for Democrats in the midterms." Once Trump is gone, she continued, "they could easily return to their natural home in the Republican Party."

"Over the longer-term," Sawhill continued,

as millennials and minorities become an ever-larger proportion of the party, it will have a natural constituency that supports a new and bolder agenda, but the concentration of those voters in urban areas that are underrepresented in our electoral system will be a continuing drag on the party's prospects.

The extensive support among prospective Democratic presidential candidates for Medicare for All, government-guaranteed jobs and a higher minimum wage reflects the widespread desire in the electorate for greater protection from the vicissitudes of market capitalism — in response to "increasingly incomplete risk protection in an era of dramatic social change," as the political scientist Jacob Hacker put it in "Privatizing Risk without Privatizing the Welfare State: The Hidden Politics of Social Policy Retrenchment in the United States." Support for such protections is showing signs of becoming a litmus test for candidates running in the 2020 Democratic presidential primaries.

Polling by the Pew Research Center shows sharp movement in a progressive direction on key issues among many Democrats.

Take liberalized attitudes on immigration as an example. From 2008 to 2018, the percentage of Democrats who said the government should create "a way for immigrants already here illegally to become citizens if the meet certain requirements" grew from 29 to 51 percent, while the share who said "there should be better border security and stronger enforcement of immigration laws" fell from 21 to 5 percent.

Similarly, the percentage of Democrats who agreed with the statement that "racial discrimination is the main reason many blacks can't get ahead these days" rose from 28 to 64 percent from 2010 to 2017.

Paul Starr, a sociology professor at Princeton, warns against putting too much stock in the ascendance of progressive Democrats. In an essay in the American Prospect, Starr argues that there were "two distinct developments" in the 2018 elections:

While progressives have gained ground in long-held Democratic areas, more centrist candidates have won the more competitive districts. This second development will limit how far to the left the party can go. The more the party expands into the suburbs, the more dependent it will be on those relatively centrist votes — and that dependence will become a constraint on the policies that Democrats are able to agree on.

In addition, while acknowledging the rise of the progressive wing, Starr pointed out that a separate December 2018 Gallup survey found that 54 percent of Democratic voters would prefer their party to become "more moderate," while 41 percent said they would like the party to become "more liberal."

Along similarly cautionary lines, David Graham wrote in the Atlantic last November:

There's clear leftward movement among Democratic voters on a range of issues, and there are more progressive candidates running than ever. But this doesn't amount, at least yet, to the socialist groundswell that advocates pine for and critics fear. The actual policy positions, and number of leftist officeholders, will remain limited — at least for now. What happens in 2020 could be more telling.

Graham's conclusion:

The Democratic Party is moving left, but it might not be clear quite how far left for two or even six years. The revolution is coming more slowly than its champions hope and its critics fear.

Matt Grossmann, a political scientist at Michigan State, noted in an email that the leftward

movement is across the board on policy, ideological identification, and values, but remains furthest left on specific policy. The public movement seems to be strongest on race and gender issues as well as any proposal tied to Trump.

Women, according to Grossmann, "are becoming a bigger part of the Democratic electorate and more supportive of women primary candidates."

The 2018 primary elections revealed the deepening strength of an anti-establishment insurgent faction, largely young, white and minority urban voters who turned out in droves in Democratic primaries from Omaha to Tallahassee and from the Bronx to Boston.

Michael Capuano, a former mayor of Somerville, Mass. and a ten-term member of the House, learned the hard way how much the Democratic electorate has changed. As mayor in the 1990s, Capuano presided over the gentrification of the once scruffy, working class town. Initially, the city was grateful.

When Capuano first won election to Congress in 1998, he owed his victory in the 10-candidate Democratic primary to his hometown. He carried Somerville with 7,852 votes, more than the total vote for all nine opponents, 6,253, while losing to other candidates in Boston, Belmont, Cambridge, Chelsea and Watertown.

The impact of gentrification is striking.

By 2017, 61.2 percent of Somerville's residents 25 or older had at least a bachelor's degree, compared with 30.9 percent nationwide. The median household income was $84,722, compared with $57,652 nationally.

Somerville had moved from downscale to upscale, not to the level of Brattle Street in Cambridge or Boston's Beacon Hill, but still many steps up the ladder.

In the process, Somerville left Capuano, a white working class Democrat in the mold of Tip O'Neill, behind.

In 2018, twenty years after first winning his House seat, Capuano could no longer count on Somerville. Despite his deep roots — his father had been mayor before him — the vote there was a wash. Capuano received 8,423 to 8,286 for his opponent, Ayanna Pressley, an African-American Boston city councilwomen.

Pressley swept Cambridge and Boston to crush Capuano, 60,046 to 42,430 districtwide.

The same pattern emerged in the widely publicized defeat of Joe Crowley, another 10-term incumbent, by Alexandria Ocasio-Cortez in the Democratic primary in a House district that straddles the Bronx and Queens.

Steven Romalewski, who runs the mapping service at the CUNY Center for Urban Research, wrote me by email that "Ocasio-Cortez did best in areas such as Astoria/Steinway and Sunnyside, which happen to be more white than other parts of the district," a point he elaborated upon in a story quoting him posted on The Intercept:

> *You can also see that most of her votes, the strongest vote support, came from areas like Astoria in Queens and Sunnyside in Queens and parts of Jackson Heights that, number one, were not predominantly Hispanic, so they're a more mixed population, and are areas where — this is kind of a term of art — are in the process of being gentrified, where newer people are moving in,*

Grace Segers, writing in July on the City & State website, noted that Crowley

> *fell victim to gentrification and that force may upend expectations in Democratic primaries throughout Manhattan and western Brooklyn and Queens. And the rise of younger voters who are newer to their districts and unattached to incumbents could power insurgent candidates throughout New York City.*

David Freedlander, writing in Politico Magazine, captured the unanticipated voting patterns that gave rise to Crowley's defeat. "Ocasio-Cortez's best precincts," Freedlander wrote, were

> *highly educated, whiter and richer than the district as a whole. In those neighborhoods, Ocasio-Cortez clobbered Crowley by 70 percent or more.*

Conversely, Crowley did best in "the working-class African-American enclave of LeFrak City, where he got more than 60 percent of the vote." In fact, Crowley

> *pulled some of his best numbers in Ocasio-Cortez's heavily Latino and African-American neighborhood of Parkchester, in the Bronx — beating her by more than 25 points on her home turf.*

Jerry Skurnik, a New York political consultant, describes gentrifying communities outside Manhattan as experiencing an influx of "people who really want to live in Greenwich Village but can't afford to."

This younger, well-educated constituency — predominately but not exclusively white — is hostile to cautious establishment Democrats, especially to older white men, and they are determined to engineer an intraparty cultural and ideological insurgency.

The emergence in force in 2018 of these insurgent Democrats grows in part out of the Sanders presidential campaign. Sanders mobilized millions of voters, many of whom did not want the Democrats to nominate a candidate with deep ties to party regulars and to the major donor community.

Maps of primary voting patterns in 2016 and 2018 produced by CUNY's Graduate School of Journalism and the Center for Urban Research show that Sanders beat Clinton in just a handful of New York City neighborhoods. Many of those Sanders neighborhoods are in Ocasio-Cortez's district and they are the communities that provided her biggest margins of victory.

Sanders also carried Somerville in 2016, 12,247 to 9,016, where support for Capuano imploded two years later.

If the turnout patterns in the Ocasio-Cortez and Pressley districts are even modestly predictive, the Democratic Party may be changing in significant ways.

Tom Kiley, who conducted polling for Capuano, described in an email the shifting makeup of the Democratic electorate in the Seventh District of Massachusetts:

> *Mike did best among older, white, non-college educated Democrats who, for the most part, still described themselves as liberals or moderate liberals.*

Pressley's base, Kiley wrote,

> *was overwhelmingly made up of liberal, college-educated, white voters, especially those under 45 who did not have a history of voting in off-year*

elections. We were expecting what we considered a robust turnout of 75,000 for the day after Labor Day. In fact it ballooned to over 100,000, largely on the strength of this younger white cohort.

While the Boston-Cambridge-Somerville district is far more liberal than the national average, Kiley argued that trends there are likely to be replicated in many regions of the country. "These new voters will have a major impact in the Democratic nomination process in many states," he wrote:

The desire for change in general is huge, and Trump is a powerful accelerant. I have to believe these new voters aren't going to just retreat after electing new members of Congress; they'll come out in droves in the primaries next year. And they'll be voting for change.

While primary voters are normally predominately committed partisans with a long history of voting, in the Pressley-Capuano contest more than half of the voters had no record of previous primary voting (24 percent) or were recorded as voting in only one previous primary (29 percent).

"If the Pressley campaign was banking on turnout, they certainly cashed in," wrote Maeve Duggan, research director at the MassINC Polling Group, in an article posted on the website of WBUR, Boston's NPR news station.

"Some 106,556 voters in the 7th Congressional District cast ballots in the 2018 Democratic primary, compared with just 61,725 in 2014," she continued, "and among the district's 2018 primary voters, only 37 percent had also voted" in 2014 primaries, according to voter file analysis.

Duggan and the MassINC Polling Group analyzed the demographics of the first-time voters and found:

They were predominantly women and young people: Fifty-five percent were women, and 66 percent were age 44 or younger (including 34 percent who were 18 to 29 years old).

The surge of young voters had a powerful impact, increasing

> *the overall proportion of voters 44 or younger from 25 percent in 2014 to 42 percent in 2018. Combining age and gender, women ages 18 to 29 made up the largest group of new voters, at 20 percent.*

The new voters, she found, "were more likely to be Asian or Hispanic, compared with the 7th's repeat voters," but, she noted, the state's only majority-minority congressional district "still has a predominantly white voting base."

A July 2018 pre-election survey of voters in the Capuano-Pressley district conducted by WBUR-MassINC makes clear the importance of growing political participation among young voters. The survey found striking generational differences not only on the candidates but on issues.

18-to-29-year-olds favored Pressley over Capuano 41-23 while those over 60 backed Capuano 59-28. Asked if they would be more or less likely to support a candidate who "made abolishing ICE a major priority," young voters said "more likely" by 48-18 while older voters said it would make them "less likely" by 25-23.

Both young and old supported a national health care program, but the margin of support versus oppose was larger (90-2) among young voters than among their elders (71-16).

In a postelection analysis of the Ocasio-Cortez-Crowley contest, the Global Strategy Group found:

> *White gentrified liberal areas went big for AOC and surged. Younger, white liberal areas contributed heavily to the margin of Ocasio-Cortez's victory. Ocasio-Cortez won Hispanics.*

At the same time, according to their analysis, voters Crowley thought he could depend upon — "expected people, especially older primary voters — did not show up."

Joshua M. Zeitz, a historian whose most recent book is "Building the Great Society: Inside Lyndon Johnson's White House," argues that contemporary Democratic progressives are not insurgents, but in full accord with party tradition.

In an essay in Politico, "Democrats Aren't Moving Left. They're Returning to Their Roots," Zeitz argued that

> *What pundits today decry as a radical turn in Democratic policy and politics actually finds its antecedents in 1944. With the country fully mobilized for war, President Franklin Roosevelt called for "a second Bill of Rights … an economic Bill of Rights" that would entitle all Americans to a "useful and remunerative job," "the right to earn enough to provide adequate food and clothing and recreation," the "right … to a decent home," "the right to adequate medical care" and the "right to a good education."*

Sawhill looks at the ideological shifts in the Democratic electorate less from a historical perspective and more as a response to contemporary economic and social dislocation. Among both conservatives and liberals, Sawhill argued, there is "an intellectual awakening about the flaws of modern capitalism" — a recognition of the failings of "neoliberalism, the idea that a market economy with a few light guardrails is the best way to organize a society." This intellectual climate may result in greater receptivity among voters to more radical proposals.

The willingness of voters to support Democrats who are pushing initiatives like these will depend in large part, however, on the ability of candidates to assure the general electorate that their agenda is beneficial to all and not just to favored liberal constituencies. This will be difficult, given the fact that what is being proposed is a much larger role for government, and that those who are most in need of government support are in the bottom half of the income distribution and disproportionately minority — in a country with a long racist history. As a presidential candidate, Barack Obama was able to overcome this barrier twice, but the challenge should not be minimized.

THOMAS B. EDSALL has been a contributor to The Times Opinion section since 2011. His column on strategic and demographic trends in American politics appears every Wednesday. He previously covered politics for The Washington Post.

Abolish Billionaires

OPINION | BY FARHAD MANJOO | FEB. 6, 2019

A radical idea is gaining adherents on the left. It's the perfect way to blunt tech-driven inequality.

LAST FALL, TOM SCOCCA, editor of the essential blog Hmm Daily, wrote a tiny, searing post that has been rattling around my head ever since.

"Some ideas about how to make the world better require careful, nuanced thinking about how best to balance competing interests," he began. "Others don't: Billionaires are bad. We should presumptively get rid of billionaires. All of them."

Mr. Scocca — a longtime writer at Gawker until that site was muffled by a billionaire — offered a straightforward argument for knee-capping the wealthiest among us. A billion dollars is wildly more than anyone needs, even accounting for life's most excessive lavishes. It's far more than anyone might reasonably claim to deserve, however much he believes he has contributed to society.

At some level of extreme wealth, money inevitably corrupts. On the left and the right, it buys political power, it silences dissent, it serves primarily to perpetuate ever-greater wealth, often unrelated to any reciprocal social good. For Mr. Scocca, that level is self-evidently somewhere around one billion dollars; beyond that, you're irredeemable.

I cover technology, an industry that belches up a murder of new billionaires annually, and much of my career has required a deep anthropological inquiry into billionairedom. But I'm embarrassed to say I had never before considered Mr. Scocca's idea — that if we aimed, through public and social policy, simply to discourage people from attaining and possessing more than a billion in lucre, just about everyone would be better off.

In my defense, back in October, abolishing billionaires felt way out there. It sounded radical, impossible, maybe even un-American, and even Mr. Scocca seemed to float the notion as a mere reverie.

But it is an illustration of the political precariousness of billionaires that the idea has since become something like mainline thought on the progressive left. Bernie Sanders and Elizabeth Warren are floating new taxes aimed at the superrich, including special rates for billionaires. Representative Alexandria Ocasio-Cortez, who also favors higher taxes on the wealthy, has been making a moral case against the existence of billionaires. Dan Riffle, her policy adviser, recently changed his Twitter name to "Every Billionaire Is A Policy Failure." Last week, HuffPost asked, "Should Billionaires Even Exist?"

I suspect the question is getting so much attention because the answer is obvious: Nope. Billionaires should not exist — at least not in their present numbers, with their current globe-swallowing power, garnering this level of adulation, while the rest of the economy scrapes by.

I like to use this column to explore maximalist policy visions — positions we might aspire to over time rather than push through tomorrow. Abolishing billionaires might not sound like a practical idea, but if you think about it as a long-term goal in light of today's deepest economic ills, it feels anything but radical. Instead, banishing billionaires — seeking to cut their economic power, working to reduce their political power and attempting to question their social status — is a pithy, perfectly encapsulated vision for surviving the digital future.

Billionaire abolishment could take many forms. It could mean preventing people from keeping more than a billion in booty, but more likely it would mean higher marginal taxes on income, wealth and estates for billionaires and people on the way to becoming billionaires. These policy ideas turn out to poll very well, even if they're probably not actually redistributive enough to turn most billionaires into sub-billionaires.

More important, aiming to abolish billionaires would involve reshaping the structure of the digital economy so that it produces a more equitable ratio of superrich to the rest of us.

Inequality is the defining economic condition of the tech age. Software, by its very nature, drives concentrations of wealth. Through network effects, in which the very popularity of a service ensures that it keeps getting more popular, and unprecedented economies of scale — in which Amazon can make Alexa once and have it work everywhere, for everyone — tech instills a winner-take-all dynamic across much of the economy.

We're already seeing these effects now. A few superstar corporations, many in tech, account for the bulk of American corporate profits, while most of the share of economic growth since the 1970s has gone to a small number of the country's richest people.

But the problem is poised to get worse. Artificial intelligence is creating prosperous new industries that don't employ very many workers; left unchecked, technology is creating a world where a few billionaires control an unprecedented share of global wealth.

But abolishment does not involve only economic policy. It might also take the form of social and political opprobrium. For at least 20 years, we've been in a devastating national love affair with billionaires — a dalliance that the tech industry has championed more than any other.

I've witnessed a generation of striving entrepreneurs join the three-comma club and instantly transform into superheroes of the global order, celebrated from the Bay Area to Beijing for what's taken to be their obvious and irrefutable wisdom about anything and everything. We put billionaires on magazine covers, speculate about their political ambitions, praise their grand visions to save the world and wink affectionately at their wacky plans to help us escape — thanks to their very huge and not-in-any-way-Freudianly-suggestive rockets — to a new one.

But the adulation we heap upon billionaires obscures the plain moral quandary at the center of their wealth: Why should anyone have a billion dollars, why should anyone be proud to brandish their billions, when there is so much suffering in the world?

As Ms. Ocasio-Cortez put it in a conversation with Ta-Nehisi Coates: "I'm not saying that Bill Gates or Warren Buffett are immoral, but a system that allows billionaires to exist when there are parts of Alabama where people are still getting ringworm because they don't have access to public health is wrong." (She meant hookworm, she later corrected.)

Last week, to dig into this question of whether it was possible to be a good billionaire, I called up two experts.

The first was Peter Singer, the Princeton moral philosopher who has written extensively about the ethical duties of the rich. Mr. Singer told me that in general, he did not think it was possible to live morally as a billionaire, though he made a few exceptions: Mr. Gates and Mr. Buffett, who have pledged to give away the bulk of their wealth to philanthropy, would not earn Mr. Singer's scorn.

But most billionaires are not so generous; of the 2,200 or so billionaires in the world — about 500 of whom are American — fewer than 200 have signed the Giving Pledge created by Bill and Melinda Gates and Mr. Buffett.

"I have a moral concern with the conduct of individuals — we have many billionaires who are not living ethically, and are not doing nearly as much good as they can, by a wide margin," Mr. Singer said.

Then there is the additional complication of whether even the ones who are "doing good" are actually doing good. As the writer Anand Giridharadas has argued, many billionaires approach philanthropy as a kind of branding exercise to maintain a system in which they get to keep their billions.

When a billionaire commits to putting money into politics — whether it's Howard Schultz or Michael Bloomberg or Sheldon Adelson, whether it's for your team or the other — you should see the plan for what it is: an effort to gain some leverage over the political system, a scheme to short-circuit the revolution and blunt the advancing pitchforks.

Which brings me to my second expert on the subject, Tom Steyer, the former hedge-fund investor who is devoting his billion-dollar fortune to a passel of progressive causes, like voter registration and climate change and impeaching Donald Trump.

Mr. Steyer ticks every liberal box. He favors a wealth tax, and he and his wife have signed the Giving Pledge. He doesn't live excessively lavishly — he drives a Chevy Volt. Still, I wondered when I got on the phone with him last week: Wouldn't we be better off if we didn't have to worry about rich people like him trying to alter the political process?

Mr. Steyer was affable and loquacious; he spoke to me for nearly an hour about his interest in economic justice and his belief in grass-roots organizing. At one point I compared his giving with that of the Koch brothers, and he seemed genuinely pained by the comparison.

"I understand about the real issues of money in politics," he said. "We have a system that I know is not right, but it's the one we got, and we're trying as hard as possible to change it."

I admire his zeal. But if we tolerate the supposedly "good" billionaires in politics, we inevitably leave open the door for the bad ones. And the bad ones will overrun us. When American capitalism sends us its billionaires, it's not sending its best. It's sending us people who have lots of problems, and they're bringing those problems with them. They're bringing inequality. They're bringing injustice. They're buying politicians.

And some, I assume, are good people.

FARHAD MANJOO became an opinion columnist for The Times in 2018. Before that, he wrote the State of the Art column. He is the author of "True Enough: Learning to Live in a Post-Fact Society."

Glossary

austerity An economic policy that cuts public services in order to lower deficits.

authoritarian An approach to government that prioritizes obedience to the state over personal freedom.

bellicose Being warlike or willing to fight. The term can apply to individuals, states or forms of rhetoric.

bimetallism An economic policy of treating both gold and silver as legal tender, a policy strongly advocated by the populists.

Bolsheviks The communist group that led the Russian Revolution and established the Soviet Union.

bond A long-term, stable investment often used to finance municipal projects.

capitalism An economic system based on free enterprise, emerging during the Industrial Revolution.

communism A political ideology calling for the overthrow of capitalist society and the establishment of a workers' state.

corporate state A term in fascist ideology, where the state appoints representation of corporate groups in the working of government.

demagogue Someone who persuades voters by appealing to their emotions and prejudices.

extremist Someone whose strong religious or political views lead them to advocate extreme or excessive action.

fascism A political ideology advocating a militaristic and nationalistic state, controlled by a strong central government.

globalization An economic process where communications and trade take place on an increasingly international scale.

Grange movement A farmers' advocacy movement, which with the Patrons of Husbandry and Farmers Alliances helped organize the populist movement.

greenback A paper currency not backed by gold or silver; a currency advocated by the populists.

Hakenkreuz The symbol of the Nazi Party, also known as a swastika.

husbandry A term synonymous with agriculture.

ideology A system of political or economic beliefs either knowingly or unknowingly adopted by individuals and groups.

monopoly The control of a particular product's market held by a single person.

moribund In a state of decline or lacking energy to progress.

nationalism A political ideology of strong support or identification with one's country, often seen in competition with others.

nativism A prejudice against immigrants, in favor of people born in one's country.

petit bourgeois The lower middle class, especially in France, comprising shop owners and laborers.

political Islam A form of fundamentalist Islam with the goal of establishing a state on strict Islamic principles.

reactionary Being strongly opposed to social changes.

tariff A tax paid on imports, usually to encourage native industry. Proponents of free trade wish to lower tariffs.

trade union An organization of workers in a particular field to advocate for their collective interests.

trust A business practice of appointing someone to oversee a property, often used to create corporate monopolies during the 19th century.

Media Literacy Terms

"Media literacy" refers to the ability to access, understand, critically assess and create media. The following terms are important components of media literacy, and they will help you critically engage with the articles in this title.

angle The aspect of a news story that a journalist focuses on and develops.

attribution The method by which a source is identified or by which facts and information are assigned to the person who provided them.

balance Principle of journalism that both perspectives of an argument should be presented in a fair way.

bias A disposition of prejudice in favor of a certain idea, person or perspective.

byline Name of the writer, usually placed between the headline and the story.

chronological order Method of writing a story presenting the details of the story in the order in which they occurred.

credibility The quality of being trustworthy and believable, said of a journalistic source.

critical review A type of story that describes an event or work of art, such as a theater performance, film, concert, book, restaurant, radio or television program, exhibition or musical piece, and offers critical assessment of its quality and reception.

editorial Article of opinion or interpretation.

feature story Article designed to entertain as well as to inform.

headline Type, usually 18 point or larger, used to introduce a story.

human interest story Type of story that focuses on individuals and how events or issues affect their life, generally offering a sense of relatability to the reader.

impartiality Principle of journalism that a story should not reflect a journalist's bias and should contain balance.

intention The motive or reason behind something, such as the publication of a news story.

interview story Type of story in which the facts are gathered primarily by interviewing another person or persons.

inverted pyramid Method of writing a story using facts in order of importance, beginning with a lead and then gradually adding paragraphs in order of relevance from most interesting to least interesting.

motive The reason behind something, such as the publication of a news story or a source's perspective on an issue.

news story An article or style of expository writing that reports news, generally in a straightforward fashion and without editorial comment.

op-ed An opinion piece that reflects a prominent individual's opinion on a topic of interest.

paraphrase The summary of an individual's words, with attribution, rather than a direct quotation of their exact words.

quotation The use of an individual's exact words indicated by the use of quotation marks and proper attribution.

reliability The quality of being dependable and accurate, said of a journalistic source.

rhetorical device Technique in writing intending to persuade the reader or communicate a message from a certain perspective.

tone A manner of expression in writing or speech.

Media Literacy Questions

1. What is the tone of the story "Bigots in a Legislature: The Farmers' Alliance Idea of Lawmaking" (on page 19)? Based on the story's descriptions of populist candidates and of segregation, does it show the journalistic principle of balance?

2. The article "Coxey Without His 'Army': He Comes to New-York as a Horse-Dealer." (on page 24) is an interview story. What insights does this interview provide for understanding Coxey's motives? Based on his statements, what seems to be the public opinion on the movement?

3. T. R. Ybarra's article, "Italy's Frankenstein and His Monster." (on page 52), attributes several lengthy quotes to an unnamed American observer. How would you evaluate the reliability of this source?

4. Examine the angle of Sir Oswald Mosley's article, "Fascists Plan Corporate State in Britain, Mosley Declares" (on page 66). Mosley led the British fascist movement. How might this perspective inform his argument?

5. F. Raymond Daniell's article, "A Communist From Kansas Is a National Issue" (page 73), is an interview story. Compare it with "Coxey Without His 'Army': He Comes to New-York as a Horse-Dealer." (on page 24). What stylistic similarities do they share? What questions may the reporters have asked?

6. C. Vann Woodward's article, "The Ghost of Populism Walks Again" (on page 86), uses imagery of "ghosts" and "specters." What is the purpose of this rhetorical device? What ideas might it be referring to?

7. John Vinocur's article, " 'A Man of the Right' Is Rousing Passions in France" (on page 109), is broken into titled sections. Compare the headline with the section titles. What kind of information do these titles convey about their topics?

8. Deborah Sontag's article, "In the Time of Hugo Chávez" (on page 126), is a feature story. What populist themes of Chávez's rule are explored in depth? Does Chávez's populist political style relate to Venezuela's struggles after that ruler's death?

9. Jeff Zeleny's article, "Thousands Rally in Capital to Protest Big Government" (on page 142), uses Tea Party leader Jim DeMint as a source. Based on his quote and the description of him, how would you describe DeMint's motive?

10. Matthew D. Lassiter's article, "Who Speaks for the Silent Majority?" (on page 153), is an op-ed. Lassiter is a historian. Comparing this article with Sir Oswald Mosley's article, "Fascists Plan Corporate State in Britain, Mosley Declares" (on page 66), how do these figures' backgrounds inform their analysis of their subject matter?

11. What is the tone of Owen Jones's op-ed, "Brexit's Bitter Winners" (on page 180)? How does the tone give readers a sense of what his opinion is?

12. Patrick Kingsley's article, "How a Liberal Dissident Became a Far-Right Hero, in Hungary and Beyond" (on page 185), is written in chronological order. Why did Kingsley choose to write it in this way? How does this approach help convey the angle of the story?

Citations

All citations in this list are formatted according to the Modern Language Association's (MLA) style guide.

BOOK CITATION

THE NEW YORK TIMES EDITORIAL STAFF. *Populism.* New York: New York Times Educational Publishing, 2020.

ONLINE ARTICLE CITATIONS

BROWN, CYRIL. "New Popular Idol Rises in Bavaria: Hitler Credited With Extraordinary Powers of Swaying Crowds to His Will." *The New York Times*, 21 Nov. 1922, https://www.nytimes.com/1922/11/21/archives/new-popular-idol-rises-in-bavaria-hitler-credited-with.html.

DANIELL, F. RAYMOND. "A Communist From Kansas Is a National Issue." *The New York Times*, 11 Oct. 1936, https://www.nytimes.com/1936/10/11/archives/a-communist-from-kansas-is-a-national-issue-the-two-major-parties-a.html.

EDSALL, THOMAS B. "Alexandria Ocasio-Cortez Is Leading and Following at the Same Time." *The New York Times*, 23 Jan. 2019, https://www.nytimes.com/2019/01/23/opinion/ocasio-cortez-pressley-democrats.html.

FLEGENHEIMER, MATT, AND MICHAEL BARBARO. "Donald Trump Is Elected President in Stunning Repudiation of the Establishment." *The New York Times*, 9 Nov. 2016, https://www.nytimes.com/2016/11/09/us/politics/hillary-clinton-donald-trump-president.html.

FORERO, JUAN. "Bolivia's Newly Elected Leader Maps His Socialist Agenda." *The New York Times*, 20 Dec. 2005, https://www.nytimes.com/2005/12/20/world/americas/bolivias-newly-elected-leader-maps-his-socialist-agenda.html.

GINIGER, HENRY. "Poujadistes Pitch Fruit at French Candidates." *The New York Times*, 17 Dec. 1955, https://www.nytimes.com/1955/12/17/archives/poujadistes-pitch-fruit-at-french-candidates-politicians-worried.html.

GITLIN, TODD. "The Left Declares Its Independence." *The New York Times*, 8 Oct. 2011, https://www.nytimes.com/2011/10/09/opinion/sunday/occupy-wall-street-and-the-tea-party.html.

JONES, OWEN. "Brexit's Bitter Winners." *The New York Times*, 30 Nov. 2016, https://www.nytimes.com/2016/11/30/opinion/brexits-bitter-winners.html.

KANDELL, JONATHAN. "Religious Revival Is Sweeping Across the World of Islam." *The New York Times*, 23 Nov. 1978, https://www.nytimes.com/1978/11/23/archives/religious-revival-is-sweeping-across-the-world-of-islam-left-and.html.

KAZIN, MICHAEL. "How Can Donald Trump and Bernie Sanders Both Be 'Populist'?" *The New York Times*, 22 Mar. 2016, https://www.nytimes.com/2016/03/27/magazine/how-can-donald-trump-and-bernie-sanders-both-be-populist.html.

KINGSLEY, PATRICK. "How a Liberal Dissident Became a Far-Right Hero, in Hungary and Beyond." *The New York Times*, 6 Apr. 2018, https://www.nytimes.com/2018/04/06/world/europe/viktor-orban-hungary-politics.html.

KIRKPATRICK, DAVID D. "Voter Insecurities Feed Rise of Right-Leaning Populist Politicians." *The New York Times*, 10 Dec. 2015, https://www.nytimes.com/2015/12/11/world/europe/voter-insecurities-feed-rise-of-right-leaning-populist-politicians.html.

KLEIN, NAOMI. "Rebels in Search of Rules." *The New York Times*, 2 Dec. 1999, https://www.nytimes.com/1999/12/02/opinion/rebels-in-search-of-rules.html.

LASSITER, MATTHEW D. "Who Speaks for the Silent Majority?" *The New York Times*, 2 Nov. 2011, https://www.nytimes.com/2011/11/03/opinion/populism-and-the-silent-majority.html.

LONDOÑO, ERNESTO, AND SHASTA DARLINGTON. "Jair Bolsonaro Wins Brazil's Presidency, in a Shift to the Far Right." *The New York Times*, 28 Oct. 2018, https://www.nytimes.com/2018/10/28/world/americas/jair-bolsonaro-brazil-election.html.

MANJOO, FARHAD. "Abolish Billionaires." *The New York Times*, 6 Feb. 2019, https://www.nytimes.com/2019/02/06/opinion/abolish-billionaires-tax.html.

MATTHEWS, HERBERT L. "Fascist Parallels Seen in Peronism." *The New York Times*, 23 Mar. 1951, https://www.nytimes.com/1951/03/23/archives/fascist-parallels-seen-in-peronism-slogan-praising-peron-seen-all.html.

MOSLEY, SIR OSWALD. "Fascists Plan Corporate State in Britain, Mosley Declares." *The New York Times*, 24 Apr. 1934, https://www.nytimes.com/1934/04/24/archives/fascists-plan-corporate-state-in-britain-mosley-declares-violently.html.

THE NEW YORK TIMES. "Bigots in a Legislature: The Farmers' Alliance Idea of Lawmaking." *The New York Times*, 1 Apr. 1891, https://www.nytimes.com/1891/04/01/archives/bigots-in-a-legislature-the-farmers-alliance-idea-of-lawmaking.html.

THE NEW YORK TIMES. "Bryan the Demagogue: Career of the Man Who Will Lead the Silver Fanatics." *The New York Times*, 11 July 1896, https://www.nytimes.com/1896/07/11/archives/bryan-the-demagogue-career-of-the-the-man-who-will-lead-the-silver.html.

THE NEW YORK TIMES. "Coxey Without His 'Army': He Comes to New-York as a Horse-Dealer." *The New York Times*, 22 Apr. 1894, https://www.nytimes.com/1894/04/22/archives/coxey-without-his-army-he-comes-to-newyork-as-a-horse-dealer-talks.html.

THE NEW YORK TIMES. "Furor Over Mary Lease: The Kansas Woman Orator Has a Crowd in Cooper Union." *The New York Times*, 11 Aug. 1896, https://www.nytimes.com/1896/08/11/archives/furor-over-mary-lease-the-kansas-woman-orator-has-a-crowd-in-cooper.html.

THE NEW YORK TIMES. "The Great Railroad Strike." *The New York Times*, 21 July 1877, https://www.nytimes.com/1877/07/21/archives/the-great-railroad-strike.html.

THE NEW YORK TIMES. "The National Grange: Declaration of Its Objects and Purposes." *The New York Times*, 12 Feb. 1874, https://www.nytimes.com/1874/02/12/archives/the-national-grange-declaration-of-its-objects-and-purposes.html.

THE NEW YORK TIMES. "Priest Defends His Radio Talks." *The New York Times*, 10 May 1932, https://www.nytimes.com/1932/05/10/archives/priest-defends-his-radio-talks-father-coughlin-asserts-he-will.html.

THE NEW YORK TIMES. "Roosevelt's Issues: Ground on Which He Will Stand in Campaign." *The New York Times*, 13 Feb. 1904, https://www.nytimes.com/1904/02/13/archives/roosevelts-issues-ground-on-which-he-will-stand-in-campaign-panama.html.

PHILLIPS, KEVIN. "The Politics of Frustration." *The New York Times*, 12 Apr. 1992, https://www.nytimes.com/1992/04/12/magazine/the-politics-of-frustration.html.

POORE, C. G. "Shadows That Fascism Casts Before It." *The New York Times*, 19 May, 1935, https://www.nytimes.com/1935/05/19/archives/shadows-that-fascism-casts-before-it-raymond-gram-swing-sees.html.

SONTAG, DEBORAH. "In the Time of Hugo Chávez." *The New York Times*, 2 June 2002, https://www.nytimes.com/2002/06/02/magazine/in-the-time-of-hugo-chavez.html.

VINOCUR, JOHN. " 'A Man of the Right' Is Rousing Passions in France." *The New York Times*, 29 May 1984, https://www.nytimes.com/1984/05/29/world/a-man-of-the-right-is-rousing-passions-in-france.html.

WILKIE, CURTIS. "The South's Lessons for the Tea Party." *The New York Times*, 12 Aug. 2014, https://www.nytimes.com/2014/08/13/opinion/the-south-s-lesson-for-the-tea-party.html.

WILLIAMS, HAROLD. "Bolshevism Seen as New Religion." *The New York Times*, 11 Jan. 1918, https://www.nytimes.com/1918/01/11/archives/bolshevism-seen-as-new-religion-compared-as-a-mass-movement-with.html.

WOODWARD, C. VANN. "The Ghost of Populism Walks Again." *The New York Times*, 4 June 1972, https://www.nytimes.com/1972/06/04/archives/the-ghost-of-populism-walks-again-the-new-populists.html.

YARDLEY, JIM. "Europe's Right and Left on March to Populism." *The New York Times*, 23 May 2014, https://www.nytimes.com/2014/05/24/world/europe/europes-right-and-left-on-march-to-populism.html.

YBARRA, T. R. "Italy's Frankenstein and His Monster." *The New York Times*, 29 Jan. 1922, https://www.nytimes.com/1922/01/29/archives/italys-frankenstein-and-his-monster.html.

ZELENY, JEFF. "Thousands Rally in Capital to Protest Big Government." *The New York Times*, 12 Sept. 2009, https://www.nytimes.com/2009/09/13/us/politics/13protestweb.html.

Index

This book is current up until the time of printing. For the most up-to-date reporting, visit www.nytimes.com.